Acknowledgments

First and foremost, I would like to thank Allah; The Exalted for giving me the ability to be creative. Next, I would like to thank those who helped me in the development of this book.

Rayshawn Demosthene, Sheila Sanders, Wanda Jackson, Giovanni Sterling, Kee-Kee, and Kimberly Barnes.

My sons King-Salaam, Samir and Prodigy. Their mothers Makeba and Brittny. My Parents Wanda and Universal for bringing me into existence. To all my siblings; Kayla, Deisha, Ashante, Rashaad and Shimani.

All my real family. There are too many names to name so I will just shout out to all my real ones you know who you are and if you don't your probably not one of the real ones. And lastly, to all the Phoney Homies I wish you a Lonely Life... GET CASH!!!

Introduction

Growing up in Brooklyn; could never be considered an easy life. No matter your background, upbringing, or home life; when you stepped outside you had to be in survival mode! Only the strong survive and the weak become victims. This is the story of King G, born and raised in the greatest neighborhood of Flatbush, Brooklyn. Flatbush is a world of its own! An area presented to be an American dream for immigrated West Indians. But Flatbush…you had to know how to navigate. You needed manners and respect, but you also had to show no weakness and violence was an everyday norm. People will do whatever possible to maintain their respect, which most of the time comes through violence. Envy and jealousy run through the hood rampant, so you got to stay alert for the fakes and the snakes! Keep your grass low, and a trusty side arm; because you never know who is on the creep. King G lives by many principles and codes; but the one that was etched into his mental by his father, Father G, was "whatever you do, you gotta get cash," So its money, power, respect until HIS DEATH DAY! Trust builds bridges; and lies burn them down. Life taught him that lesson! I'm here to give you his story, as well as some lessons to live by. Some of you will relate through similar experiences and some may have yet to go through these things. There is no doubt in my mind that, you will learn that PHONEY HOMIES DIE LONELY AND REAL G's DIE HARD!!!

Chapter 1

Father G is cruising down Church Avenue in his brand new '92 Cadillac Deville. All black with the peanut butter interior; Benzy Box stereo, gooseneck equalizer and two 12" subs in the trunk bumping a stone love mix. He passes him and his wife; Mama G's, Laundromat, and sees his son outside playing with his friend, Lil' Troy. Everyone calls him LT.

As he pulls over, he shouts "Hey King G, come take a ride with me."

King G runs over and says "Can LT. come with us. father?

"This is a father and son moment King, tell LT. you soon come back." Father said.

As King G bids his friend goodbye, Father G smiles at his son, because he sees the loyalty that his son has within him. He just hopes that loyalty doesn't come back to bite him in the long run. King G hops in,

"Wah Gwan Pops?" "King, you always askin' me how you make your own money. Well, I'm gonna put you onto something so you can start your own business since you think you ready and we will see how you do." "Well, what is it father!" "Just cool ya foot King! We are taking a ride to the warehouse so I can show you."

Father G can see the excitement and anticipation in his sons' eyes. He hopes he is making the right decision; he has been grooming his son with morals and principles his whole life. He knows he is ready; it's just he didn't run this by Mama G. The rest of the car ride is quiet except for the music playing. As they pull up to the warehouse, they both are thinking this; is the moment Father G unlocks the door and they step inside. He walks King to a room that's filled with chops, cookies, and candies.

"Here you go King, all this is for you," Father G says with a smile.

King is wide eyed and just staring around the room.

"Father all this is for me to do what I want?" "Yes son, but whatever you do you gotta get cash!" All the lessons I have been teaching you about counting money and saving money and investing has brought you to this moment."

King nods, he is wondering where his father got all of this; but he knows better that to ask! His father always told him,

"I will supply you with all the information you need until I think you need more." So, he says, "How much inventory is it, Father?" "It's 10,000 cases of candy, there are 10 boxes of candy in each case, and each box has 20 candy bars or 20 packs of candy in each. Then there is 50,000 bags of chips and 50,000 packs of cookies." "Father that's $2 million in candies," King says with his mouth wide open. Father G laughs: not at his son's expression, but how quick he calculates numbers. In his mind, he knows his son is ready. Father G can see King thinking and he stands there awaiting the results. King says, "Father can we get this to the house to keep in the basement so I can get to it when I need?" "Sure, son but you think you're gonna need the whole shipment at the house?" "Yes Father!" "What's your plan King?" "To get cash Father! Just watch me work. Father, I'm gonna make you proud." Father G just smiles and says, "say no more." They leave out the warehouse and King can't wait to get back to the hood to start his empire. Father G notices the seriousness in his son's face, and realizes he is more mature than he gave him credit for. He would have expected a 12 yr. old to be hyper, smiling and talking about all the things he could buy; but King was all business. As they pulled back into the hood King asked his dad to drop him off at LT's building. "Alright son, I got you. I'm going home to get that delivery set up for you. It will be here in the next 2 hours." Thanks Father, I won't let you down."

They stop in front of LT's building and King jumps out. As he enters the building, he sees LUV and Empress talking and he comes to a stop. LUV has been his girlfriend since he was 7. He knows he is in love with her and will marry her, there is no doubt! She is Trinidadian and more beautiful than a 12 yr. old should be. They are both the same age and play no games when it comes to each other. As he stares at LUV, she looks at him and smiles. Empress smiles at him at the same time too! Empress is a beautiful Black/Asian mixed girl who was 10 years old at the time, he can feel the smile creeping on his face as he looks at her. She is exotically beautiful, and he can't help but want her as his girlfriend too. He told her he liked her, but that LUV is his girl, plus LUV and Empress are friends. He walks towards them and hugs LUV and kisses her.

He looks at Empress and says, "What's up Empress?"

"What don't I get a hug too King G?" He smiles and looks at LUV, who shrugs her shoulder, so he hugs Empress. "Empress told me you told her you like her, and she says she like you too. Is that true King G?" "LUV, I told her you're my girl it ain't like I was trying to cheat on you." "I know you ain't gonna cheat on me, you ain't stupid boy! Is it true you like her though?" Yes, LUV I do, I'm sorry." "You don't have to be sorry; you know we don't lie to each other. She's my friend and she is always ready to fight girls with me over you too. I see why now." They all laugh." Well anyway I told her if you want; she can be your girlfriend too, but we all hang out together." King G looks at Empress who is smiling, "You with that Empress?" King G asks. "Yes King G. I mean me and LUV share toys, games, secrets, and clothes, so why not?" King G gets serious and says, "Ok, but I ain't playing about neither one of y'all! So don't get nobody beat up!" Can I have my kiss now, King G?" And with that King G kisses his new girlfriend. He's happy and almost gets lost in the moment, when he remembers he gotta holla at LT. "I will see y'all later I gotta handle some business." Empress and LUV, at the same time, say "later King G." He runs up the stairs. He hears Mama Judy door opening. He makes it to LT.'s apartment and knocks. LT answers and King G rushes in. "Listen Bro, I got a way for us to make some money. But I need your help and the rest of the crew." He breaks it all down to LT. "You know I'm with-it King G. I'm tired of asking my parents for stuff I want." "Ok then LT; call up the crew they should be home getting ready for our martial arts and 52 class with Barkim." "Aight Bro, I'm gonna call them now." After LT. got all the rest of the crew on the phone and on their way, they sat back and waited. "Oh, yeah LT, I forgot to tell you, Empress my girl now too. We just made it official. LUV said it was ok." "What the hell Bro, how you pull that off?" LT. asked laughing. "You don't need to know all that Bro!" Ha, Ha, I got you Bro!"

A knock came at the door, LT. opened it and in came the whole crew. Nutso, Illy, K9, TEC and Jungle. King and LT spoke first,

"What's up Y'all?" the crew replied "just chillin". Nutso was the first to speak up "so what y'all call us over here for?" "Check this out Nutso, I got a way for us to make some money Bro" King G said, "Ok Bro, how?" "I got a bunch of snacks we gone sell at school or outside. We not gonna touch the money til everything is gone. I'm gonna hold all the money and when we finish; we all gonna get paid!" K9 says, "why you gotta hold the money? And why we gotta wait to get paid?" King G started to get mad, but calmed down and said "First, because it's my idea. I'm the one bringing the business to everyone, so we all eat. Plus, I got plans for us all to have some serious money before we finish high school! Plus, you know damn well if your parents start seeing you buy too much stuff it's gonna be a problem." Everyone else agreed with King G because they trusted him. Plus, he didn't even have to put them on. After a while K9 spoke, "Ok Bro I just wanted to know what's up. Anyway, I can get bread when I need off stealing and robbing." "You don't have to do none of that Bro; trust me I got us!" King G stated. "Whatever Bro" was all K9 said. "Well look ya'll; we gotta each go out and try to make $200 a day in sales, every day. If we go hard, the faster we will be done! Now, I was thinking, we sell candies for .25 cent a piece, chips for .50 cent a piece and cookies for .25 cents apiece." "Why so cheap?" Illy asks. "Because that will make it go faster, which will keep them coming back to us faster. Oh, yeah; the chips are the big bag too, like for parties and the candies are in packs or bars" Together they all say, "we with it." "Alright y'all, this what we on from here on out. I will have everyone's $200 worth ready tonight. Ain't no lookin back. We are now the GGC Crew," King G stated proudly. TEC and Jungle say, "What is GGC, Bro?" Which King G says," Gotta Get Cash Bro, Gotta Get Cash!" C'mon y'all it's time to go to Barkim house to train," LT says.

After an hour in Barkim house training, the crew is sweaty and worked up. They all make their way down to the first floor and run into LUV, Empress and Brandy, who everyone calls Lil Brandy. Everyone greets each other. King G is sure to kiss LUV and Empress; to let the crew know what's up. They all look wide eyed at the silent statement made. King G peeps the envy in K9's eyes. But doesn't say anything.

Lil Brandy says "that ain't fair King G why I don't get a kiss?"

Brandy is visiting for the summer; she is the one who was coming out of Mama Judy door when King G was going up the stairs. She is from North Carolina. She was 9, at the time, but thinks she is as old everyone else in the hallway. They all treat her like a little sister. Especially King G and LT; they don't let anybody bother her. They always give her money to get stuff from the store. King G looks at Brandy and says,

"Now Lil Brandy; you know I can't kiss you like that; those are my girlfriends. I will give you one on the cheek." He kisses her lightly on the cheek. She smiles and says "I ain't gonna be little forever!" which gets a laugh out of everyone.

"I hear you Lil Brandy, you something else!" is all King G can say. "I'm leaving to go back to North Carolina tomorrow, so see y'all next summer." They all tell Brandy they gonna miss her. King G leaves to go home, while everyone else goes to their apartments in the building.

After King G gets out the shower, he goes to the basement where the shipment is waiting for him. The whole basement is almost full from top to bottom. He gets everyone's inventory ready and set aside. He calls them all to meet him in front of the building. He then gets Father G to drive him and the inventory to the crew. After giving it out he tells the crew:

"Monday, we start school. Let's get ready, cause everything changes after our first sale!"

King G had no idea how real and in depth his words were. As King gets back in the car, Father G says,

"I see you putting your boys on." "Gotta feed the dogs dem or they will round and bite you! Isn't that what you always say Father?"

Father G just laughs and nods knowing his son soaks up all game given. Monday comes around and King G is ready for school to start. He takes his duffle bag to school, full of inventory. You see; King G goes to a private school with about 1500 students. He knows $200 a day is too small for him, but he wants to be prepared for anything. Inside the duffle he has 4 separate garbage bags of snacks. He is gonna load 1 in his hallway locker, and 1 in his gym locker. He will also use his friend Alvino's hallway locker and gym locker. Alvino is Mexican and has all the Latinos on his side. They love Alvino. He is popular, dresses fly and is dropped off in a limo every day to school. This is the first-person King G plans on Brokering a deal with. He knows Alvino knows money and loves to make money.

After loading his lockers, he goes looking for Alvino, who he finds talking to a group of pretty Latinas. "Yo Vino, let me holla at you." "Excuse me ladies; I need to holla at my friend King G. I will catch up with y'all later. Besos" "What's up King G?" What's with the duffle bag?" "I need you to hold these 2 garbage bags of snacks for me in your lockers. Also, I got a business proposition for you." "I got you Bro. Lets go to my lockers and you can let me know what you have in mind."

After breaking everything down to Alvino, Alvino is all in. He gives King G $100 for some snacks. King G gives him his inventory and they make their way to class. By lunch Vino is back with another $100 for more. On his own King G has made $200 from his classmates. By the time lunch is over he has made another $100, and Alvino is back for another $100. They go to the locker for more inventory and both part with big smiles on their faces! When school is over, King G has made $1000 on his first day and decides that's his projected daily profit. 400 of the dollars came from Alvino, who because he had inventory in his locker, was able to grab another $100, which he gave to King G after school. King G was excited; him and Alvino had locked the school down, and everyone wanted in on the snacks.

King G got home from school; completed his homework, and then went to the building to get up with his crew. They were all on the first floor talking and smiling when King G entered.

"So, what y'all do today?" King G asked. LT stated, "You know, just went out and had to get some cash!" Everyone laughed and pulled out $200 apiece. "How did you do King G?" TEC asked. "I made $1000. You know I gotta get cash too, ha ha!" The crew couldn't believe it, they were all wondering how King G did it. "Y'all, know I go to school with a bunch of spoiled rich kids, so it wasn't that hard. Don't worry, I don't expect y'all to do no more than the $200. If we can do this daily, then we will be fine." Leave it to King G to make $1000 on the first day" K9 said but tried to laugh it off as a joke.

Again, King G peeped the envy. See King G knew that K9 chased the limelight. He needed it to feel good about himself. Plus, he stretched the truth every chance that he got, but King G didn't judge him. For one they were from the same hood; and two, they grew up together. Also, even though K9 had his faults, he would definitely have your back, if anyone was trying to cause you harm. So, for that, King G let alot slide.

"Alright y'all, let's turn in all money. We gonna do it like this every day, so we all know the count. I'm gonna put it in a safe place when I get with my father. I'm on my way to his liquor store now." "We walking you there Bro! Ain't no way we gonna risk someone trying to do anything to you," said K9.

See that was one of the good things bout K9, he was protective; especially when it concerned his benefit. After King stashed the money, he gave out inventory to the crew again. Every day they did this, and everyone easily hit their mark. After 18 days, all the cookies were gone, 17 days after that all the chips were gone.

Everything was running smoothly. King had been hanging with LUV and Empress in the building and around the hood. He also studied with them and helped them do homework. He wasn't playing with them. He truly had plans to see everyone around him succeed. LUV and Empress were smart anyway, so schoolwork was easy. It was keeping their attention from straying, that was hard. They wanted to play often, which King G could enjoy, but he wanted them to know they can't always be about playing.

"Listen, y'all I know we are young; but my father always taught me, life was serious. After you succeed, you can spend time having fun. If you spend too much time having fun before you succeed, then you are just wasting time!" "We get it King G, but just remember we are kids and we still got time to grow up. We definitely take school seriously. We take you serious too," stated LUV, which made them all laugh. "I take you serious too."

He walked them home and told Empress to be sure to tell Miss Trish he said hello. He told LUV to tell Mama LUV, he said hello too. Back at school, King and Alvino were still doing their thing. They were the go-to guys for all things snacks. Only now it was all things candy.

It was October, things were looking great on the candy front. The kids' parents were sending them to school with money to buy candy from King G and Alvino. Everyone was getting ready for the schools Halloween party. A girl named Dana Cohen was in the hall talking to her friends about what she wanted to wear when two older boys who were 14 asked Dana to the party. She kindly turned them down. As Alvino and King G were walking by, she asked Alvino if he had a date. She was interested in being his date. The two older boys immediately got upset and started calling her names and one of them grabbed her butt. This triggered Alvino to tell them to stop and push them back. Two more older guys came up and jumped on Alvino, he was no match at all for all four boys; but with King G there, the tables turned. He immediately used his martial arts training and his 52-block style to dismantle them. He basically beat all four guys by himself. When three of them were knocked out, King G and Alvino stomped the fourth guy out. Teachers rushed in to break it up, and carted Alvino and King G to the principal's office. Dana went with them and was crying and explained that King G and Alvino had saved her from being assaulted and sexually harassed. The principal wanted to hear none of it. King G and Alvino's parents were called up and so was Dana's father, because she refused to back down. When all the parents arrived, they all were escorted to the principal's office. Father G and Mama G looked pissed as did Mr. Velez, Alvino 's dad and Mr. Cohen, Dana 's dad. The older kid's parents were on their way also. After the story came out; King G's parents, Dana 's dad and Alvino 's dad was furious that the principal wanted to suspend King G and Alvino. Once the older kids' parents came in and heard what happened and questioned their kids, they agreed King G and Alvino did nothing wrong. They were upset to the extent their kids were beaten. So, they all agreed that the kids involved minus Dana should miss the Halloween party and the older boys should serve detention for two weeks.

Mr. Cohen and Mr. Velez, both thanked King G for saving Alvino and Dana. Mr. Cohen also thanked Alvino for stepping up to protect his daughter's honor. Mr. Cohen and Mr. Velez told King G; if there was anything they could do to pay him back don't hesitate to ask. Mama G and Father G were proud of their son. They took him out to eat and let him know he did well. King just wanted money. After 245 days of having inventory, they were finally done. The total amount earned was $537,500.00. King G gave Father G $250,000.00, which made Father G very proud. He wasn't even expecting that much but he said nothing to King G. King gave each member of his crew $11,071.00. He let them know he was putting away $210,000.00 for them for later on. They now believed completely in his plan and ability as a leader, when it came to money.

Chapter 2

It was now May 1993; King G was 13. All his mind could focus on was what the next business venture would be. Father G kept telling him as soon as he had something for him, he would let him know. King G patiently waited, and he gave LUV and Empress $100 apiece and told them to save it. He bought them both a pair of Jordans. Father G and Mama G opened a West Indian restaurant. At the insistence of King G, they hired Mama LUV to be the cook and run the place. Mama LUV was so thankful, and King G told her it was no problem. All he was doing was looking out for his soon to be mother-in-law, which made her smile.

Summertime hit and Father G started schooling King G more and more. He let him know that besides the businesses that him and Mama G owned, they had been ripping off truck and shipyard shipments and warehouses. He told King G when he was a little older, he would let him know how it was all done. The beginning of the summer had the crew just chilling of course. The boys bought themselves some gear, but not too much or their parents would have been suspicious. Plus, King G wanted everyone on a low profile for now. It would be their time to shine soon enough. They would hang out at the building. Lil Brandy was back and still crushing on King G. She hung out with them every day in the building, and everyone still spoiled her. Over the years, she started developing. Everyone thought it was early because she was only 10. She also had become a Lil wild child always fighting anyone who wasn't a part of her crew. King G noticed she had skills. He started teaching her, Empress and LUV how to defend themselves. As pretty girls they were sure to have haters!

That summer Princess G came back from her European Boarding school. She was King G's younger sister by one year. Mama G wanted her to have a high-class education. For two years, she had been living abroad. She would be attending school with King G in the fall. Princess G and King G were cut the same. All money and success on the brain and a no-nonsense way of handling business. Mama G was grooming Princess herself, she had big plans for her. Everyone hung out tough every day. King G, LUV and Empress relationship was going well. The two girls remained friends and loved having King G, as their boyfriend. The only other female they let around him was Lil Brandy. She wanted to be everywhere he was, and she loved having LUV and Empress as big sisters. Brandy was a triplet; she had a sister named Candy and a brother named Andy. Brandy was different than them though. She felt outcasted, which is why she stayed with Mama Judy every summer. One day while in front of the building, a boy around Brandy's age started talking to her. Right away King G and the others could tell he liked her. It was all innocent, but they kept their eyes on him.

When they were all going inside, the Lil boy asked Brandy for a kiss. Before she could reply King G flipped and said:

"Get yo Lil ass away from her, you ain't getting no kiss or nothing else!"

The boy ran off and everyone laughed. LUV noticed King G was a little too upset. She brushed it off as him being overprotective, which he was. As everyone went in, King G put his arm around Brandy and said:

"Lil Brandy, don't be letting these boys kiss on you." "OK King G, I don't want them kissing on me no way. The only boy I want kissing on me is you," she whispered. This caught King G by surprise, and all he could say was, "maybe when you're older." This made her smile.

Around the middle of July, Father G called King G out of his room and told him to come to the basement. King G made it downstairs where Father G said:

"Son, I have some new business for you. I have 5000 game boys and 10,000 games for you, you think you can handle that!" "Of course, Father, if it makes money, it makes sense." Ha-Ha I hear dat son."

King G immediately took everything to his room. He separated two games for each Gameboy. After he finished, he went to the crew, rounded them all up at the building and laid the new plan out.

"Ok, y'all, we are not in school. We gotta go out and hit the streets hard, sell to any and everyone! Hit the post office, hospitals, electronics spots, car dealerships or wherever you think money can be made. We're gonna sell them $50 a pop including two games. We can't lose, that should bring us $250,000, when we are done." "GGC" is all everyone said.

He gave everyone 10 Gameboys a piece and 20 games. They hit the ground running. LUV and Empress wanted to help out. He didn't want them outside trying to sell things. Empress told King, her uncle was always selling electronics at his job, so, King G said,

"Call him and tell him the price and if he is interested, I will meet him here." "Ok Boo. I got you" she replied.

King hurried home and called Alvino. Alvino loved the plan. He hollered at his dad, who told him that they were coming to pick up 20 Gameboys/Game combinations. King G just loved it when a plan came together. For the next five weeks the GGC crew went hard and finally sold all the electronics. Father G didn't even want a dime back, so King G stash $210,000 again. Everybody in the crew got $5,714. That averaged out to a little over $1125 a week.

They were making more than adults! Empress's uncle happened to be a blessing. While he bought Gameboys, he also talked about his racist boss, who treated him like shit because he was Asian. He told King G how his boss was expecting a big shipment of pagers which was to be distributed all over the tri-state area. He knew where and when it was coming in. If he had a way to rip his boss off, and get away with it, he would do it. King G told him he might know someone that could help and would get back to him through Empress. First thing King G did was tell Father G. He told him to offer Empress's uncle $100,000 just for the info and the rest will be handled. Of course, the uncle jumps on the hundred grand. Father G wanted to pay King G for the info as well, but King G had other plans.

"Father let me pay $50,000 to get 10,000 beepers since the load is 50,000 beepers. You still come off with 40,000 beepers and only have to come out of pocket $50,000 to Empress's uncle."

Father G could not believe how business savvy his son was. All he could do was smile and agree with the deal. After all, he was grooming, his son to take over anyway. King was passing all test with flying colors, at 13. If he was this sharp in his 20s, he would be unstoppable! Empress's uncle got the money, and the heist went off without a hitch. Summer was coming to an end and the crew wanted to go out with the bang. Immediately after receiving the 10,000 beepers. King G told the crew.

"We selling these at $20 a pop. There is no reason we shouldn't move these faster than the Gameboys. Let's go hard! It's almost time for school, and I'm sure this extra bread couldn't hurt the school shopping."

Everyone agreed and ran out to get to work. King G decided to talk to Mr. Velez and Mr. Cohen on his business venture. He knew Mr. Cohen owned a warehouse that catered to Jewish people, and he knew Mr. Velez had money. Mr. Cohen and Mr. Velez agreed to buy out all the beepers over a four-week period as they didn't want to have too much on their hands at one time. This was great news to King G. After the first two days, King G gave the boys the good news. They had sold 100 of the beepers so there was still plenty left for Mr. Velez and Mr. Cohen.

September was here and Brandy was going back to North Carolina. Everyone was saying their goodbyes. All the crew gave her $100 apiece. King G gave her a Gameboy with two games he saved for her. He had even paid for it out of his pocket. Brandy was happy, to the point she was in tears. They all hugged her and left. King G stayed around to give LUV and Empress their chains. LUV's chain said LUV G on it and Empress chain said Empress G. They were both 14k gold and the name plates were too with white gold trimming. Brandy was happy for her friend/sisters but wanted to be a part of the chain wearers too. She started to cry, and everyone wondered what was wrong. She exclaimed.

"It's not fair! I want to be King G's girlfriend too. I want a chain too; I will give back all the money and the Gameboy for it." Nobody knew how to respond. LUV said, "Lil Brandy if you want to be King G's girlfriend, you can be when you're 13. You'll be a teenager then, but only if you stop crying." Immediately, Brandy stopped crying and said "I will be 11 in December. So, another two years will be fine. Promise you won't change your mind now."

Now LUV felt confused because she really only said it to calm Brandy down. As she thought about it, she thought King G was like one of those African Kings she had read about who deserve more than 1 wife. She couldn't explain why she felt this way. It's not like he ever said these things. It's just something her an Empress had agreed on when they first decided to share him:

"Ok, Lil Brandy I promise." Brandy hugged LUV said, "thank you, thank you, thank you."

Then she looked at Empress who smiled and Brandy ran and hugged her. LUV and Empress looked at King G who asked,

"Do I have a say in this?" They both laughed and said, "that's it! It won't be no more additions to this tribe your majesty." Then Brandy said, "yeah cause I will cut any girl that even look at you funny!" King G just shook his head and said, "you might not even want me when you're 13." "I'm gonna show you King G and have my chain ready when I do." All King G could think was what he had gotten himself into.

A couple of weeks later the $200,000 was all there. He put the $50,000 back in the stash and they each got $21,428. School had started and King G was sure to tell his crew to save the money. Don't blow it all because he was looking for the next business move. King advised them to do some school shopping, but again be mindful of the parents watching. King G's eighth grade year was pretty mild. Father G hadn't come to him with any prospective business ventures.

Around April of 1994, Father G told King G he had something at the warehouse waiting for him. He could see the anxiousness in his son. He had seen how down he was when he wasn't making money. As he watched his son over the months, he also noticed he never complained or begged. He also didn't spend money without a thought. He saw King G give Mama LUV money for groceries, knowing she had five children to feed. He gave Miss Trish money for groceries, knowing she also had five kids to feed. Outside of that King G waited patiently. This would be the last lesson Father G would give his son. It was now his turn to figure it out. The shipment sitting in the warehouse had been there since winter. Father G could have given it to his son, but he wanted him to learn the lesson of patience; as well as not waiting on anyone else for your money. As Father G and son entered the warehouse.

Father G looked at his son and said, "there are 30,000 Jansport Bookbags and 10,000 North Face coats in those boxes for you. Just kick me back something decent and everyone will be happy. After this, though, you're on your own until you turn 18. Find your own way, but whatever you do, you GOTTA GET CASH!!!"

Chapter 3

It took 6 months to get rid of everything. The boys each got a Book bag and a coat. In total sales, they made $1,099,510. King G gave Father G $500,000, stashed $350,000 and each member of the crew got $35,642. The crew had each made $73,855 in personal money and had $770,000 stash. They knew now that listening to King G was the best decision ever. They had achieved this in two years and at 14 years old, who could even come close. They did all without selling one drug. Now it was time for the realest convo of the year for their young lives. King G gathered them all up at the building and said.

"Ok my brothers, that was the last ride on inventory. I appreciate y'all for trusting me and not asking where I got anything from or who was my source. I've been told I am on my own till I turn 18. With that being said, we gotta get out and make our own money; until I can figure a greater plan out. Our money is safe, but that stash is to achieve greatness! We are going to make it with our personal funds and show the world what GGC is about. Get out there and mingle. Find a way and bring it to the table."

Everyone nodded their heads in agreement. Jungle was the next to speak.

"Listen y'all, I'm moving to Canarsie. My parents bought a house out there. I'm going to see what I can do out that way, until we come up with something better or we turn 18. I'm thankful for what we do have and it's thanks to King G's brain and our execution. Everyone agreed."

They all dapped and promised to link up with ideas in progress. King G stopped at LUV's apartment and got her to come out. Then they went and got Empress. He gave each of them $350. Then they went to Mama Judy house. King gave her $300 to send to Brandy $50, and for herself.

"Boy, why are you giving me all this money for my grandbaby? Thank you for the money for me" Mama Judy stated. "Mama Judy I just wanna make sure Brandy is good. I've been saving up."

Brandy hadn't come for the summer. She told LUV she wanted to be closer to 13 when she came back. Now baby, don't think Mama Judy is slow, I have been hearing how you been handling your business. Mama Judy doesn't miss nothing; but Mama Judy don't run her lips either.

"You are a real man King and still ain't nothing but a boy. You gonna make a real good husband one day." "Thank you, Mama Judy. I hope to live up to your expectations." King G said. "You will baby, you better. The way my grandbaby and them 2 pretty girls you got with you, be sniffing round you, you gonna darn well need to be! Ha-ha."

King G, LUV and Empress all laughed then wished Mama Judy a good day and left. As they were walking away; the Super came in the building with Crazy Joe right behind him.

"What's up Super, what's up Crazy Joe?" King said, they both said what's up to King G and the girls. The Super said, "nothing much. Bout to take old Crazy Joe to take a shower and feed him. Had him working round the building with me all day." Crazy Joe you still ain't got no place to stay?" asked King G. "No son, I don't, but Crazy Joe's gonna be all right. I was 17 years old in 'Nam in 1971. If that ain't killed me the streets out here sure ain't!" King G shook his head. He liked Crazy Joe!

He knew Crazy Joe wasn't crazy. The war just had him shell shocked. Joe had lots of sense and he protected the children in the neighborhood. He wouldn't let nothing happen to them. King G remembered one time a man was in the hood trying to kidnap some kids. Every time Crazy Joe saw him, he would chase him away with a machete. Joe knew what he was up to. Everyone thought Joe was crazy, till one day that same man, tried to snatch King G in front of the building. Joe almost killed that man, saving King G.

"Hey Super, you still got that empty studio apartment in the basement?" King G asked, "Yeah, King why you ask?" "Put Crazy Joe in there for a month or two. I will pay you $500, since you ain't using it no way" "You don't have to do that King. You ain't nothing but 14, where you get that kind of money?" asked Crazy Joe. "Never mind that Joe, I got it, you know my dad got money."

King G handed the Super the money, the Super just shrugged his shoulders and said:

"God bless your heart King, you sure are a different type of teenager. Looks like you got a place to stay for a couple of months Joe. C'mon let's go."

LUV and Empress looked at King G with astonishment, then LUV said:

"See that's why you deserve more than one wife. You really are a King!"

They both kissed King G on the cheek and he told them he would see them later.

King G was racking his brain trying to figure out what to do for money. He came up with a proposal, an idea for Mr. Cohen. King figured he could put two soda machines in Mr. Cohen's warehouse to make some money. Father G had four of them at his warehouse just sitting not being used. He would holla at him and then see if Mr. Cohen would agree. After talking with Father G, who agreed to give the machines to his son, King G called Mr. Cohen. He agreed to the terms. Mr. Cohen loved the fact that this young man was business minded and far from an average street punk. In two days, King's Vending Corporation was up and running. King G had gone to a wholesaler and bought enough sodas and canned juices to last three months. He asked Crazy Joe if he could fill the machines when needed. Of course, Joe agreed, after all this young man had gotten him a place to live. After 30 days King G was making a consistent $1400 a week with the two machines. They had to be refilled twice a day. He paid Joe $400 a week.

Then one day, Father G told King G he had no use for the warehouse and that it now belonged to him. Father G cleared it out and handed the keys to his son. Now King G was trying to think of a way to make money from the warehouse. The warehouse was in Canarsie not far from a police precinct, a medical facility, post office, and private houses. Instantly King G thought of turning it into a garage space. This he thought could work. He took a cab with Crazy Joe to the warehouse and when he got inside, he was able to see the whole place. Anytime he had been there before it was full of inventory. He decided he needed some paint. He went to the rooms lined along one side upstairs and downstairs to see what they could be used for. Upstairs was a break type room with a kitchen and sink and everything. Then there was another empty room next to it and then a bathroom. He instantly decided Crazy Joe would live here. The downstairs rooms were the same as upstairs, but without the kitchen and bathroom set up. In the last room there were cases and cases of canned sodas and juices. King G just smiled and secretly thanked Father G and God for giving him the best dad in the world. He told Crazy Joe; upstairs was his new apartment and that the warehouse will become a parking garage. He had Joe paint the walls, gray with a black stripe running horizontally on the wall and paint the ground full black. Joe told him legally he was ordained as a minister of his own church called Holy Church of Vietnam Vets. He said that anything under the church's name was tax exempt. King G just laughed and told Joe.

"The warehouse and vending company are going under that name and be sure to put me on the board of directors."

Now King G was set. He would do 30 cars at $150 each month 10 motorbike at $125 each month, which includes weekly washes provided by Crazy Joe. That would amount to $5750 a month. He would pay Joe $1750 a month for washing and looking over the cars. Instantly, the spots were filled. Everyone was on a year-by-year contract. Now King had a yearly plan for income. He was still going to school and getting good grades. He had Joe handle his businesses, and Joe was functioning fine. Who would have known, all Joe needed was some weed to level him out! King G had his father help him downsize the $770,000. He turned all smaller denominations into all $100 bills. He ended up with 77 stacks of $10,000 stacks; and put it back into the ground safe in his warehouse that his dad had built, nobody knew about it except him and Father G.

Chapter 4

Then in January 1995 on his 15th birthday, Mr. Velez pulled up at the school. He picked up Alvino and he asked King G to go for a ride. King G knew an opportunity when it presented itself, so he hopped in.

"King, you are a very intelligent young man and a true businessman. I respect your ability to acquire money and your ability to protect those and what you value. I am a man of many resources, but my main one is cocaina. Do you know anything about this?"

King G looks at Alvino and then Mr. Velez then says:

"Sir I know what it is. It is not something I am familiar doing business with." "It's all a numbers game King," Mr. Velez states. "It's a product you get for a number and sell for a higher number. Simple business! I have never forgotten what you did for my son. With that being said, I am willing to provide you with Kilos of pure cocaine for $10,000. Right now, you can sell for $30,000 and have people running you down for more." "I will think about it Mr. Velez and I appreciate the offer. If I do decide to take your offer, I need you to know it may not be consistent." "It's ok King. Something tells me if you do embark on this journey, you will not disappoint as the dollars are concerned. Let me drop you to your home and please get a cell phone so we can keep in touch." "Thank you, Mr. Velez, it's an honor."

As soon as King G got home, he got the crew together to see what's the updates on what they had been doing. Jungle was the only one not available. LT had an update on him. LT gave his Uncle Ernie $8,000 for the 10 pounds of weed a month. His uncle had also given him a worker fresh from Jamaica who he pays $880 a week. LT makes $2,000 a week and he will see $96,000 in a year. K9 is robbing dice games, illegal number spots and homes. He says he sees about $10,000-$20,000 a month and he is cool with that. He doesn't have to spend money to make money. Illy gave his Uncle Big C, $50,000 to invest in a construction company. He says his uncle promised him $100,000 at the one-year mark and $50,000 a year for four years. He is also gonna buy him his first car.

"My mom was getting real suspicious, so I just invested. Plus, I got a job at the construction company and my uncle pays me $500 a week for labor work; It's hard work but it keeps my mom off my back." Illy says.

LT says Jungle, (who now goes by Jungle Fever because he loves the white girls in Canarsie, and they love him.) has found a candy wholesaler. He has printed fake school candy sale catalogs. He got 5 white girls going door to door selling the candy. He requires them to make $100 a day each, which brings him $3500 a week. He says Jungle only wants to do it six months out of the year, and at this rate will make $84,000 in six months.

"Oh yeah; he only spends $2,000 a month on them and they love it" LT states.

TEC has come up with a fake basketball team donation bucket and sign in sheet. He collects $100 a day. He says at this rate he will make about $36,500 in a year. Finally Nutso says,

"I started the snow shoveling business. It's $100 a block, I got five blocks. I'm on my way to making $30,000 for 60 days work."

King lets them know; he is on course to making $96,000 in his first year with his two businesses. Everyone is happy with their individual hustles and their stash is safe.

"Sky's the limit Brothers! But we tryin to see space, and whatever we do." They all say, "we gotta get.

Cash GGC!!!"

After leaving the meeting King G stops at Empress' apartment. Miss Trish answers and says,

"Hey King G, with your cute self. Let me get Empress for you. Hey Empress, ya Boo at the door" *"Hey Boo* I miss you. You been really busy lately" Empress states." "Just trying to secure our future Boo. Where Wakeel at?" "He inside, what you want my brother for?" "I need to holla at him bout something and tell him to come here please." "I got you Boo, Wakeel!!! King G at the door for you." "What's up with you King G?" Wakeel states, "Yo, you still going upstate to get money?" King G asks. "Yeah, why? What up you trying to go with me?"

Wakeel is about 17 but looks 20 and is about his paper. He really ain't seen no big bread. He is happy with making $1000 a weekend, and then blowing half of that right away.

"Nah, I ain't trying to go. I got a whole thing for $30,000. It's raw too. If you do the right thing, there is more for you. You can get rich, but no games Bro." Wakeel smiles and says "One thing for sure King G. I ain't a game player. Plus, I know your pops. I watch you come up and I respect the hustle. Let's do it though. It will take me a few weeks. I got to put it out there, since I only been moving G packs. Let me know when you ready, Wakeel states." "Gimme two days and I will meet you back here. I got some things to take care of," King G says. "Aight bet King G, I will be ready." Wakeel walks off and Empress comes back "I love you King G." I love you too Empress G.

I gotta go, but we're gonna make time to go to the movies this weekend." "Happy Birthday my King "she kisses King G on the lips, and he spins off to go check LUV.
After knocking on LUV door, she answers and pulls him inside.

"Hey baby, Happy Birthday my King" "Thanks baby. I just stopped by Empress's house to holla at her brother bout business. We gonna go out this weekend to the movies, just us three." "Ok baby."

For the first time King G notices LUV is in her robe and it's see-through. All she has on is a panty and bra. He is instantly aroused, and LUV can tell. She grabs his hand and pulls him into her bedroom.

"You ready for your birthday present King G" "You sure you about this LUV?"

They are both virgins by choice. LUV wanted to wait till she was ready. King G was too occupied with getting money that he didn't mind waiting. Even though he had two girlfriends; it was a fact, he would lose his virginity to LUV.

"Yes, I'm sure my King."

And with that she dropped her robe and peeled off her bra and panties. King G jumped out of his clothes and then thought he should shower first. He ran to the bathroom, jumped in the shower and took a five-minute wash. When he came out LUV was just smiling.

"I wanted to be clean for my queen." "That's why I love you King G, you always make me feel special."

They laid down together kissing passionately. LUV pushed him on his back and kissed him down to his full-on erection. In her mind she was thinking, ain't no way I can suck this, and put it inside of her. When she looked at the excitement on his face, she said, fuck it! It's my Kings birthday! She began sucking on the head and licking around it, and up and down his shaft. King almost lost his mind! He never felt anything like this before. She started sucking further down, till her mouth was full. She couldn't get it; all but King G didn't care! She thought to herself, I'm going to do this every chance I get, till I can get it all. When it started feeling too good; he reversed their positions and then he began kissing and licking her virgin pussy. Her hips started bucking. After two minutes, she was screaming her way through an explosive orgasm.

"Oh my God, oh my God!"

King G grabbed himself and guided into her. She was so tight. They both wanted it so badly. She opened wider and he pushed harder; and penetration was finally achieved. He worked his way in and out of her slowly for about 10 minutes. When he couldn't hold back, he pulled out and came on her stomach. They were both happy. There was some blood, so they showered together. LUV said:

"Baby that was wonderful! I can't wait to do it again. Right now, you gotta go, before my sisters and Brother get here with my mom." King G quickly dressed, kissed her and said, "Thank you LUV G, I love you." "I love you too King G," with that King G was out of at the door.

All the way home he felt high. Suddenly, he remembered he had to call Mr. Velez. Losing his virginity was great; but even after that, he still got to go get cash! Mr. Velez had the kilo delivered that night. King G was nervous to have it in the house; but he knew it would be gone in two days. Two days later, he met up with Wakeel. He sent Empress to holla at LUV, and then commenced business with Wakeel. As soon as

Wakeel got the work, he let King know he was on his way upstate to get started.

King went to LUV's apartment; and gave each of his girls $100, to get something to wear to the movies. After the movies, he decided they needed a car. This taxi stuff wasn't working! He dropped them off and then he had the car take him to the warehouse. He entered the warehouse.

"Yo, Joe you in here?" "Yes, son where else I'm gonna be?" "Hey Joe, you got a driver's license?" "Yeah King, I sure do. I just ain't got nothing to drive." "OK, well check it, Joe I want to buy a car. You gonna drive it though and it's going to be in your name." "You got it boss!" Joe says. The only person King G knew to go to about a car, was Father G.

"Hey Father, I want to get a car and put it in Crazy Joe name and, have him be my driver. I don't like cabs. I feel as a businessman; I should have reliable and dependable transportation." "Well said son. I was just about to buy a new Chevy Tahoe. So, I tell you what; you can have the cadi. My gift to you!" "Thanks Father! That's perfect and don't worry, one day I'm going to give you a car."

All Father G could do was laugh. After Father G took care of the papers and got Crazy Joe to the DMV; King G was on the road. First ride in the car, King G went and bought five cell phones. He gave one to each of his girls, one to Joe and one to LT. He let LT know to have the rest of the GGC to buy one.

Chapter 5

Thirty days after giving Wakeel the work; he got a call from Empress:

"Hello" "Hey my King; my brother wants you to come over." "Tell him I'm on my way."

King G made it to the building. As soon as Wakeel saw him, he smiled and handed him a Bookbag with $30,000 in it!

"Yo, King G, I got shit jumping out there! That work is fire! Let's keep this going." "No problem, Bro, but is it always gonna take a month?" King G asks. "Nah Bro, I told you I had to open it up. Now that everyone knows I got it. I can probably do double in 30 days." "Aight, Wakeel while we are doing business, please don't be flashy. I like for all my business to be under the radar." King G spoke the words his father taught him proudly. "I got you King G. As long as you are helping me come up, I have got no choice but to respect it. I'm gonna take my brother Abdul with me so we can spread out. Just do me a favor; keep an eye on my little Brother, Karim and my sister Sahara while we're gone." "I got you Wakeel, we family. I'm gonna get up with you later tonight. Oh yeah, by the way get a cell phone so we can talk direct."

Wakeel nodded and King G left to call Joe to pick him up. Then he called Mr. Velez and put in an order for two. He was happy! He had made $20,000 in 30 days. Even though drugs weren't his thing; he knew numbers, and this made sense. He also knew; his days of hands, on were limited. Once he took care of Wakeel, everything was smooth sailing. Every month, as promised, Wakeel cashed out $60,000. King G sent him back on the road with two more.

Between the vending machines, the warehouse and Wakeel; King G had a lot of free time. He decided to spend more time fight training with Barkim. That extra time: got King G even sharper with his fighting and helped him pack on 15 pounds of muscle, after four months. He was now 15 years old 5'9" tall and weighed 165 pounds. He also spent a lot of time learning more life lessons from Barkim, who also introduced him to Islam. King G was really intrigued. Religion wasn't a big thing at his house. All he knew, there was a God. Throughout these lessons, King G decided to take his Shahada and become Muslim. He also talked to Barkim about wanting to marry LUV and Empress.

"That's very noble of you King to be thinking that way at 15. If you truly want to do this, when you are ready, I know a mosque where we can make this happen."

Barkim explained how it could be done and told King G to explain it to his future wives. The girls agreed. Empress helped LUV understand the religion, because her dad and older brothers were Muslim.

It was now summertime and the crew had been doing well. They were all together more often, now that school was over. Everyone had a safe stashed and was happy with their lives. They all were in the park chilling, when Empress called to say Lil Brandy was back. They immediately left to go see their adopted lil sis. When they got to the building, Brandy was in Mama Judy's house. They all just chilled in the hallway talking. Then they heard the apartment door open. Out stepped Brandy! But she wasn't so little no more. She was 5 feet even and had filled all the way out! She had on some wedge sandals, a jean skirt and a tank top. Her nails and toes were painted hot pink. Her hair was out, looking wet and curly. Everyone's mouth dropped! They couldn't believe it as she walked towards everyone smiling. They all noticed that her walk was now very sexy. She waved at everyone and walked straight to King G. She gave him a hug and said:

"Damn! Close ya mouth King G before your jaw fall off!" "Damn Lil Brandy! You done grew up a lot! You ain't so little no more" King G. stated. "You like how I've grown?" Brandy asked with so much sex appeal. King G 's head was spinning. "Damn Brandy can't nobody else get a hug?" K9 asked. "Of course, but I had to hug my future husband first." She proceeded to hug everyone. Then they all kicked back and chilled. All that was on King G's mind, was how sexy Brandy had become! The next day King G popped up at the apartment building early. He called Empress and LUV before he came and told them he was going to holla at Brandy. He knocked on Mama Judy door and she answered,

"Hey King, bet you came here looking for my grandbaby huh?" she said with a laugh. "Yes, Mama Judy I did. I got something for her." "Well, I hope it's a wedding ring! I sure hope she don't let you pass by." King G just laughed.

Mama Judy got Brandy. Brandy came to the door in some short shorts and a halter top. King G was mesmerized:

"Hey, my King. Why are you looking at me like that? You see something you like?" Brandy stated while licking her lips. "Of course; I had to, or I wouldn't be here. Why are you dressed like that though? Where are you going looking like that? "I ain't going nowhere King G. Me, LUV and Empress bout to take pics and we all got the same type outfits. We taking them for you. Boo." "Is that right? Well, who taken the pics?" Mama Judy taking them Boo," Ok. Just don't be going nowhere dressed all sexy without me. I don't need niggas looking at my future wife like that!" This put a big smile on Brandy's face. All she could say is, "Ok Daddy, you got it." "Anyway, I came by to give you a cell phone and $100. We all gonna go have a cookout at Prospect Park later. I'm gonna be thru with Joe to pick y'all up around 2." "I got something to tell you King. I'm not going back to North Carolina. I'm staying up here with Mama Judy. I'm gonna need help finding the right school and learning my way around. I'm not gonna always have y'all to be around." "Don't worry I got you Brandy." He gave her a kiss on the cheek, then a hug, which she used to press her body against his and whispered in his ear. "Thank you for the money you gave to Mama Judy for me King G. I will be 13 in December, so you can start making me earn it then."

With that, she walked away with her million dollars walk. All King G could do was shake his head.

They were all at Prospect Park, the whole GGC crew and LUV, Empress, Brandy and Princess G. Joe was doing the grilling. Everyone was spaced out on the grass. King G put a blanket down. LUV, Empress and Brandy were on it with him. They were all laughing and talking. The girls all had on tennis skirts with tight polo tops and Jordan sneakers. They were all rocking ponytails. Empress hair was almost to her lower back; LUVs was in the middle of her back, and Brandy 's was just passed her shoulders. King G felt so lucky to be surrounded by them. Princess G was dressed in some biker shorts, that came to the mid-thigh, with a matching crop top and some air max's on. She was hanging with Joe at the grill helping him cook. She loved to chef it up. The rest of the crew was hollering at females and just kicking it. K9 stares at King G and the girls and says:

"That nigga thinks he special. He thinks he can just have everybody love him and get all the girls. He thinks he's better than us" Illy hears this and says, "Bro, you're bugging. You know King G ain't like that. You sound like you jealous or something" "I ain't jealous, jealous for what? That nigga doesn't look better than me and I'm the one out here in the streets doing gangster shit. I take money and what I want, been doing that." "Yeah, you take money. King G makes it and not for himself, he do it for all of us. Ain't none of us ever thought about doing anything for the whole crew! And what you trying to say King G ain't gangsta? Cause he definitely down to fight and have our backs. Making all this money at a young age and making sure all his boys do the same is some gangsta shit! If you ask me." Yeah well, I ain't ask you nigga; but I can't argue with your points either. I still think he thinks he better. Bet if I took one of his shorty's, he wouldn't feel so special." "Man, you tripping Bro! You better not do no shit like that." Illy, stated.

The whole time TEC could hear the convo, he filed it away in his mind. He knew that if it came down to it, he would ride with King G.

As they were leaving the park, the girls were walking ahead. Bout Three dudes were trying to holla at them, but Princess G shouted:

"We good thanks though" "Well fuck y'all bitches then! We should come over there and slap y'all. You must not know who you talkin to!"

This pissed Princess G off:

"Try it then nigga! We will never be half the bitch ya mother and daddy made."

King G and the crew started running towards the girls as the dudes stepped up to Princess G.

"What you said bitch!"

But talk time was over! Princes G stepped back, and front kicked the first dude in his hip. Which put him on his ass and all the girls began stomping him. King G and the crew got there just in time to start the whoopin on his homies. King G ran up on the biggest dude and punched him in the throat. Then reached down, grabbed his ankles, and flipped him upside down. Before his head could hit the floor, he punts kicked him to sleep. LT kicked the next dude in the shin; and as he fell forward, he uppercut him and knocked him out. TEC and Nutso hit each of their opponents with a vicious six-piece combo that consisted of two jabs, an overhand left, two hooks and an uppercut. This left the opposition sprawled out on the street. K9 spit two razors out of his mouth and cut the man closest to him across the face. He tried to runoff and was leveled by a spinning flying roundhouse from Illy. The last guy was not trying to fight these young scrappers, so he pulled out at 380 and shot it in the air. Everyone froze! King G try to defuse it:

"You got it my nigga! It ain't even that serious. Let's me and you work this out."

As the gunmen focused on King G; he never saw Joe walking up behind him. King G had peeped it though:

"Fuck all that working it out. You see what y'all did to my homies? Nigga this Hoody Lyfe y'all fuckin with. I should smoke your bit..."

That was all he got out; before Crazy Joe gave him a vicious elbow to the temple, that crumbled him to the ground.

"Let's go y'all" was all Joe said.

He loaded the girls in the car along with Jungle and K9. The rest of the crew hopped in a $1 cab back to the hood.

King G had swiped the 380 off the ground before they left. As they rode back, he thought about how to get them some guns. Crazy Joe stopped in front of the building and the kids all exited. The girls were all excited by how it all went down. Everyone thanked Joe. As the girls were going in the building, K9 pulled LUV aside, and said:

"Y'all handled yourselves well. If anything, ever happens to King G or he messes up, just know that you got me." This drew a look of disgust from LUV who said, "All I need to have me, is King G! So, try that with one of them other chicken heads." "I ain't mean nothing by it, LUV. I was just saying I got you." "Mmm hmm whateva" was the only reply LUV gave as she went in the building.

The rest of the crew made it to the building, excitedly talking bout the episode that just went down. King G wasn't feeling it.

"One of us could have died back there y'all, we did our thing in that fight. We need guns just in case of situations like that. I got some homework to do. I'm out!"

As King G walked off, they knew something had changed. Of course, it only took King G two days to put together an artillery which Mr. Velez helped him acquire. He was now looking at a Bookbag with seven Taurus .380s, 2 TEC 22s, and 1 sawed off. He had 200 rounds of assorted ammo, for all the guns he had. He called the crew, and they met up at the building. He gave everyone their personal 380's and put the other guns at the warehouse. The rest of summer was uneventful. Money was still rolling in, but there was no drama.

King G decided to pay the tuition for Brandy to go to school with him and Princess G. It went from 6th through 12th grade. It cost him $12,000. It was ok to have Brandy safe. He gave LUV, Empress and Brandy $2000 a piece to go school shopping. He let LUV and Empress know next year Brandy would be in the school with them, since this was her last year of junior high. Empress was a freshman and LUV and King G were sophomores. Of course, King G let it be known Brandy was off-limits at school, so the boys left her alone. All she wanted was King G anyway, so it didn't matter.

King G was still having as much sex with LUV as he could. One day after a sex session in King G's house LUV began to speak:

"King, I love you so much and I'm still ok with you having Empress and soon Brandy too. I can tell by how you look at her you want her. I know they love you and will do anything and everything for you; like I will. We all feel safe and cared for by you; but Empress is feeling some type of way, that she doesn't get to have sex with you too. She would have said something to you herself; but I told her it would be better if I spoke to you. Do you not want to have sex with her? Brandy knows we have sex too. She hasn't said anything because she isn't your girl, but she may feel some way when she becomes yours." "Well LUV, I haven't even thought about it I have been enjoying you and focusing on all our future's. I figured she would let me know when she was ready, the way you did. I will talk to her about it. As for Brandy, I figure we will cross that road when it's time. The deen got me treading lightly too! Even though I know, if y'all are gonna be my wives, we aren't exactly old enough to get married on our own. As soon as we are it's on! Now let's make love one more time before I get you home" and that's just what they did.

Chapter 6

It was now November 27, 1995, Empress was turning. 14. King G had given Miss Trish money to take Empress to get her nails and hair done; then to Macy's to get her a DKNY outfit with the shoes to match. Mama G always told him to treat the woman you love like she is the world, and that's what he did. While Miss Trish and Empress were out, King G, Kareem, Sahara and LUV cleaned the house and decorated it for the surprise party. They had about 100 chicken wings, 12 large pizza pies, and an assortment of drinks. He had a cake 3' x 2' with Empress face on it, wearing a crown with a G on it. The whole GGC arrived and two of Empress' and LUV friends from school. Miss Trish called King G's phone to let him know they were on their way. He called Brandy and Princess G to wait in front of the building for Empress. As Empress got out of the cab, Princess G and Brandy said,

"Happy Birthday, Birthday girl!"

Empress was absolutely beautiful in her DKNY dress and shoes. Her hair was bone straight into her lower back and her nails were French tip:

"Girl, you look So fly" said Princess "Yes Empress you need to be on somebody's runway!" said Brandy. "Thank y'all, but let's go inside.

Miss Trish started to open the door then told Empress go ahead and she would be in in a sec. As soon as she stepped in, everyone yelled:

"Surprise!"

Empress was overwhelmed. She cried happy tears. She hugged everyone and thanked everybody. Miss Trish was happy to see her daughter happy. She looked at King G and mouthed thank you. He nodded. Empress knew this was all King G's doing and thanked him. She kissed his lips in front of everyone, with no shame.

After the party was over King G told Empress to get her brand-new fur coat on, so they could go to the movies. They departed telling everyone bye. Crazy Joe was outside waiting and drove them to the warehouse, where one of the bottom rooms were set up with candles on a small dining table. There was a full-size bed in one corner and two place settings at the table. King G went upstairs and came back with two pots: one with oxtail and the other with rice and peas. He served Empress and they ate. When they were done, she said:

"Thank you so much Boo, this has been the best birthday ever! Only one thing could make it better…" "and what's that Boo?" "If you would take my body and make me a woman."

King G didn't hesitate. He removed her clothes slowly, then let her remove his. He laid her on the bed and proceeded to make her a woman. When they were done Empress said:

"That was as good as I thought it would be. I can't wait to do it some more" which made King G laugh, "I got you baby. That was just as good as I thought it would be too. Your body feels so perfect against mine. Let's get back to your house before it gets late."

They dressed, kissed and Crazy Joe got them back to the building. King G walked her to her apartment. When they came in Miss Trish, LUV, Brandy, Princess G, Sahara, and Kareem were all in the living room. Everyone could tell it was something different bout Empress now. All Miss Trish could think is my baby is all grown-up. She was just happy Empress had such a good young man like King G to do right by her.

Two weeks later, on December 12, it was Brandy's birthday. She was turning 13. King G had just left the jewelry store getting her, her Brandy G chain. Crazy Joe drove him to the building. He called Brandy's phone, and she came outside. She had told him she wanted to go shopping for her birthday outfit with him on her birthday and go to the movies. She didn't want a party or nothing. They went to Macy's where she picked out a DKNY knitted sweater with some DKNY Leggings, DKNY sneakers and a DKNY down coat. She put the outfit on right in the store! King G gave her the chain. She jumped for joy and kissed King G shoving her tongue in his mouth in the middle of the mall.

"Thank you so much Daddy! This was the best part of my birthday; now I'm your girlfriend. I don't need nothing else!" "Well, we still got a movie to catch Brandy G." "I changed my mind King G, baby I just wanna chill with you. Give the movie tickets to Crazy Joe. He can take Mama Judy to see it." "Ok baby let's go then." was all King G said. Crazy Joe dropped them off at the building and invited Mama Judy out. After waiting a while, she finally came outside.

"I know y'all kids ain't playing matchmaker. Are y'all?" "Lol, no Mama Judy, just thought it would be nice to get you out of the house." King G stated. "Well ok baby. Y'all stay out of trouble now" "yes Ma'am" was both their reply. They went into Brandy's home and watched TV, kicked it, cracked jokes and bonded. Brandy was a lot more mature than King G expected. She had dreams of being successful. She let King G know she was gonna play her part as a queen and not leave all the work to him. King G dug that and at that moment, he realized he was in love with Brandy too and told her so.

"Brandy G, I love you for real. You stuck with me, like how I stuck with you." "I love you too Daddy. Now come give your Lil mama some sugar!" "Ha-ha you something else but I got you." As they kissed, it started to get intense. Brandy let him know that she was ready for sex. "Are you sure baby? You just turned 13" "I got to tell you something King G; I'm not a virgin."

This instantly pissed King G off and Brandy could see it.

"Please, let me explain. My Dad had a friend, I called him Uncle Marc. Before summer, he took advantage of me and raped me. I told my parents and my dad said I was lying and was too hot in the ass. They didn't believe me. I was so pissed, so before I left to come here, I told Mama Judy. When she picked me up, we went to Marc's trailer, and I set it on fire. Mama Judy told my parents she was keeping me. That's why I moved here."

By now tears filled Brandy's eyes.

"I promise; one day I'm going to do something to dat bitch nigga and let you watch for what he did to you." "Ok Daddy. I didn't get to choose my first time, but I'm choosing you now, to make it right and be my first choice!" All King G could do was give her what she wanted.

Chapter 7

It was January 3rd, 1996, King G 's 16th birthday! Wakeel had called him to bring him his money and to talk. King G had him meet at the warehouse.

"That's $60,000 cash Bro" Wakeel said, "Look it's been a year since we started. I done Brought for you $690,000. I'm all the way up. I bought two houses upstate for me and my mother and siblings. I got a car and a stash I never could have imagined! I'm ready to up the score." "What you got in mind?" King G asked. "I wanna get like 20 a month I will pay you for 10 upfront and you front me. 10 After I move 100 of them, I'm out. I'm trying to chill and do real estate." "Ok Bro, give me about a week to get everything together and I will get at you." "Aight bet, As Salaam Alaikum," "Walaikum Salaam."

Immediately King G called Mr. Velez for a meeting. Mr. Velez told him to meet at Marine Park in an hour. Crazy Joe got him there in 45 minutes. As Mr. Velez entered the park, he spotted King G walking around the track. He strolled up next to him and says,

"You never disappoint King. You're never late and your money is never short! What can I do for you today?" "I have a need for a specific number, that I was hoping you could fulfill." "What is that number my friend?" "100!" "Ah, so you have entered the big leagues I see. I knew I was right about you." "This may be the only order for a while Mr. Velez I cannot promise to keep this date up monthly or even yearly." "It's ok King. If you don't mind me asking, are you sure you can handle that much?" "Absolutely Señor Velez" "Ok mi amigo, since you're getting so much at one time I will give you a discount, the total price will be $770,000." "I have the cash on hand. Do you think we can do an exchange at one location?" Sure, send me the info and I will have Alvino come see you in my limo with everything" "Gracias Señor Velez" "De nada King."

Three days later, King G was $770,000 poorer but 100 Kilos richer. Alvino met him at the warehouse, and he had made the exchange. He then stacked the bricks in empty boxes and took 20 to Wakeel. He let Wakeel get them at $20,000 a piece, which he was so happy to hear. He gave King G $200,000, shook hands and they departed. Three days had passed since his birthday, and he hadn't celebrated. But he was fine with that. This last move would put him at $2,000,000! He would put that all in the stash for the crew. They would be surprised he had done this for them.

That weekend the girls wanted to celebrate his birthday. So, he gave the super $300, for a vacant apartment for the weekend. Paid $500 for a King-sized bed and bought about 20 $10 plastic chairs for people to sit in. LT also put his futon in the apartment. The whole GGC crew came through and blessed him with gifts. They knew he loved Polo; So, everyone got a Polo shirt. Mama LUV cooked Bully beef and rice with sautéed carrots and cabbage mixed in and some fry bake and Chicken Vienna sautéed with onions and tomatoes. That's all King G wanted to eat. Mama G also made a pot of Hominy Corn Porridge. They played music, danced and had a good time. Of course, everyone's parents could stop by and check any time, but Mama Judy and Mama LUV assured them they would keep an eye out. Sunday morning LUV, Empress and Brandy came to the apartment and found King G in the shower. They all got naked and laid across the King size bed. When King G came out, he was surprised to see them all there in their glory, but he didn't hesitate. Each one gave him a birthday to remember; one at a time, while the others just watched, until they were all too tired to move!

It was now March; King G had made all the stash money back plus, some. Wakeel was a man of his word; they were now 60 Kilos in, with only 40 to go. $2,000,000 would be achieved in five months. King G still wasn't touching the vending machine or warehouse money. He had $690,000 put up from his year run with Wakeel and another $96,000 off the warehouse and vending machines. Not to mention, about $60,000 from the business ventures with Father G. He was basically a millionaire! Mama G and Father G, still did their jobs as parents, taking care of him.

The whole GGC was actively profitable. They were so busy they hardly would see each other. They knew once high school was over, they would be full-time on a money mission together. King decided he would study hard and test so he could skip a grade. He wanted out of High School immediately! It was too much money to be made. He talked to LUV, Empress and Brandy and told them to do the same. He told them that for every grade they skipped, he would give them $10,000.

"Listen y'all, if we do this, we can all be on our own. We can be living a life our parents will like and respect our drive and support our decisions. I'm trying to get us a house and start our own life." King stated seriously to them. Brandy was the first to jump up, "I'm on it baby, the school stuff easy! I see your vision. You know if you lead, we gonna follow. After freshman year in high school, I'm going straight to the 11th grade. So have dat bread ready!" she stated laughing. "But serious, nonetheless, after 10th grade, I'm going straight to senior class!" Empress said empathetically. "Well, my King; whatever you on, we on! So, I guess me and you graduating a year early, which is fine by me" stated LUV.

Chapter 8

It was already May 23, 1996, LUV's birthday. King G was on a high. Just yesterday Wakeel dropped the last of the money off. This helped King G to achieve $2 million in the stash. 20,000, $100 bills neatly packed in his safe. He had Crazy Joe rent a limo for the day. He bought a Ralph Lauren suit, and had it tailored to fit. He got LUV a DKNY gown tailored to her measurements, which he got from Mama LUV, with some shoes to match. He had Mama G, Princess G, Empress and Brandy, decorate the diner in LUV's favorite colors blue and purple. Mama LUV cooked Curry lamb chops, sweet plantain, white rice and dumplings. This day would be perfect. Princess G took LUV her dress and helped her get ready. When the limo arrived, outside the building, King G went in to pick up his date. Brandy and Empress were in the hallway with baskets of rose petals. He smiled at them, then knocked on the door. When LUV opened the door, she was staring, and she thought her King was dapper. He held her hand, kissed her and said:

"Happy Birthday, my LUV"

As they walked out Empress and Brandy threw rose petals at her feet. She smiled and winked at them. They were genuinely happy for her. She was happy they were there to share the moment.

The sight of the limo had LUV feeling on cloud nine. They got in and drove off. When they got to the Diner, King G walked her. She was taken aback by how beautiful everything was! There were candles everywhere. A dozen roses was in the center of the table, with her name on it. They were seated at the table. Mama LUV served them their meal. She kissed LUV on the cheek, then kissed King G and left out. King G and LUV enjoyed their meal. Mama G came out with a bucket of ice with ginger beer and sorrel in it.

"King G you thought of everything" LUV stated. "I tried my LUV; this is your special day."
King then extended his hand and asked for a dance. As she stood up, the sweet sound of Soca music began to play. LUV laughed and they began to dance. After they were done, they jumped in the limo and drove to downtown Brooklyn and parked under the Brooklyn Bridge. King G gave the driver $100 to give them some privacy for an hour. He walked off. Behind the tint, King G and LUV had a private viewing of the water and the city lights. They made love to end the night. King G got LUV home safely. He walked her to her door and kissed her good night. As she entered her home, her mother was smiling with tears in her eyes.

"Why are you crying ma?" "I'm just happy for you baby, you look so beautiful. You are lucky to have a young man that cares for you the way he does. You two better get married" "We will ma, you can trust that!" "There is something waiting for you in your room."

LUV ran to her room and opened the door. There she found 120 roses and a big card that said to a King's LUV. All she could do was smile. She knew more than ever she chose right.

Since money was coming in steady; all King did was study, train, workout and plan for the future. He challenged the GGC to complete school early. Almost everyone said they would give it a try, but K9 wasn't with it. He said he was dropping out. He had too much money to worry bout school. King G didn't even bother trying to convince him of anything else.

Summer hit but King G didn't lose focus; him, the girls and Princess G attended summer school. By August they were ready to be tested but had to wait till September, when school started. K9 got locked up the end of August for a robbery attempt. He didn't want a lawyer because he was caught in the act. The crew all paid for one. He got a deal for two years juvenile which he was lucky to get.

School started and LUV and King G were promoted to seniors. LUV got her $10,000. Birthdays came around again and King and the girls did as usual and celebrated. March 1997 LUV, Empress, Brandy and King G were in Time Square, when they spotted TEC.

"Yo TEC what's getting Bro?" King G stated. "Cash Bro" TEC replied. "What you doing out here?" asked King G.

"Just working my donation hustle. You see that kid over there with down syndrome? That's my Lil homie Mikey but I call him Magnet cause he's a money magnet! I'm doing the same scam like the basketball team, but now it's for college tuition for kids with mental retardation. I'm seeing like $100K a year. I slide magnet $20K and we good." "You something else Bro" King says laughing "Magnet my homie for real tho. I hold him down. Plus, I teach him how to fight and dress and make sure he's good" "That's what's up Bro. We out tho! Keep getting money like a cash register" "U already know King G. Later Lady G's." That's what the girls were known as now and they loved it. King G and the girls went to eat, and LUV dropped a bomb, "I think I'm pregnant y'all" "For real?!"
Brandy and Empress said clearly excited. King G was smiling so hard. LUV said:

"Say something baby" "After we eat this food you gonna get tested. If you are, we gonna celebrate!" "You mean you want me to have the baby?" "What you think my LUV. Allah don't make no mistakes, of course I want our baby" "Not to interrupt this moment, but I got something to say too. My mom is ready to move upstate. Wakeel finished fixing the house for her. She is taking Sahara and Kareem. She wants me to go, but I don't want to. She says if I don't have nowhere to stay, I gotta go" Empress stated sadly. King stated. "Nah we gonna figure something out I'm gonna holla at Miss Trish. Let's go get this test done and get back to the hood."

Sure, enough LUV was pregnant. They got Mama G, Father G and Mama LUV altogether and explained the situation. King G and LUV decided they should also know about their arrangement with Brandy and Empress. After a thorough explanation, Mama LUV and Mama G said:

"So ya'll girls are having sex with each other too?" "No way Ma and Mama G! I ain't got nothing against nobody who do that, but that ain't for us. We all gonna marry King G when we old enough or have parental permission. We gonna do it at the Mosque. King already got it pre-planned for when the time come." "Well, if anything, y'all are quite thorough and have thought this out" Mama LUV states! "Don't worry Mama LUV, I have enough money to take care of the baby and my wives. I have saved up and invested well." "What you got boy a couple thousand and you think you're rich?" Mama LUV asked. "Actually, Mama LUV I'm a millionaire. The only reason I'm telling you this is because 1. I respect you and 2. your daughter is pregnant for me." Mama LUV jaw is just hanging open she looks at Father G and Mama G and says "Did this boy just say he is a millionaire? He ain't but 17" "He has been making his own money since he was 12, Mama LUV. We teach our children to be business minded at an early age" says Father G. "Well, I know all yuh is responsible and you in your last year of school, which you accomplished early so you have my blessing." "And ours too" Father G and Mama G say together.

Father G excused himself and King G, "So son why didn't you tell me you were a millionaire. You've been busy since we last spoke" "Father I was just doing what you said and finding my own way" "Well son I'm proud of you and I know you have what it takes. When you turn 18, me and your mom are retiring and turning everything over to you and your sister. Your mother is training her. You will need to work together with your sister, to be at your best!" "Ok Father. Could you tell Mama G to also teach LUV, Empress and Brandy, please? They will be a part of this family, Son. I trust your judgment if that's what you want, then so shall it be" "Thanks Father" Quick tip son; start cash businesses, so you can run your stash through the business." "Got you father. One more thing, Miss Trish is moving upstate and wants to take Empress. Empress doesn't wanna go. Miss Trish says if she doesn't find somewhere to stay, she has to move. I was thinking of asking Mama Judy to keep her and I will pay her rent for a year. Once I graduate in June, I'm trying to buy a house for me and the girls and the baby." "Well son you gotta man up and holla at Mama Judy. So, let's go see Mama Judy and see if she will agree."

After getting Mama Judy on board, Empress was finally able to stay. Only stipulation Mama Judy had was, King G had to promise to take care of Brandy, marry her and treat the girls right. Which wouldn't be a problem. King G and LUV graduated with honors. Brandy and Empress attended summer day school and summer night school to gain more credits. LUV wasn't allowed to do much. King G babied her all summer not letting her lift a finger. It upset her but she knew he meant well, and Mama LUV loved it. Meanwhile, King G made sure the whole GGC dropped $2000 apiece on K9's books. He would be good, and they also sent him packages. He stayed straight! Illy and Princess G started dating, which made King G happy. He knew Illy was a good person and smart. They would go far together.

School was back in; Empress went straight to her senior year! The big surprise was Brandy, who was basically a senior too. All she had to do was night school throughout the school year and she would have the credits to graduate. King G gave them each $10,000 with a promise to give Brandy another $10K if she indeed graduated with Empress.

October 1997, King G bought a home in Long Island for $250K cash. Of course, Father G 's name was on all the papers, but it belonged to King G and his girls. It had four bedrooms, a completed basement and an attic. He spent another $50K decorating it. LUV gave birth to their son Royal on November 6, 1997, he weighed exactly 8 pounds.

Life was good! June 1998, Empress and Brandy graduated. Empress was 16 and Brandy was 15. It was a good day. King G gave Brandy a Louis V bag and $10K in it and Empress a Gucci bag. Mama Judy and Miss Trish were so proud. They all rode out in a limo back to the house in Long Island. Phase 1 complete.

Chapter 9

King G was proud of everyone's accomplishments. Now, it was time to start the next phase of life. He needed to marry his girls and go full throttle on getting cash and having his whole crew on the same path to success. One day LT called King G inquiring about some business, so they met up at the building.

"What's getting LT?" "Dat cash Bro, you already know. Look my uncle trying to get his hands on that thing your boy Alvino people got." "Oh, yeah well, I can see what I can do. What he tryin to get?" "He said he got $60K he trying to get two. He says everyone else got trash and I told him I might know where something good was" "Aight Bro, let me see what I can do; I will holla at you later. "Crash or get Cash," "Crash or get Cash Bro," LT replied before they departed. King G was about to call Alvino when Wakeel rang his line.

"As Salaam" Alaikum Wak" "Walaikum Salaam King G. Listen, I know I told you I was chilling from messing with them chicks, but my people say they asking for me. I wanted to see if you wanted to maybe check the shorty's out." "What them Broads talking bout Bro?" "My man say they keep it a hunnid around his way. I should be down your way this weekend and you could ride with me to see if you like any of them." "Aight Bro just call when you get here." As Salaam Alaikum" "Walaikum Salaam."

Wakeel hadn't called bout no girls. He was letting King G know it was some business on the work and he could make $100K off one but would have to do it himself. He knew Wakeel wasn't on bullshit, so he thought it through and came up with a plan. He called Alvino who he told to meet him at the building. Once Alvino arrived, he broke everything down to him:

"Listen Vino I got a play for $60K, I'm gonna give you all that! I don't want nothing off that. Since you charging me $10K for each, just take the $60K off the two brick sale and give me four more for me. The deal is with my Bro LT's Uncle. He good peeps. Y'all can link and keep it going. I don't need to be in the middle and trust, Bro, he about his cash!" "Ok King G, you know I trust you, that ain't no problem. Plus, that will show Dad I'm able to handle business. I will have that to you in a couple hours. Meet you at the warehouse?" "Yeah Bro."

Later, at the warehouse, Alvino gave King G six keys. Uncle Ernie pulled up, handed the money over, and King G slid him two keys and did the introduction between Alvino and Uncle Ernie. He was done with that part of the business, so they all departed. That weekend, Wakeel let him know Vermont was where the business was at! He had a greyhound bus driver who would take the work up there, while King G flew into town. He wanted King G to meet his homie P-Nut. He felt King G needed someone like him. He was dependable to get cash and as a shooter, if necessary. The driver required $5000 for the move; he was only that cheap because he was love struck by Miss Trish.

"Listen Wak, I got four of them things. Is that cool?" "Yeah Bro it's whatever. P-Nut the one with the spot but he's gonna let you do your thing. Just look out" "I got him Bro. Don't worry, if I like his vibe, he gonna definitely be good!" King G let the girls know he was going to be away for a couple of weeks. He had Mama Judy come stay at the house and Crazy Joe was on call if they needed to go anywhere. Arriving in Vermont, King G was picked up by P-Nut who was driven by an older white man in a taxi.

"What's up King G?" nice to finally meet you Wakeel told me a lot about you, says you're the reason for his success." King G looked at P-Nut and nodded towards the white man suspiciously "oh don't worry about Fred, he works for me. This ain't even a real taxi. I had Fred start a taxi service just so he could drive me around. He does little jobs here and there, but he is my driver. He knows everyone in town. They think I'm his worker" he says with a laugh. "Oh, ok P-Nut. I see you got your ducks in a row. I like that! We got a few hours before we gotta make dat pick up so let's go get some food and chop it up." They went to a local pizzeria and ate and chopped it up."

King G dug P-Nuts vibe. After they met the bus driver and paid him, they went straight to the trap. From the door, P-Nut told him, they would only sell grams for $100 each.

From the first sale they were booming nonstop. In five days, they had sold a whole brick. The people were loving it. The work was so pure, they could double the gram and make their money back and still get high. Once the word got out, hustlers started to want to cop. Four days later, they had run through another brick! King G was ready to go home. He had $200K in a bag and two bricks left. While they hustled King G decided to put P-Nut down with the crew. Every business needed to expand, and he could tell P-Nut was the real deal.

"Yo P, I'm about to bounce. I gotta get back home to the fam. I'm gonna take this money and leave you the other two bricks. Dat's all you" "You serious King G? that's gonna bring another $200K" "I know Bro. Welcome to GGC, Bro" King G said proudly. "Yo King G, I promise you I'm gonna show you what loyalty in real money getting looks like." He gave King G dap. "Now I need to get this money changed to $100 bills" They counted out all the hundred-dollar bills and he came up to 500 of them. They still need to change $150K. "Let me call Fred, he knows all the bankers and rich guys around here." P-Nut said.

After 3 hours of ripping and running, they had changed all the money. King G now had 2,000 $100 bills. Standing at 6 feet tall, weighing 240 pounds of solid muscle, King G was a big guy. He decided to duct tape the money around his legs. He wrapped the money in plastic after separating them into $10K stacks and taped them to his legs. He put on some baggy jeans and wore a simple wife beater.

"Aight P-Nut I'm out, holla at me when you're done. Crash or Get cash, Crash or Get cash King."
After Fred dropped King G at the airport; he got a ticket and made it through security, with no problem.
Back at home and riding in the car with Crazy Joe, King G told Joe:

"It's time I get a whip Joe." "You already got this Cadi, King G." "Nah, this is your car Joe. I need something for me and my family. I think I'm gonna get me a Chevy Astro Van. Let's go to the dealership in Long Island." "You got it King G."
At the dealership King G picked out a Charcoal Gray 97 Astro van with gray cloth interior. He decided to finance it to build his credit up. He put 9K down, his payments were $120 a month, total price of the van was $19K. He went and bought a system and tint for the car, which he would have Crazy Joe put in, he was a beast at anything to do with a vehicle. Next was a rim shop. He bought some Titanium Gun Metal 17" BBS rims and new suspension, that also lowered the van. He put in an order for a body kit as well. King G would drop $5K at the shop. The kit will be in the next week. They would mold it to the van and paint it. King wanted everything done at one

time. He would have the rims and suspension done before he left. He spotted a GT steering wheel, which was all wood, and told them to add that in too! Next, he went to a jewelry store and purchased 3 1-carat princess cut diamond solitaire engagement rings, that ran him $4,500. Back at the house, him and Joe pulled into the driveway and hopped out.

"Hey Joe, please hook the system up for me and do the tint. I got you when you're done" "Please King G, you don't owe me nothing. I will do that out of love. You forgot; you got me off the street, gave me a place to call home, two jobs that make me $100K a year and you just gave me your Cadi. I ain't no charity case son, let me work for some of these blessings." King G laughed "You got it Joe."
LUV, Brandy and Empress all ran outside to greet King G hugging and kissing him.

"We missed you, my King" LUV was the first to say, "yeah Daddy we sure happy you back" came from Brandy next. "Who you were showing all your muscles off for, huh?" Empress said with her hand on her hips which made everyone else laugh. "Well King!" Empress said impatiently. "Girl, you know Daddy ain't crazy stupid," "Brandy was quick to say. "Man, Empress, you know I ain't checking for no other females! I got the best wives in the world. Now where my son at?" "He in there with Mama Judy" LUV said.
King G ran inside to see his son. He picked him up and hugged and kissed him. He was 8 months old and crawling around and

trying to walk already. Mama LUV would always say he was hurrying up for the next one.

"Damn can Mama Judy get some love" "My bad Mama Judy."

King G hugged her and gave her a kiss. He put Royal down then turnt to everyone:

"I'm glad y'all here, I have something I want to say." King G walked up to LUV, Empress and Brandy and sat them down on the couch.

"I will be right back" he said leaving everyone looking confused.

He went outside and came back with Crazy Joe. King G had his hands behind his back. When he was back in front of the girls, He got on one knee and presented 3 open ring boxes and said,

"Will y'all do me the honor in making me your husband for eternity?!" they all screamed "Yes!!!" at the same time and started to cry.

Mama Judy was so impressed by this young man. Even though she couldn't imagine sharing a man she had to admit these youngins made it work and look good! King G slid the rings on their fingers and kissed them all passionately.

"I guess congratulations are in order" Mama Judy said. "Congratulations y'all" Crazy Joe said. "Thank you both from all of us" King G stated. Then King G took them all outside to show them the van they clearly missed when he pulled up." This is our vehicle. I didn't want nothing too flashy. It can fit all of us in it." "Ok, Daddy that's fine but when we getting married?" Leave it to Brandy to get straight to it. "How bout this week? We can have 3 separate marriages and then one big party, ya'll with that? King G asked. They all agreed.

They all went out to the mall in the Cadi, while Joe worked on the van. They went to an African shop in the mall, where King G, picked out a Dashiki with a matching Khufi and 3 long-sleeved floor-length Dashiki dresses with matching scarves. He bought them all some black air Force ones. After, Barkim arranged everything at the mosque. The Imam talked with King G and everyone's parents. King G and the girls were married that week! Only one set of legal marriage papers were filled out between King G and LUV, which was only for tax purposes and the government. All the marriages, under Allah's eyes, were what was most important, to all of them. The party went well. Everyone attended and was happy. LUV's younger siblings, Adore who is 9, the twins Amor and Amore' who are 8 and Desiree who is 7, were the spark of the party, as they showed everyone all the latest dances.

"Yo, King G, I can't believe you really married all of them girls. You something like a pimp!" said LT. "Nah Bro; I'm a man, who values my queens. That's all" I respect it Bro, you know I was just kidding, I'm happy for you though. I'm too young to bust dat move I got too many girls running me down." "Yo King G, can I holla at you?" Illy says. "What's up Bro?" "I wanna propose to Princess G, but I want your blessing." "Of course, Bro." "Thank you, King, I'm not gonna do it now, I want it to be private"

The night ended happily, and King G went home with his wives.

A week later King G dropped off the van and jumped in the Cadi with Joe.

His phone rang, "What's getting P-Nut?" "Cash King G straight cash, I need to see you Bro" "Ok Bro just make sure when you come, get my $40." "Of course, Bro. I got it in my pocket. I should be through there tomorrow" "See you then Bro. Crash or get Cash" "Crash or get Cash." King hung up and immediately called Vino, "Yo Bro, you think you can get me 4 strippers to party with me?" "Of course, mi amigo, got some fine ones too" "ok, meet me tomorrow at noon, so we can do lunch" "Got you hermano" "Peace Bro."

The next day P-Nut showed up with the $40K and King G gave him 4 keys:

"Just kick me bac $50K P-Nut and we good" "Nah Bro, I got $100K in a shoe box in the truck for you I'm bout to turn this 4 into 6 keys. I told you I'm gonna show you real cash getting and loyalty."

P-Nut went to the car and popped the trunk and handed King G the shoe box.

"Say less P-Nut and from now on it will be dropped directly to you. No use in taking risks. You will have to pay $20K more on your end for delivery. It will be at the Mexican restaurant in Rutland" "Got it King G. Let me get outta here. I will holla at you when I'm ready. Fred's niece will be flying out to meet you with your money. She is a flight attendant." "Aight Bro, that will work. "Crash or get Cash" "Crash or get Cash."

King G walked back in the warehouse and Vino was upstairs in the kitchen.

"So that's your new cash cow hermano?" "Nah, that's my new GGC money earner. Just make sure you stack up your people in Rutland. Dat boy game be ready for every 10 days!" "That's what I like to hear. Old tio Ernie, done seen me 3 times since that first meeting. He just spent $90K with me three days ago. when he gets to copping 4 consistently; I'm going to drop the price to $25K for him. He has a large need for bud, that I can fill. I will be cheaper than his old connect and better quality, I have you to thank for this." It's all good, Vino, this is what we do. We gotta get cash or nothing else. I need to go get my whip. Let's Bounce."

Chapter 10

King G was driving in his Astro and loving the way it looked and rode. He stopped at the crib to get the girls when he got out Joe told him:

"You need to let me put bigger headers in that engine and air intake kit and wider dual piping under there and put silencers in the muffler. She will really ride correct" "Aight, Joe if you think that's what it need go ahead. For now, I'm headed to Brooklyn to take the girls and Royal to see Mama G."

His wives and son came out and loaded up in the van and they pushed out.

At the same time, upstate at the nearest juvenile facility, K9 was talking to a dude named Chip from Flatbush (who is from Foster Avenue) and Gauge (a dude from uptown in the Bronx.)

"Yeah, my nigga, I'm telling you, I got a crew I run called GGC. We getting mad paper! Why you think my Books so stacked up and I'm getting all these packages? Them niggas know to pay the big homie homage" "Oh yeah, K9. So how can we get down?" asks Chip "Man, trust me, once we get home next year you in. I'm gonna introduce you to all my crew and tell them y'all in. If ya'll really get money ya'll good" "Man K9 I told you I can lock down the weed in my hood" Chip says. "That dope game jumpin for me in the X.

Every one of the fiends know Gauge. My moms are with a big-time hustler out there." "Ok nuff said, when we get home it's on. I got one homie, named King G, thinking he is running the show. I just let him think that! He really my lil man. But he good with numbers." "It don't matter to us, we know you really the top dog K9," Chip says sounding like a true dick rider.

King G and his family stepped in Mama G crib:

"Mama G, where you at?" "Me deya inah di kitchen King" "Hey Mama G" the Lady Gs says simultaneously "Hey my daughter in laws. Where is my handsome grandson?" Mama G snatches up Royal and kisses him all over." Mama, I know the time is coming for us to take over. I want you to know the girls dem ready to focus all the way in and learn everything" "You late King; whole time you was away, me and yuh sister did teach dem nuff tings," King G looked surprised "well nobody told me this" " well I told the ladies, we don't mingle inah big mon business and big mon shouldn't inah big womon business neither!" Everyone bust out laughing "Seriously tho Daddy, we wanted to surprise you, and show you how ready we really are" Brandy announced. "Alright well check it out, Mama says Princess soon graduate. Me and the girls are going on a lil vacation/homecoming down south for two weeks. When time we get back, we movin full speed ahead." "Alright son be careful out there on di road.

Who keeping my grandson?" Well, you and Mama LUV can share dat Mama" says King G. "Alright den son."
They enjoyed the rest of the day with Mama G then headed back home.

The next morning: King G woke up in his California King size bed, with all his wives next to him and Royal in his crib. He headed to the kitchen and found a note on the table next to the Cadi's keys from Joe; letting him know he took the van to work on it. King G decided to cook breakfast for his wives. He made waffles, turkey sausage, scrambled eggs and honey ginger tea. He piled it all on a tray in 4 plates and a thermos for the tea and went to his bedroom.

"Wake up sleepyheads.' Breakfast is served!" The Lady G's got up "Aww you so sweet my King, Thank you Daddy, with yo fine ass. You sure know how to make a girl feel like an Empress for real" As they were all eating; King G's phone went off, "what's getting P-Nut?" "Dat cash King G! I wasn't expecting to hear from you so soon Bro" "I already kno, listen I had a one-night stand with a fire broad. She was acting wild. Her homegirl is trying to go today; so, I'm getting ready. Fredericka said she trying to see you tomorrow, if you're free?" "Ok bet, Yeah, tell shorty we can meet up and wear something tight" "Bet Bro" "oh yeah P-Nut, I'm going away for a couple of weeks. I will hit you when I'm back" "Ok Bro Crash or get cash" "Crash or get cash."

P-Nut had just told King G he finished the whole thing in one day and was about to do another one. He was sending Fred's niece to see him, which means he had already seen Alvino's people in Rutland. King G shook his head and said:

"Damn this boy better than I thought." "Daddy why do you want some chick wearing some tight shit for you?" Brandy was steaming. "Baby, that was my way of telling the Bro to have the money banded up neatly. Ha-ha your crazy girl" "Why y'all looking at me like that!" Brandy said while looking around the room, "y'all know I don't play bout our husband" "Neither do we, but you know he don't play bout us. Do calm ya crazy butt down. Dat man ain't trying to lose all this" LUV said, "That's right baby! Give me, your King some credit." King G said laughing, "Ya'll get dressed we going to get tatted."

They pulled up at the tattoo shop and King G immediately gave the owner $4k and said:

"We trying to get done up now. You got enough artist here?" "We only have 2 available" Ok, I need one to work on me and the others can take care of them. Whatever they decide is what they get." "You got it boss" The money made the man not even ask for ID. After 3 hours, they were all sitting in the lobby. King gave the artist a $100 tip and they left. "So, what did y'all get?" "You will see when we get home my King." "What did you get?" "You gonna have to wait too" Joe was back at the crib when they pulled up and so was Mama Judy.

"What's up Joe. Hey Mama Judy" they all said "Hey y'all. I see y'all bandaged up y'all must got tattoos" "Yeah Mama Judy" the Lady G's replied. "Well let's see them."

The Lady G's all pulled the gauze off their arm to reveal their tats. They all had a Queens crown linked to a Kings crown. The queens crown had heart shaped jewels in it and the Kings crown had money symbols and above it said a Kings Queen.

"That is so sweet y'all," said Mama Judy. "Damn y'all; I like how y'all got the same exact tats. "That's fire" King G said and kissed his wives. "Well Mama Judy wanna see what you got too, ain't that right girls?"

King G took off the first gauze on his right upper arm. It was a portrait of Royal and above it says a King's Life.

"Aww" everyone said "No fair, I would have got that too, my King, but I ain't have a pic of Royal with me" LUV pouted. "Chill my LUV, you can always go back."

Then King G pulled of the gauze on his left upper arm all the females in the room eyes got glossy and they gasped. It was portraits of LUV, Empress and Brandy and above it said, "A Kings Heart." The Lady G's rushed him kissing him and crying. Then they all held his arm staring at the tattoo. Crazy Joe winked at King G, Mama Judy said:

"Boy I tell you, King you something else. They don't make'em like you" "Thanks Mama Judy" "Come on Judy, let's leave the man with his wives."

Joe and Mama Judy drove off in the Cadi, back to

Brooklyn. King G and his wives all sat around cooling and playing with Royal. King G knew he had it made.

The next day: King G was headed to Queens to the airport, to meet Fred's niece. He had to pick up his money! He had to admit, the Astro Van was moving really nice. Joe had done his thing. King G pulled up to Kennedy Airport and saw only one stewardess at the Delta curbside.

"Hey, are you Fred's niece?" "Only if your King G," she said with a smile. "Yeah, that's me. Hop in"

Now King G had to admit the white woman was fine. He stayed focused. She wasn't worth risking his happy home for.

"Here you go King G." She handed him the bag with the $100K. "My name is Lauryn, if you ever need me for anything, I'm willing to help" "Thank you Lauryn and I will keep that in mind." He went into his pocket and gave her $1000. "I've been taken care of already" "Then consider that a tip." She smiled and got out "Bye King G," "Bye Lauryn;", and with that he pulled off.

On the way, home King G stopped at the jewelers, and got himself and his wives wedding bands with ½ carat in ice across the top of the band. As he walked into the house, he put $15K in front of each ring and $5K in the middle of the table.

"Hey, has anyone seen my wives?" The Lady G's came running down the steps. "Hey Baby," they said together.

He gave them their rings and money then handed LUV the $5K.

"This is for Royal. We leave in two days for our trip. I thought we would go to Myrtle Beach, South Carolina" "Daddy can we stop in North Carolina on the way back? I want to see my sister and brother," Brandy asked." "I got you Brandy."

Two days later, after dropping Royal off, they headed to Myrtle Beach. They enjoyed a week there having fun in the sun. While they were vacationing, LT ran into a problem.

"Yo, Polo, so you mean to tell me one of them Hoody Lyfe niggas robbed your mom?" "Yeah Bro I'm looking for any of them niggas right now!"

Polo was LT's Lil homeboy. He was 16, but very much about his business. They called him Polo because that's all he ever wore.

"Let me call the crew up so we can see about this" LT said.

At the same time, Princess G and Illy were at Kings Plaza mall getting some fresh chocolate chip cookies. A dude in a hoodie bumped Illy.

"Watch where you standing homeboy, before ya lil pretty girlfriend have to save you."

Illy turned around quickly, taking a fighting stance. He noticed the dude had a hat on that said Hoody Lyfe. Princess G saw two more guys stepping up. She stepped up, to put space in between them and said:

"What y'all tryna do?" "Oh shorty, a gangster huh? One of them said. Illy replied, "Homie you might wanna chill. We already had to deal with a few of your homies at Prospect Park, a few years back. We would hate a rerun of that show!" The Hoody Lyfe dudes looked shocked. They had heard that story; but never knew who the crew was their homies were up against. They tried to save face and step up. But play time was over! Illy pivoted and hit the first one with a left hook that sat him down. Then in one motion, swept the feet out from the next one, as Princess G kicked the other one in the knee, bending it the wrong way and snapped it. Illy grabbed her hand, and they ran out of there. Before they left, Illy told the one with the foot swept.

"Y'all gonna stop playing with GGC." Illy and Princess G jumped in his 1998 Infiniti Q45. "Damn Boo, we showed them niggas what time it is," Princess G said excitingly. "You already know baby, but I think them dudes gonna be a problem."
Just then Illy phone rang, and it was LT. After Illy told him what just went down, LT told Illy to come to the hood. Illy pulled over quickly, looked at Princess G and pulled a ring out.

"I was waiting for the right time, Princess but I can't wait. Will you marry me?" "Yes!! Illy, baby yes!"
They kissed and headed for the hood. In the hood, the crew was all at the building. LT was the first to speak.

"Listen y'all these Hoody Lyfe niggas is doing too much! I know we on money, but after our first situation with them, and now Illy and Princess G situation. Plus, they robbed my little man Polo's mom's. We need to see about them." "I know where they be at" said Nutso "I got a little Shorty that live on the block. She always talking bout how they always trying to holla at her." "Aight bet, we at them then. Since they like to show off for females, we gonna line them up." LT said. Jungle, who was all full-fledged pimp now said:

"I got some of the coldest pink toes out. You know there ain't none in the bush; so, we can use them to draw them out." "That's a bet." LT replied. "Look y'all, let's wait till my brother gets back from his vacation. He's gonna be mad if we do this without him." Princess G interrupted! Everyone just stay strapped in case we do see them. I think Jouvert will be the best time to catch them."

Everyone agreed with Princess G, as soon as King G got back it was on.

Chapter 11

King G and the Lady G's had just reached Wendell, North Carolina. Brandy had gotten a call that Mama Judy was there. She wanted to support Brandy because Mama Judy knew how this could go, after not dealing with her parents for three years.

"Turn left here Daddy, that's where Mama Judy is staying." Brandy stated.

It was a small, outdated home, it looked clean though. Mama Judy came outside and greeted everyone.

"Hey y'all, Glad you're here safe." "Hey Mama Judy" they replied. "Whose house is this, Mama Judy?" King G asked. "This is the house I grew up in. My grandmother left it to me when she passed. Whenever I visit, this is where I stay. My cousin Betty lives here on a regular though. C'mon y'all, let's go in."

As everyone turned to go in, King G looked across the road and noticed a burnt down trailer. Brandy seen where he looked and whispered,

"That was that dirty nigga Marc's house."

King G could feel his blood boil! Mama Judy called her daughter to inform her Brandy was here, and to bring Candy and Andy up the road to see her and then hung up.

"That should give us bout 10 minutes to relax till they get here. Now Brandy you stay calm and control that temper of yours." "Yes ma'am." Five minutes later Mama Judy jumped up saying, "now I never told that damn daughter of mines to bring her husband ass over here!"

King looked out the window and saw four people walking up a dirt road. He didn't know they lived that close.

"Well, y'all, let's go outside to meet them" Mama Judy said. Outside Candy and Andy ran to their sister, hugging her, then hugged Mama Judy. "We miss you sis" "I miss y'all too. Y'all look so different now" "You do to. Looking all fancy with your high fashion New York clothes on and all dat pretty jewelry! Ooh, let me see" Candy shouts.

As Brandy's siblings are admiring her, her mother and father walk up.

"Oh my God Brandy! You looking so pretty, come give yo mama a hug. How's New York treating you?" Brandy's face turns serious, but hearing Mama Judy clear her throat, she hugs her mother and says,

"New York is treating me great. I love it" "You ready to come back?" "Never!" Brandy's reaction shocks her mother, but she tries to avoid an issue, "Well ok, how do you like school?" "I done finished school mama I just graduated in June" "Whaaaat? You hear dat Chris our baby's a genius" she states to her husband who still hasn't said anything up until now. "Yeah Brenda, she must be, "Look Brandy, I know you still upset with us, and we apologize. Dat no good nigga Marc tried to do the same thing to your sister. When she told us, we knew that you had been telling the truth. So, I took a bat to his ass and ran him from round here!" In a flash Brandy lost it, "Oh so when Candy says something you jump to believe her; but I was all kind of lying, fast and hot in the ass. This is some bullshit, Candy. I'm not mad at you. I'm glad you ain't go through what I did! I just wish I could have gotten the same response out our father you did." Brandy's dad stepped toward her and shouted "Now you might be still upset, but you watch your mouth! You ain't too big for me to slap you in it."

He raised his hand while saying this, Mama Judy instantly panicked, because she knew what could happen next. Before she could react, King G had run over and put Brandy behind him. LUV and Empress were at her side in a flash.

"Sir I understand that's your daughter; but won't nobody be putting hands on her around me!" "Who the fuck are you?" Brandy's dad shouted. "I'm King Greene, and I'm her husband."

Brandy 's mother and siblings jaws dropped!

"Tell him again Daddy" Brandy shouted. Brandy's dad laughed, "Young man you real funny. My daughter ain't old enough to have no husband. Now back up out of my face before we have a problem!"

King G was unmoved. The Lady G's all fanned out next to King G. King G leaned in and said:

"Sir, I respect my elders, but you might wanna rethink that…"

Brandy's dad knew he had been challenged in front of his wife and kids, and he swung. King G weaved it and prepared to attack but heard Mama Judy yell,

"No King no,"

He grabbed Brandy's dad's arm, slammed him on the ground and put him in an arm bar.

"Mr. Banks. I don't wish to fight you, but I can't allow you to put your hands on me either."

The girls had formed a semi-circle around King G blocking anyone from getting involved.

"You got it, you got it! Let me go!" screamed Mr. Banks. King G let him go. Just then Mama Judy ran up and pulled King G back and said, "Thanks for not hurting him." "No problem, Mama Judy," She then looked at Mr. Banks and said, "Chris you are out of line. Now first off, that is her husband. I gave them permission to be married; because of King she graduated school early. He also got her and these lovely young ladies and his son a house. Brandy has over $40,000 in her own bank account. He treats her like a queen and would die before he let any harm come to her as I'm sure you can tell. Before you ask, no he ain't no drug dealer!"

Mr. Banks was shocked by what he heard. For one, he couldn't do the same for his own children or his wife. He hated to admit it, but he felt good his daughter had someone like that.

"I apologize Mr. Banks. Things shouldn't have gone that far. I'm just very protective of mine." King interceded. "No King I apologize. Brandy I'm sorry too," Mr. Banks conceded.

After that they all sat down and talked. Mama Judy helped explain King G and the Lady G's situation. It was hard for Brandy's parents to understand but they also couldn't argue. Especially after seeing the rings and tattoos. Brandy's mom pulled her aside and said:

"You got a real one Brandy! Mmm you better do what you gotta do to keep him as long as he doing right." Says Ms. Banks "I know Mama trust me he ain't going nowhere."

They spent the next couple days hanging out.

Andy had a fascination with guns and was a real sharpshooter. He taught King G how to shoot accurately. He offered King G two P89 Rugers with extended clips for $200 apiece.

"I want them Andy, but I can't be driving back to New York like that" "You ain't got no stash box Bro?" "Nah" "Well I can get you a nice one for your van for $500" "ok but it gotta be done today. We are leaving tomorrow. Who I gotta pay?" Andy just smiled and said "I'm gonna do it. Just take me to get the parts I need. You gonna learn city boy, us country boys are good with our hands."

Back on the road, two guns heavier in his new stash box, King G couldn't wait to get home. Mama Judy had rode back. He had helped driving. 8 hours later, he was looking at the "Welcome to Brooklyn" sign.

King G woke up the next day ready to get business started. He called up the crew and called for a meeting at the Diner. Stepping into the diner, King G was glad to see everyone there.

"What's getting y'all?" King G said. "Cash" everyone replied. "Look Bro before you get into what you called this meeting for, we need to holla at you bout them Hoody Lyfe niggas." LT stated.

After LT and the crew broke it down, King G agreed something had to be done.

"Listen Jungle; since these dudes got a sweet spot for females, we will use your white girls to distract them. Then we will take them out! We will have the perfect disguises. You let me take care of that. Nutso you get all the info from the lil shorty that's on their block. We got money to get to and no time for these bullshit issues. After this, we all getting our CDL 's, so we can implement the next phase of this money empire."

King spoke calmly, but he was boiling inside. There wouldn't be a third time his sister would have to deal with these motherfuckers' disrespect, indirect or directly. They all got up to leave. King G called Jungle back.

"Yo Bro you ever think bought legitimizing your Pimpin?" "How the fuck I'm gonna do that?" "I was thinking; instead of you risking police contact, we could start a porn company. You use the same girls and get you some more. We make it all legal and we watch the m's role in" "If you think it can be done let's do it! But I don't know nothing about making movies. You set it all up, and I will bring the talent!" "Aight Bro and I think this will be the business we can all eat off of. We can take our stash and make it jump. Let me work everything out and get back to you," King revealed. "Bet Bro. Crash or get cash" Crash or get Cash."

King G sat back lost in thought. He got up, when he remembered Mama LUV made costumes every year to play mas at the Labor Day Parade. He walked into the kitchen,

"Hey Mama LUV, you think you can make me some masks for J'ouvert for me and the guys?"

It was the night of J'ouvert. The whole GGC was posted on Flatbush and Church Ave, along with LT 's lil man Polo. They were all wearing black shorts, all black Air Force Ones and demon masks. They were covered from head to toe with black shoe polish, and all had on fanny packs. King's phone rang.

"Hello, it's go time King G"

King G hung up. Him and the crew made their way up Flatbush towards Parkside. Jungle's hoes were walking down from Empire, clad in. tight mini dresses and sneakers. They were all of Sicilian heritage. They had sexy hips, round butts and big breasts that the dresses did little to hide. Loud music blasted from everywhere. They all seemed to be enjoying themselves. When they got to Parkside, a group of guys, in open spring jackets with hoods and no shirts underneath, approached them.

"What's up ladies? Damn y'all some fine white Broads. You trying to party with some real gangsters?" One of the white girls called Butterfly said, "What y'all got in mind?"

Before they could get an answer; the Hoody Lyfe dudes, peeped a group of guys covered in black wearing masks jumping up and down throwing that powder.

"Listen up guys, they're just having fun" Butterfly stated.

The group of Powder throwers grabbed the white girls, as if to dance with them. King and the crew were really moving them out of the way!

"Hey, you niggas get your own hoes! Them white girls with tonight."

Those would be the last words any one of the niggas would speak that night! King G and LT came out their fanny packs with the Rugers and started shooting. There were about 30 of these Motherfuckers on the corner. The rest of the crew and Polo unloaded the 380's on them. Body after body dropped! All you heard and saw was screams and people running. The white girls took off. After the last body dropped, the crew took off down Parkside towards Rogers Avenue. They busted a right on Rogers, and all jumped in the back of a panel Van. As the door closed Crazy Joe pulled off smoothly. Joe drove them to the hood, where they all used the hose in Polo's backyard and some Dawn dish detergent to get the polish off and any gunshot residue. They had left a change of clothes in the backyard too. Everyone changed up! They bagged up all the clothes and masks and put the guns in a separate bag which Joe took in the panel Van.

"Ain't nothing to speak on."

Was all King G said. They all understood! Joe had left to discard the guns, masks and clothing. After an hour everyone went their own way. King G was back in his van headed home.

Chapter 12

November 6, 1998, came around real quick. Royal's first birthday was here. By now things were getting closer for the crew to kick off phase 2. Everyone had their CDL 's. The Lady G's and Princess G were officially GGC. Polo had been Brought in by LT; but any members outside of the females and the original crew, were kept at a need-to-know basis. At the moment, Polo just sold weed. LT paid him $1500 a week. Polo still had to prove himself as a cash getter. For now, King G and his people were focused on Royal's party. King G had rented out a Hall to have his son's party. Royal loved Elmo, so LUV insisted on an Elmo theme! There was a real live Elmo there! which was a midget in an Elmo costume. The hall was decorated to look like Sesame Street. There was a ball pit, a balloon artist, a photographer, an Elmo cake that could feed 100 people and cookies that had Elmo's face on it. Everyone came out and Royal got a lot of gifts. All Royal did the whole party was chase around the live Elmo. The DJ entertained the bigger kids and the adults. It was a joyous occasion. After all the guests left, Mama LUV took a sleeping Royal with her. GGC conducted a meeting.

"Check this out everyone; starting top of next year we will have our own trucking company and the logistics will be handled by LUV, Empress, Brandy and Princess G. Jungle, we will use some of your ladies to help get us some shipments to take. The bulk of our "takes" are gonna come from our logistics department. They are the brains behind our trucking business. My goal is to have legitimate businesses that are for everyone here. Remember we can't do wrong forever." Everyone trusted in King G's words, so nothing needed to be said, King G closed the meeting "Crash or get Cash" y'all "Crash or get Cash" everyone shouted.

When King G and the ladies got home that night and emptied the van there was an unopened present in the back for Royal. They went inside and opened it in the living room. There was a box of money with a card that read:

Hey King G, this is a present for Royal. It's $100K. Small things to a giant, love P-Nut, "Crash or get Cash." King had to smile; P-Nut was truly a real one! Once he had collected $2 million from P-Nut, he told him he wouldn't accept any more money from him. He also had P-Nut go down south with Brandy's Brother Andy, to get away from Vermont and open a new business. P-Nut's expression of loyalty to Royal meant a lot to King G.

In December of 1998, King G purchased 7 Peterbilt trucks, a warehouse with a lot attached and started the trucking company, "All4One trucking service." January 1999, they were in business. Princess G and the Lady Gs were set up in the warehouse office. Mama G had told them all the ways to look into what trucking companies had the contracts, for what companies. The best way, she said, to get info was to get the men working logistics. She had said the fat, ugly and little dick ones were the best! But any man could be seduced out of information. The females of GGC had inked enough "for real" and solid contracts to keep the men on the road, while they went out to do their homework. As it stood, the contracts would bring in close to $1 million a year right now, with the seven trucks on the road. The "takes" would be the real Bread winners! Mama G and Father G turned over the liquor store, diner and laundromat to King G and Princess G. They had officially retired! They left their home to Princess G. They moved to Reading, Pennsylvania, into a four-bedroom home on a half-acre of land. The first set up for the crew was put together by Brandy. She went into a major trucking firm scouting prospects. She found a skinny, balding white man talking logistics to the boss. She backed out of the building and called Jungle for one of his chicks. He sent Butterfly. Butterfly pulled up and Brandy got in.

"Hey Butterfly." "Hey Brandy" "Listen girl, we gonna wait for this skinny lil white man to get off. When he comes out, we gonna ask for help with directions. Flirt with him. Then get him to come with us to eat." "Ok got you."
The plan went off without a hitch and he was eating out their palm. Brandy's knowledge of logistics loosened his tongue up significantly. He started bragging, like he was a big man in the company, and how they handled large accounts. He let it

slip that he was responsible for the entire East Coast supply for Wilson's leather, this week.

"Yup, Thursday morning; I will be inspecting the trailer and handing over the manifest to the driver, to deliver 50,000 coats to three different Wilson leather stores in Virginia." "Wow, I have never met someone so important. Important men really turn me on. It's all the power I think" Butterfly stated flirtatiously. The white man, who they learned name was Albert, blushed. "Let me get your number Albert. I will give you a call. Maybe we can spend more time together,"

Albert quickly gave Butterfly his number. Brandy waved goodbye and Butterfly hugged him and squeezed his butt. Albert was elated. Right on time Thursday morning, LT watched the driver get on the road and followed him. He called Nutso and TEC, letting them know the truck's description and tag number. When the driver stopped at a truck stop in Delaware; TEC distracted him with trucker talk, while Nutso climbed in his truck. He spiked his coffee with crush sleeping pills. An hour later, off and exit in a rural part of Maryland, they relieved a sleeping driver of the contents of his trailer and drove back to New York. That score brought the crew $1 million. King G gave the leathers to Mr. Cohen, who sold them out of his warehouse for $50 apiece wholesale. This got Mr. Cohen a cool profit of $1.5 million. LUV and Princess G scored them a Toys "R" Us and Babies "R" Us, shipment which netted them a total of $1.3 million. They would have gotten more; but King G wanted to keep all the diapers and formula. Then Empress came through in a major way. She snuck her way into a manager's office at a major shipyard company, when she flirted with the manager and asked to use his bathroom. She had made copies of the shipyard's shipping container inventory listing. She only got a copy, one sheet! That sheet would bring them seven containers, that earned them $4 million over a 12-month span.

June 1999, K9 was finally home! King G threw him a big Party. K9 brought Gauge and Chip with him. K9 told the crew he put them down with GGC. Nobody was feeling their energy; but as long as they got the money, they would value K9's opinion. King G handed K9 the keys to a 1998 Jaguar XK8 with 18" Momo rims. The rest of the crew handed him a duffel bag with $150K. Princess G had got him Iceberg jeans and a T-shirt with some Airmax 95s to match. He was wearing that outfit for the party.

"Yo, y'all really know how to bring a nigga home in style" K9 said.
Everyone gave him a gangsta hug. He saw the Lady G's playing the back, so he walked up. He was admiring how beautiful they were. LUV hips had spread a lot since he last saw her. She couldn't hide that 36- 24-48 frame. Then Empress was so exotic looking; with her light skin, chinky eyes, and black features with a perky set of breasts and hair to

her ass. Then Lil Brandy was no longer little for sure! Her bow-legged stance, bubble butt and slim, thick frame was alluring.

"Hey ladies" "What's up K9?" they all said with a blatantly fake smile. "Damn big Homie who are these beautiful sisters?" said Chip, while smiling. "We are the beautiful sisters known as King G's wives. Excuse us," said Brandy; as she pulled her sister wives and walked away, leaving Gauge, Chip and K9 staring at them.

King G walked past his wives, straight to K9, staring at them.

"Check this out. Let that be the last time y'all lust after my wives without an invitation! Are we gonna have a problem?"

Princess G played her brothers side and the Lady G's weren't too far behind.

"They didn't know who they were King G" said K9. "Ok now they do; but what's your excuse?"

King G wasn't feeling the disrespect!

"Chill Bro, yo a nigga just got out! I ain't mean nothing by it. They are just the first females I seen my bad." King walked away and everyone else followed, leaving K9 and his Lil crew behind.

"What's up with that fool?" Chip asked, "Ain't nothing I can't handle, just chill and let's get to this paper." Said K9.

King G's wives let him know they were not feeling K9 and his peeps and didn't trust them.

"That nigga ain't really ya friend, my King, and you bought that nigga a Jag" LUV said shaking her head. "I got this, my LUV. He's still the Bro and when one eats, we all eat." "Whateva!" was all he heard from his wives.

July came around fast. King G and the Lady G's anniversary was coming up on the 30th. He had plans to buy them all cars and a new house. He wanted to give Mama LUV the house in Long Island. Crazy Joe had just bought a home in the Poconos, Pennsylvania and told King G about the homes out there. King G drove out there with Joe and found a six-bedroom mini mansion on an acre of land for $400k. It was perfect. It had a full basement, and attic Jacuzzi in the backyard and enclosed pool and land as far as the eye could see. King G put it under the liquor store business name because that line of credit was well-established. He dropped $50,000 on it. His mortgage was $1200 a month. With that settled; he now had to find the cars to put in the four-car garage. He decided on three 2000 Mercedes-Benz ML 320's. He got one in navy blue with Peanut butter interior, a silver one with gray interior and a black on black one. He had to drop a little extra to get it early. It was worth it. The man at the dealership promised it would be delivered to their new home on 29th of July. He paid some contractors to do upgrades he wanted and to repaint. He bought all new furniture, that would be delivered on the 28th. He was now set. When he got back to Brooklyn, he let Mama LUV know what's up. She was so happy. She hugged him and kissed his cheek and said,

"I watched you grow from a boy, and I love you like my own son. You are truly a blessing to those you love!" "Thanks Mama LUV and so are you. I need you to be up in the Poconos on the 28th and 29th for the deliveries. Let me get up outta here, I will catch you later."

As King G reached the door, he looked over his shoulder and said:

"Oh yeah, the Diner is yours now" and walked out leaving Mama LUV with her jaw dropped!

There is a four-bedroom house available across the street from the crib in the Poconos. He called Illy and put him on. Immediately he jumped on it. The rest of the crew had all bought homes, except for K9. He was cool in a condo. King G doubled the rent on parking spots at the warehouse, and none of his renters batted an eye. After all, people were paying $600 a month for parking spaces; so, if King G wanted $300, they weren't gonna complain. Then he switched from cans to bottles in the vending machines and doubled the price and his income too. Life was good. Illy closed on the house by July 15th. He called King G to let him know.

"Yo, what's getting King G?" "Cash Illy, what's up Bro?" "Listen I closed on that house. Got it for $350K. Me and Princess are getting married in five days. We ain't doing nothing big just going to the courthouse. That's the way she wants it. She wants you and the Lady G's there and of course y'alls parents. I was thinking; since you tryna surprise your wives with the house we could go out there on the 30th to me and Princess crib and then you could surprise them!" "Yeah, that'll work Bro bet. I have been having K9 chilling. You think I should bring him in on the trucks?" "Listen Bro; I ain't feeling how he is moving with them new niggas. Whatever you choose you know I'm with you" "I dig that Bro. You're right! I'm just gonna put him on to some shipments. He can jack. That way, he stays fed but don't know the ins and outs. I will tell the rest of the crew what's up. See you in five days." "Crash or get Cash" "Crash or get Cash."

Princess G and Illy got married just the way they wanted. Princess G announced she was pregnant, which everyone congratulated. King G called P-Nut and told him to rent a private jet and fly Brandy family in for their anniversary. Mama LUV and LUV's siblings would already be there. King G told Wakeel to bring Miss Trish and the rest of the siblings. The 30th came and everyone except for K9, was pulling up at Illy and Princess G's new home. It was beautiful and well-furnished. All day, all King G had given his wives was a dozen roses, mixed in with a dozen lilies to each of them. New iced out chains that said, "King's Queen."

This morning they all got a message. After exploring Illy and Princess G new crib King G said:

"Hey y'all, let's go for a walk in the neighborhood." Brandy asked, "Since when you like to just walk around Daddy?" "They got some nice houses out here. I thought we might find something" "I could go for a walk" Mama G said. So, everyone got up, they went outside and crossed the road into a cul-de-sac. King G was walking straight up the driveway to the front door, of a home.

"My King, you buggin! You trying to get shot?" LUV asked. King G was looking through the window "ain't nobody even home my LUV. Y'all come on." "No way, I am not tryna get shot." "Well, y'all just some scary people we going in" said Father G holding Mama G's hand. Illy and Princess G were next. "Man, y'all crazy Boo" Empress stated, "But since everyone else with it, come on!"

They all held each other's hands, as they passed through the doorway and closed the door. The house was dark, King G flicked on the light and that's when everyone hopped out yelling:

"Surprise!!!"

The Lady G's all grabbed at their hearts shocked. When they recognized all their loved ones, they laughed and started punching King G's arm.

"Happy Anniversary" my queens this is y'all new home."

To say the Lady Gs were happy was an understatement. After they ran through the house viewing every room upstairs and downstairs; they went to the backyard and stood on the patio amazed by the space.

"Daddy this is perfect," "Yes, my LUV you did that" "For real Boo can't nothing top this!" LUV exclaimed. "Don't speak too fast" King G said.

He led them to the front door, everyone followed. When they were all standing in front of the garage, he pressed the opener. All the doors went up and there were three brand new Benzes. The girls all looked confused, til he threw them each a key. They screamed to see which SUV belonged to who! Mr. Banks walked up to King G and said:

"Well done son-in-law. I'm trying to be like you when I get older" "thanks, Mr. Banks, I got a feeling thing will change for you soon."

Miss Trish and Mama LUV both kissed King G and hugged him. He felt on top of the world; LT shouted,

"That's my Bro right there!" I taught him everything he knows," which got a laugh from everyone.

Chapter 13

Back in Brooklyn, while the crew worked, King G and the Lady G's stayed at his old house. King G turned the basement into a studio for the porn company. Which they named "Porno Pimpin Entertainment." They had all the latest video cameras, Boom mics and lighting. They were decorating the rooms differently to shoot multiple scenes. Jungle had at least 10 white girls and five Asian girls. He only made interracial films with titles like "Jungle Fever," "Ebony and Ivory," "As the swirl turns," "Ragin Blasian in Hong Kong," "Black Dong and "Oh me so horny," to name a few. He made Butterfly a talent scout and she was all business. K9 told King G that he needed some weed and dope, to put the Bro's Chip and Gauge on.

"Gimme a couple of days and I will see what I can find out for you Bro" King said.

K9 felt like King G was being funny, but he decided to see what happens. LT and King G discussed this. LT said he would handle it. Uncle Ernie had been dealing with Alvino steady and could get his hands on anything, so he grabbed 5 pounds of Bud and A whole brick of Pure Dope. K9 met up with LT and picked up the work then went and hollered at Chip and Gauge.

"Yo Chip these 5 pounds of that fire. We gone split the money down the middle Dat's $11,200 apiece. Gauge that's a whole joint. I need $50,000 back. Now that's pure. So, you can double it and still get $100 a gram easy." "Say less Big Homie, I got you" Gauge replied. "Yo, K9, I should be done with his Bud in 10 days. Yo, where you get all this from?" Chip asked. "Come on now Chip you know the big Homie got connects, I make shit happen!" K9 bragged. "Word Big Homie. my bad" At the end of August, King G got a call from Alvino that woke him out of his sleep. "Yo, Vino what's up?" "Sorry to call you so early hermano, but I need to meet with you ASAP!" "Say no more. Where do you want to meet?" "Come to my home in two hours" "Got you Bro. see you in two. Peace" "Adios "

King G and Alvino were sitting out on Alvino's back porch enjoying the weather.

"Listen King G, I have a problem; I think you could help me solve and will benefit you too. I have planted a spy in my competitors' ranks, who knows the comings and goings of drug shipments. With your trucks; snatching them there should be no problem! I will pay you handsomely for the entire shipment." "How handsomely are we talking?" "How many shipments are we talking, as well." "To start, two shipments. I do not want to expose my spy's whereabouts. The pay is $1 million per shipment. All you have to do, is drop it off in Long Island City, Queens for me. I will handle the rest." "Sounds good to me Bro; but between me and you, how much do you stand to make?" "I won't lie to you hermano, I will probably see $5 million total. With them out the way, my own sales will jump tremendously. Also, I need you to jack the shipment in Texas. So, it looks like another competitor did this, which will further Boost my sales." "When do you need this done?" "The two shipments will be coming across the Mexican border September 14."

King G let Alvino know he would take care of it. King G decided TEC and Nutso would do this move with him as, he formulated his plan.

Something in the back of King G's mind was bugging him. He knew he wanted legit businesses and had enough success to continue that path. He also knew not all the Bros would be on the same vibe. He needed a safety net for them all, because if he was honest, he probably wouldn't pass on opportunities like the one Alvino was putting him on to. Since it was easy money. He had been contemplating this for a while, so he decided to implement a plan. He grabbed his phone and made a call.

"Hey Lauryn, it's King G. I got a proposition for you... you can't refuse!"

A week later King G is riding through Long Island City in Queens to check out the drop off location for the shipments. He notices there are a lot of warehouses out here. He parks at the end of the dead-end street and just watches what's going on. The dropoff location is about a block away. As he is looking through his binoculars, he notices quite a few

Mexicans walking around. He figures this must be Alvino or Mr. Velez's people. Everything looks fine. It's not that he doesn't trust Alvino, he is just thorough. Just then, a side door to a warehouse opens on the block he is on. He sees two Dominican men carrying two seabags a piece coming out. One of the bags slipped off the second guys shoulder and hits the ground. He quickly picks it up! King G notices a large bag of weed sticking out the top. Now King G knows it must be more of that inside the warehouse. How much, is the question. He also notices, there is no camera in front of the door. They just come out of. He waits til the men pull off and decides to follow them. They make it to Bushwick in Brooklyn and unload their vehicle into the basement under a bodega. Some people make it so easy! King G didn't want to rob them. It just made him feel good to notice a way to get cash in everything he saw. He would give this info to K9. As much as he didn't like some of his ways, that was still his Bro. He didn't like his additions to the crew. There was no need to call K9. King G knew he would be posted up on Church Avenue, with the top down on his XK8. Playing a big man, a role!

"Yo K9, hop in I gotta holla at you" After they cruised the Ave and King G put him on, K9 only wanted to know one thing, "What I got for you?" "Nothing Bro this is all you. You can do what you want with it. Matter fact: put your two homies on, so you don't gotta do shit but get da cash!" "Ha-ha I know that's right King G. Hey King G, about that shit at my coming home party my bad! You have got three beautiful wives and I'm happy for you. They some good women too. I would take a bullet for you, but I would never try and take a woman or should I say women from you." K9 said, with a slight chuckle. "I hear you, Bro. I ain't sweating that. Let's get this cash."

One thing for sure King G knew K9 would take a bullet for him. Probably or mostly, so he could brag about it and blow up his gangster image. The trying to take his woman part, he couldn't go for. He knew his homie. He had a complex and needed to shine above everyone. He just hopes his complex wouldn't expose him as a Phoney Homie. King G, TEC, and Nutso were sitting in a 1999 Chevy Lumina in Brownsville, Texas. They had been waiting for the two trucks to come across the border and hand over the trucks to the two American drivers. They had already spotted the American drivers waiting. The drivers were the only two people who were around all day like them. Finally, two trucks pulled up and the Americans got out of their pickup and switched with the Mexican drivers. The GGC was ready to make their move when King G noticed the Mexicans didn't leave. As the trucks pulled out, the Mexicans followed in the American drivers Chevy Silverado. King G immediately followed. This was a change in the plan. He knew there was a tracking device underneath the trailers of the trucks, so why were they following the trucks? King G decided to be patient and just follow. When they were about 50 miles outside of Houston, TEC said,

"Man, they gotta stop for gas soon, that Silverado gotta almost be empty!" "Yeah, you're right" said King G. "When they stop, Nutso you take down the Mexicans. Me and TEC will get the drivers" "Sounds like a plan to me, I been fiending to get this over with."

They pulled into a truck stop in Houston. King G pulled up to the opposite pump from the Mexicans. All the while keeping an eye on the drivers, who went to the pumps for the trucks. One of the Mexicans started pumping gas as the other went to the counter. Nutso eased out the car pulling his trucker hat down and went inside. After paying for the gas, the Mexican went to the bathroom and that's when Nutso made his move. As soon as the Mexican cleared the door; Nutso rushed in and tased him, before he could even look back! When he hit the ground, Nutso kicked him in the head. He was out cold and had pissed all on himself. Nutso dragged him into a stall, pulled his pants down and sat him on the toilet. After about five minutes the other Mexican came in. Nutso was positioned behind the door by the air dryer, pretending to dry his hands. As soon as Nutso noticed it was his target, he put the laser to his neck and put him to sleep. He did the same with him, as his partner, in another stall. He fished the keys out of the driver's pocket and also took their IDs. Whenever the police came, these two would be going to immigration for a while.

Nutso made it outside and found the Silverado parked on the side of the building. He noticed the Lumina empty and ran to it. The keys were in the ignition, so he hopped in. Looking around, he saw King G and TEC coming from underneath the other trucks. They were walking fast to the target trucks. They made eye contact with Nutso and Nutso pulled up out of there. As they crossed the state line into Louisiana, they pulled to the back of a rest stop. King G and Nutso hopped out, went to the passenger side of the truck and lifted both men out. They took them into the woods, behind the rest stop, and tied them to a tree. One behind the other in just their underwear. Nutso was standing outside of the car looking around when they emerged from the woods.

"What the Fuck, Bro? I thought y'all left them hillbilly's back in Texas" Nutso said. "Nah, we caught them in the truck and tased them and just slid them in the passenger seats. Had to tase them a couple more times before we got here. They won't remember shit." TEC offered. "Aight. let's get the fuck home!" King G exclaimed. Back in New York after dropping trucks off and then making it home; King G called Alvino and said "mañana" and hung up.

After picking up two suitcases with $1 million apiece; King G called a meeting with the GGC. He let K9 know it was only for day ones. They went to LUV's old apartment. The rent had been paid for the rest of the year, so this was where they had their meetings. King G had already split the $2,000,000 into seven separate piles of $285,714. Once everyone was there King G spoke:

"Each one of y'all grab a stack of this money. I know y'all entrusted me with the stash we made 5 years ago. This is to show my appreciation for y'all trust and patience!"

They all thanked him. K9 was impressed and shocked. He was sure King had been trying to swindle them out of their stash; and was waiting for the day to come, so he could turn everyone against him. Seeing King G be such a stand-up dude, made him feel proud. But the fact he couldn't compare to King G's realness, still ate at him! Nevertheless, he had to give him his props.

"Yo King G! One thing you know is money, I got to give it to you Bro. But you forgot one thing." "What's dat?" "How the hell we supposed to carry all this money out of here?" That got a laugh out of everyone. King G produced seven gym bags and said "There ain't much I forget!" K9 sensed a hidden message behind his statement but shrugged it off. "Alright now to the business. Jungle we gonna register Porno Pimping offshore in Barbados, so we can incur no taxes on that money! We gonna keep the trucking company as clean as possible. We made off good this year so far with the extra income. No need to push it! I'm thinking we should start promoting parties on the GGC banner. Also, next year, start employing more drivers for our trucking business to free up our time for other ventures. What y'all think?"

Everyone liked the ideas.

LT spoke up and said, "I can handle the parties. I got a homie named Chef, from the Bronx, who is big on the party scene in Manhattan and the Bronx. He might be good for the GGC crew too; since we are recruiting now." he said looking at K9. "I recommend Polo too. Let's take a vote" King G said. Everyone voted yes to Polo. Everyone else agreed to wait and meet Chef, and see if he was about his business, before he was accepted in.

"Speaking of new members my cousin's, Money and Legend, have a clothing company called GTI. It stands for "Getting To It." It's based on getting money, which all the designs reflect. They definitely bout their paper. I think with us backing it, it could bring in some good cash and open up another lane. Oh, yeah, and Legend also has a CDL," "TEC stated. Sounds good to me," said King.
Everyone else nodded in agreement. Before they closed the meeting, King let them know he wanted to throw a party for Empress for her 18th birthday. They decided to make it GGC entertainment's first event.

"Anything else anyone wanna discuss before we go?" asked King G. "Oh yeah Bro, dat situation you put me on to; got me 100 pounds of purple haze; 10 bricks of heroin and $85,000 in cash! I really appreciate dat! Nobody else got purple haze in Flatbush right now I'm killing it. Matter of fact.... K9 reaches in the gym bag and counts out $85,000.

"that's for you. I know you said I ain't owe you, but it's only correct!" Everyone was surprised at that. "Thanks Bro" King G, said "oh yeah, before I forget, I want P-Nut apart of GGC. Dat Brother's a cold money getter."

Everyone agreed and they all left. King G went to the crib in the hood where his wives and Princess G were waiting. He counted out $92,903 four times and gave it to each of them.

"Put that away that's a lil something to help build y'all stash."

They all thanked him and hugged him. There were no truck routes needing to be driven so he decided they would go home to the Poconos for a couple of days. They picked up Royal from the diner with Mama LUV and drove home.

Chapter 14

K9 had Gauge and Chip working overtime. The demand for the work they had was so high. They hung on to every word K9 said. They desperately wanted to impress him. Chip had just copped a 1998 BMW 323 CI convertible. You couldn't tell him nothing! Gauge had a 1997 Chevy Tahoe. LT and K9 met up with them on Fulton Street, in downtown Brooklyn, at Bargain Bazaar. K9 had just picked up a new 18" Cuban link chain with an iced out GGC piece. Chip was the first one to comment.

"Yo Big Homie you killin them with that chain!" "Yeah, I know and we gonna be killing them. The jeweler got two more chains just like this waiting for y'all. Go ahead and pay the man!"

After getting their chains, K9 explained about the first GGC Entertainment party and how they had to shut it down. Chip and Gauge ate it up and agreed they would stop the show that night.

King G took the shipment of diapers and formula and gave Princess G a six-month supply of everything. He also went around the hood to all the mothers with babies or expecting a six-month supply until he ran out.

November 6, 1999, Royal turned 2 years old, and everyone came out to celebrate. Father G hollered at King G afterwards,

"Listen son try hitting up Atlantic City for shipments to knock off. A lot of truck drivers stop there for prostitutes or to gamble. They drop their trailers in the urban areas and then drive the cabs to the casinos. You can lift the trailers and haul them off or catch a driver who has blown it all in a casino and buy him out of his cargo. All he will do his report a robbery to cover his ass." "I will keep that in mind Father."

Empress's birthday was approaching. King G decided to make it a costume party to attract more party goers, instead of those just looking for trouble. Empress went to a tailor to design her costume. She would not tell nobody what she was getting made. The men of GGC, except K9, decided on coming as characters from the movie "Coming to America." Of course, King G picked Jafi Joe. Everyone else picked one of the many characters Eddie Murphy and Arsenio Hall played. LUV and Brandy decided to come as Catwoman and Mystique from the X-Men. The night of the party was a big turnout. It was at a club called The Ark. Everyone had their finest costumes out. The GGC crew pulled up, three limos deep. The first limo had K9, Chip and Gauge in it. They stepped out dressed as Wesley Snipes in Blade, Demolition Man and New Jack City. They all had their make-up and hair on point, just like the movies. Of course, they had their GGC chains on. Next was the rest of the men from GGC, who all looked like the characters in Coming to America. King G had a real lion head across his chest. The crowd waiting outside was impressed. The last limo contained the ladies of the GGC. First Princess G stepped out as Jessica Rabbit; her make-up had her even looking like a white woman. You would've thought the red hair grew out of her scalp. Then Brandy stepped out in a latex bodysuit, that clung to her body so tight, you could see every curve! She had a Catwoman mask made of latex. Her nails really looked like claws and she had some custom-made latex Boots on. LUV was next to come out. She had a blue bodysuit on that made her appear. It was tight in every nook and cranny. It blended with her blue make up and red hair. She had some Air Force ones on, that were painted the same color blue. Then the birthday girl stepped out into a Geisha gown, with her hair pinned up with chopsticks. The gown was completely see-through, except where her private parts were concerned, but left a little to the imagination! Her 4-inch heels and the split in her gown elongated her legs. She truly looked like a model. King G escorted his wives inside. It was time to party. LT introduced Chef to the crew that night. He was dressed as Biggie in the Coogi sweater, jeans and timbs.

"Nice to meet y'all. LT has told me a lot about y'all." "Nice to meet you too. You and LT definitely did y'all thing promoting and get this party ready. It's packed!" said King G. "That's the only way to run dat money counter up," Chef said. King G liked his answer. "How was that money counter looking?" "Oh, by my calculations, we should make a profit of $8K tonight. That's after security and the bartender is paid!" "No more business talk Boo this is my night." said Empress, while prying him away. "Excuse me Chef the Mrs. has spoken, we'll get up."

That night all of the crew left with a shorty on their arms except Illy and King G. They had all they needed. That night, Empress got her husband all to herself and he tried to knock the lining out of her. She couldn't get enough! A couple of weeks later Brandy's birthday came. All she wanted was a normal day in the Poconos with her sister wives, Royal and King G. That's exactly what she got. King G loved how simple and easy-going Brandy was. He would make sure her 18th was one to remember. King G was trying to wrap up things for the upcoming holidays, so everyone could do what needed to be done. LT and Chef were planning a New Year's bash at Club Speed, in the City. Jungle had finished filming and editing 10 movies, so they had to get ready to distribute. Jungle was taking the girls on a tour to promote, for three months. King G sent TEC and his cousin Legend, to case out Atlantic City. If Legend did well, he was in. King G was already feeling him and Money's clothing line and their hustle. King G was looking to buy a car. He had gotten into collecting and car races, after hanging out with Barkim's nephew, Flex. He was on his way to check out some rides with Flex, out in Queens, some Italians were selling. They pulled up at a car lot in Astoria full of classics. King G saw the car he wanted instantly. Him and Flex walked to a 1972 Chevelle SS.

"This the one Flex, I gotta have her!" King G stated excitedly. "Say no more King G, I'll be right back" 10 minutes later Flex came out with some 30-day tags, title and keys in his hand. "Let's ride Bro. It's all taken care of."

Summer 2000, all the Lady G's were pregnant. Business and the hustle were jumping. All money flow was improved and steady. Porno Pimpin was projected to bring in $6 million in sales, by the 1-year mark. TEC and Legend had made $500K, off lifting trailers, in Atlantic City. That was after, catching two loads that King G had sitting in the warehouse, that wasn't such hot commodities.

Chapter 15

The whole GGC was out at a car race in Queens, watching Flex race his '98 Dodge Viper GTSR – GT2.

"I ain't racing for nothing but pink slips and big chips! So, if you talking anything less go find a Go-Kart to race," Flex shouted. "I hear you talking but what are you driving be like?! shouted a guy in a '77 Porsche 930 RUF. "All gas no brakes. Place your bet or step," Flex replied. "I got my pink slip and $30K, dat my Porsche walk ya viper." "Dats a bad!" Flex said excitably. "I'm taking side bets on my nigga Flex whip," shouted LT." "I got $40K on my man 930P against your boy!" shouted a dude in an All-white Moschino outfit. "That's a bet," shouted LT.

They lined up at the light. When the sexy Puerto Rican Mami waved and dropped her scarf, they took off! The race was for three city blocks. For a block and a half, it was neck and neck. Then Flex hit the NOS and left 930P in the dust! As they pulled back to the start Flex jumped out,

"That's how a motherfuckin GGC bad boy drives! Big Brooklyn Shit. Now hand over my slip and dem chips, so I can have my chick drive her new Porsche home" Flex said while laughing.

As LT counted his money; from the side bets 930P, hopped out his Porsche mean mugging.

"Here go your little $30K for the race homeboy, but let's run it back for the slip" said 930P "Nah Fuck dat! Hand me them keys and the pink slip partner. You placed dat bet now pay up," shouted Flex.

King G peeped at the inevitable about to take place, so he made his way over. K9 peeped the move and circled around, in the opposite direction, with Chip and Gauge right behind him. The rest of the crew stood next to LT.

"Listen Brothers we don't gotta get into no unnecessary shit. Just pay the man so we can be on our way," said King G. "I ain't ya brother! Who the fuck is you to tell me what to do?" said 930P. King G laughed and stated, "You right, you ain't my brother. But you gonna pay my homie or your already bad luck is gonna get worse!"

At that moment, 930P homies stepped up next to him. Their body language spoke aggression. Before anything could happen; K9, Gauge and Chip, backed out their posters from behind 930P and his boys. K9 put his burner to 930P head and said,

"You might wanna have your boys rethink their next move or we all gonna be viewing your thoughts, in 3D" "You got it homie. Just be cool. Here take the keys, the pink slip is in the car" 930P said clearly shook! As Flex handed his shorty the keys and told her to drive 930P said "I'm SouthSide Mafia nigga. My homies ain't just gonna let this ride." "Well then tell them niggas come see bout it then." LT stated, before gun butting 930P to sleep.

Gauge and Chip kept their guns on the rest of the niggas as the GGC Homies backed up outta there. They all headed back to the hood.

King G woke up the next day unable to shake the feeling dat shit was about to get crazy. He explained to the girls to stay away from the hood and to always stick together. Still focused on business King G drove to the warehouse, loaded a trailer and drove the truck to the hood. He stopped at the dinner and unloaded 100,000 bottles of water and told Mama LUV,

"All these are for you Mama LUV, do what you want. All the money goes to you."

He kissed her on the cheek and pushed on. He stopped on his old block and called Lil Kenny over and said,

"Gather up four more of your homies. I got these bottles of water for y'all. Lil Kenny ran off and came back with his homies. "So, what you want us to do with the water?" asked Lil Kenny. "Y'all gonna take these waters to sell them. Here is $100 go buy some coolers and ice and fill them up with waters. Two of y'all gonna do the selling, two gonna be security and one of y'all gonna be in charge of the money. All the money is y'all's. After that, you gotta figure out your next move. Whatever you do, Gotta Get Cash! Anything less, I will never help y'all out again." "Damn King G, thanks big

Bro. We gonna show you we can get this done. Nobody never gave us a chance like this. But why us?" asked Lil Kenny. "Because y'all from where I'm from and we take care of our own. Y'all stay up and come grab these cases out the trailer until you got 150,000 bottles. I gotta bounce." "Where we gonna put all of them cases King G?" Lil Kenny and his crew ask at the same time. "Y'all got cribs, y'all better figure it out," King stated. After they got everything out, King G pushed off. He had 250 bottles left. He went to the shelter on Atlantic and Bedford, opened the trailer and started unloading them on the sidewalk. "Hey yo, y'all help me get these off the truck!" King G told the homeless men.

After the truck was unloaded, he went to check Alvino. It was time to get some artillery for the beef he knew was cooking!

"Yo Vino, I need something I can really count on to get the job done," King stated. "Hermano, I got you," replied Alvino. "I have plenty of guns at my exposure. You tell me what you need and what you want, Cabrón." "I need something that holds a lot of rounds and packs some power too," said King G "Well hermano, I have some P89's with 32 shot clips, calico 9 mm dat holds 100 rounds, and some Glocks dat hold 17. Oh, yeah and I just received some Taurus millenniums, dat hold the same as the Glock" "Alright let me get 2 Calico's, 2 Glocks, 2 Taurus's and 8 Rugers." "I will have the guns dropped in an hour hermano" "Ok Vino. Dat's a bet! How much do I owe you?" "Please don't insult me hermano, just be available for delivery and leave the rest to me." With that taken care of King G departed. He pulled out his phone and made a call. "What's getting Bro?" LT answered his phone saying, "That cash Bro! Listen meet me by the warehouse, I need to holla at you" "Aight I need to holla at you too King G" "Aight see you there "Crash or Get Cash" "Crash or Get Cash." "At the warehouse, LT and King G arrived two minutes apart. "Yo LT, I got some straps on the way. Vino looked out. I got a feeling this shit with the SouthSide Mafia gonna get bad," "I feel you Bro. That's why I hollered at Chef to see what he could find out about these dudes. He says they a team of street niggas, who hustle and got shooters. They be shining in a lot of the clubs and events. They also keep some fly shorties around them." LT stated "Aight Bro but do Chef know where they lay their heads?" "Nah Bro, but he knows they got Jamaica Avenue on smash. Down by the mall." "Aight bet. I got an idea. We should send Butterfly out there and see if we can get one of them to bite. What you think?" asked King G. "Sounds like a plan to me King G. We can never be too careful and if it works out and they move wrong, we will have the drop!" "Cool, so what's good with the next party, you and Chef working on?" asked King G. "It's a go Bro. Everything is on schedule and next weekend is gonna be epic! I rented four Hummers for our crew, so we can pull up strong" replied LT. "A'ight yo, I think this is the delivery pulling up right here," said King G.

After securing the guns, they were ready to ride. King G told Jungle the plan, and he got Butterfly on the job. Jungle promised she wouldn't disappoint. True indeed, Butterfly came through. King G pulled up on her at Green Acres Mall.

"What's up Butterfly?" "Ain't nothing King G. So, listen, I finally snagged one of them southside dudes. He was on my heels. I guess he the muscle, his name is Sheisty. We were talking out on Jamaica Ave, by the pizza shop, across from the mall. Anyway, while we are talking, a dude pulls up in a '00 Porsche 911. He hops out, wanting to know who I am. I had told them my name was Butter, and that I was from L.I., just doing some shopping. Anyway, the one in the Porsche asked me if I knew who they were. Of course, I said no. That's when these lames start bragging bout being SouthSide Mafia and having the city on lock. Blah, blah, blah. I asked old dude in the Porsche, what is his name and acted like I heard of their lil crew. He said he was 930P; but now he go by 911P, since he upgraded his Porsche. They ask for my number. Talking bout they ain't never seen a white chick with a face or body like mine. Anyway, I gave it to them. They want me to come chill whenever I want" "You did good Butterfly, and you know I got you? "You don't gotta give me nothing King G. I love y'all. If it wasn't for y'all, and particularly you, then I would just be a pimp's recruiter! You showed me I could do more. I'm happy to do this for the team. If you need me for anything trust, I got you!" "Say no more

Butterfly. Keep in touch and keep me updated. I will holla at you later." Bye King G"

Chapter 16

The night of the GGC party, the whole crew pulled up in the hummers. Everyone was rocking all white Gucci tees with Gucci belts, Gucci jeans, and Gucci sneakers. They were literally Gucci down to the socks! Jungle had all the porn stars arrive in two limos. King G had Butterfly park the Astro van by the club earlier that day, with a few hammers in the stash in case of anything. Butterfly emerged from the limo and immediately hooked King G's arm.

"Hey Butterfly, what are you doing?" "Oh sorry, King G. Your wives said to play you close and keep the hoes off their husband. I'm your stand in wife for the night!" Butterfly said with the sexy smirk.

Butterfly had a body like Ice T's wife Coco, but natural. She had the face of a pageant beauty with the bluest eyes and full sensual lips. She was wearing an all-white Gucci mini dress and some 4" heeled Gucci sandals. King G thought, not bad for a stand in!

"My wives are crazy; They know it's no need for that." "I agree King G, but they are pregnant and hormonal. They said, if I didn't do all I can to keep the hoe's away from you they would jump me after they have the babies. I ain't tryna get my ass whooped King G," "Aight, Butterfly, c'mon."

Everyone was in VIP and the place was packed. It was clearly more females than males in the place. King G left everyone in VIP to walk around the club to see if any SouthSide Mafia nigga's was in there. On his way back to VIP, he still hadn't noticed any that night. While walking, he was approached by a beautiful Spanish Mami, who was trying to Holla.

"Hola Papi. My name is Pinata. Would you like to beat me with your stick?"

All King G could do was laugh, but before he could answer, Butterfly was right there. She grabbed his hand, put it on her ass then grabbed his dick!

"This stick is spoken for Miss Pinata. So don't get ya head busted open for it; cause I'm sure candy won't fall out." Before Pinata could say anything, she noticed 10 other white girls behind King G, looking just as ready. She decided to just walk away.

"Sorry King G, just doing my job. Now I see why your wives asked me to be the hoe repellent for the night! That's quite a nice weapon you're packing."

King G didn't even know what to say. He just started walking back into VIP. He thought about how good Butterfly's ass felt and the way she had gripped on his dick. He quickly got his thoughts together because he knew he loved his wives. The night was over, Butterfly and the girls got in the limos and the rest of the crew was leaving out.

After LT and Chef counted the money; As they were walking to the car, a car came screeching to a stop in front of the club and they heard.

"Southside Motherfuckers" Boom, Boom, Boom, Boom, Boom rrrrrrrrrrrrrrrraaaaaa. Everyone hit the ground." The car peeled off as King G started running to the Astro van. He hopped in and chased the car down, but he had lost them. He pulled back by the club. He could see the crew gathered in a circle and someone was on the ground. King G jumped out and ran over.

"Yo what the Fuck happened?" he asked "Nutso got hit in the leg King G, "said Illy. "Put him in my van I'm taking him to the hospital."

After dropping Nutso to the hospital, King G met up with the crew.

"Listen y'all we taking it to these niggas immediately! But we gone do it correct. Nutso should be good. He probably gonna be on crutches for a week and then a cane for bout a month. Bro said he want a piece of the action. We already got a drop on these fools. So, we gotta execute!" "Man, I ain't waiting. They touched the Bro, so it's on!" K9 said. "Chill Bro, they gonna be on point right now. It's gonna be hard for our insider to draw them out." said King G. "Man listen, King G, them niggas hang on Jamaica Ave. They ain't gonna suspect nobody to ride down. I'm taking Chip and Gauge. We gonna catch them tonight, on some humbug shit! Make it look like a robbery. Let us get the TEC 22's you have stashed, and I will bring my P89. You can still plot and wait for Bro to get out of the hospital and all that" stated K9. "Aight, Bro. Fuck it! If you wanna do it like that, it makes sense. Ride out there tonight but be masked up. I don't want them to know it came from us. Make sure you scream out Lefrak City or something, so that they think it's local. TEC you go with them. I want you there watching K9's back. No disrespect to your boys, Gauge and Chip, but I don't know them like that. I'm not trusting them with your life K9." said King G." It's whatever Bro. I don't care who comes. They bout to know what beefing with a Flatbush nigga gonna get them." K9 said emphatically.

Everyone Broke out, King G drove to the Poconos to see his wives. As he came to the door, they bombarded him with questions.

"Are you ok, my King?" "Is Nutso ok Daddy? Do you know who did this, Boo?" "Y'all calm down. Y'all should not be overwhelming yourselves in your condition. I'm ok. Nutso will be fine. He just got hit in the leg. He should be good as new in 30 days. Some niggas from Queens did it, but it's gonna get handled." "Y'all be careful, my King. "We don't want nothing to happen to nobody else," LUV said meaning every word. "Yeah Daddy be careful but somebody gotta feel it!" "For real Boo" Brandy and Empress let it be known. "Ha-ha, y'all chill out, Lady of Rage and Gangsta Boo! We got this. Y'all just worry about having babies. "King said "Oh yeah, and what's up with giving me a watchdog. Or should I say a watch butterfly, at the party?" "Oh Daddy, we just had to make sure everything was good, since we couldn't be there to do our jobs. We had to make sure a sexy bitch kept them hoes off you." stated Brandy" "Y'all know, I ain't on that though, so wasn't no need." "Yeah, we know you not, my King, but that don't mean them hoes ain't!" "Yeah Boo, we heard all about Pinata wanting you to beat her with your stick!" Ha-Ha-Ha," they all laughed together at King G. "Oh, so you heard about that?" "Yeah, we heard about it, Daddy. Butterfly filled us in on the whole night." "Well did she tell you that she grabbed my dick and put my hand on her ass when she pressed Pinata? Bet she ain't tell you that!" "Actually Daddy, she did. See I told y'all my King would come home and keep it real with us." said LUV. King was shocked! He couldn't believe they all knew and was so calm. "So y'all knew and ain't mad?" "Nah, Boo, we ain't mad. For one, we told Butterfly to do all she had to do to keep them hoes away and she told us you ain't grip her ass when she put your hand on it. She also let us know she was impressed with our husband's package." Empress said with a smile. King G just shook his head and said "Y'all crazy." "Crazy bout you!" they all said. "We fuck with Butterfly! We ain't trippin my King." "I'm going to bed, I'm tired and I gotta handle some business later." King said shaking his head.

That night, K9, TEC, Gauge and Chip all drove in separate cars on the Van Wyck Expressway. They exited, found their way down Jamaica Ave and cruised up and down Guy Brewer. They were stopped at a light when they heard some dudes talking. So, they cracked their windows and listened.

"Nigga we really down with SouthSide Mafia. Fuck we gotta lie for Dat nigga 911P, sent us on a mission out in Brooklyn. We handled that" said a dark-skinned dude in a wife beater. "Word, Bro. Pinata told us, them niggas was in all-white, riding in Hummers. We got up on them and let dat heater do the talking." said a light skinned in a black tee.

They were shooting dice and talking shit to four other dudes with SouthSide Mafia T-shirts on. That was all the GGC Homies needed to hear. They spun around the block and parked up. They got out and readied themselves to walk up.

"Listen, we gonna get up on these niggas, back them down, rob them, and then shoot'em. Make sure y'all scream out, Lefrak city in this bitch!" K9 stated.

Everyone nodded their heads in agreement. As they got near the corner the mask came down and it was all action.

"Y'all niggas know what the Fuck it is! Run them pockets and all jewelry now!" said TEC." "Nigga get on the wall and don't move," screamed K9. "Yo, Looney and Crazo, relieve them of their belongings." said K9 to Gauge and Chip. After doing so, K9 spoke, "now don't none of you motherfuckers move and you'll be fine." "You know who you fuckin with homie this SouthSide Mafia," said the one in the wife beater. "I don't give a fuck! You Southside Tilapia right now we came here to eat!" said TEC. "Yo check their whips Looney" Gauge came back with two hammers and some money out the cars. "Tell ya Homies, Lefrak City in this bitch! This the takeover!"

LT said, before shooting dude with the wife beater in the jaw. As soon as the shot fired, the rest took off in separate directions. Gauge, let the TEC spray and cut down the one in the black tee; as K9, TEC and Chip chased the ones in the mafia tees. Chip was shooting erratically with the other TEC. He was the closest but couldn't hit shit! He managed to finally graze one of them in his calf muscles. TEC and LT decided to take over. They shot the other three in the back, causing them to fall to the ground. They put two in each of their heads. Leaving no recognizable facial features. Chip was still chasing the other one who was limping. Gauge pulled up in one of the Southside niggas' whips. TEC and K9 jumped in, then pulled up to Chip.

"Jump in nigga! Let dat nigga deliver the message," said K9.

They drove down the street from their whips. TEC pulled a bandana out of his pocket, stuck it in the gas tank and lit it on fire. Then they all jumped in their whips and pulled off smoothly. Two blocks away they heard an explosion. Then and only then, did they mash the gas headed back. Back in

Brooklyn, they set the cars on fire in Bushwick, where they had the females, who they swapped the cars with, pick them up. They drove to the chick's crib. They dropped the broads off, who complained.

"What about our cars? "Why would y'all burn them up like?"
K9 wasn't trying to hear no complaining. They had caught bout $80K from the SouthSide Mafia niggas. Not to mention four Rolex's and six chains with iced out pendants and iced out bracelets.

"How much your bum ass '92 Honda Accords cost y'all?" K9 asked. "First of all, our Honda's wasn't no bum ass cars. Me and my girls is fly! Everyone knew our crew for having the same whips, same rims and all," said a chick named Keisha. "Check this out Keisha, we burnt them shits cause can't no Broads that fuck with the GGC ride around in no shit like that! Take this lil $80K and go cop 4 '98 BMW 3 series. Then get all matching BBS rims and we will pay for them. Then y'all can have a real crew GGC, Girls Got Cars." He handed them the money. All they could do was stare as the crew pulled off. "Call us!" shouted the females.
TEC drove to Canarsie Pier; broke all the guns down and threw the parts in the water, as far out as his arm would allow. That was the only instruction King G had given him. Now he had to go tell King G about this guy Chip and his lack of aim.

King G, TEC, and K9 sit down in the warehouse discussing the events; TEC says.

"Ayo, K9, what's up with you man J. Reid and the fucked-up aim? I swear he was missing on purpose." Ha-ha. Yo Bro, you called him J. Reid, from dat movie, "In Too Deep." I ain't gonna lie, he did look like dat motherfucker missing all of them shots! But nah, that's my homie. He just can't go hunting with me ever again! K9 said laughing. "Yo, y'all did good, regardless of J. Reid's performance. I will handle the next move." Said King G. Let's go check on Nutso."

Chapter 17

After seeing about Nutso, King G went to holla at
Butterfly. They met at a Pool Hall in Canarsie on Flatlands
Ave.

"What's good Butterfly?"
Butterfly had shown up in a white polo shirt and some khaki
pum-pum shorts; that looked like they were painted on, white
polo socks, and all white air force ones. King G couldn't
understand why this white girl body was so stacked!

"What's good King G, Let's play some pool cause the
way everyone staring at us I think we should do something
while we talk" "Aight I will get the balls, you get the table all
the way in the back? Ladies first so you break."
Butterfly bent over to break, and King G couldn't help but
notice how bubbly her ass was. He just shook his head and
chalked his pool stick.

"So, Butterfly, I think in a week you should call up
911P and Sheisty. Tell them to bring 4 of their homies cause
you and your friends are having a get together at your house.
Let them know your friends don't fuck with the help. As I see
it, they are gonna come strapped and be happy to be able to
bring people along. More than likely, you should say the get
together is a week after your call. Insinuate that whatever
happens that night, is up to them." "I got this King G; you
know I know how to mesmerize a man" she said with a wink

and a bite of her bottom lip. King G felt his dick rise and said "Yeah, you do Butterfly, my bad. Wasn't trying to insult your skills." "It's cool King G. I know you meant nothing by it" "Aye, I was thinking after this, I would like you to come work with and for me and the Lady G's. It's time you started to make more money." "Whatever you need me to do King G." After two games they were tied 1-1 "Well let's get out of here I'm not gonna let you have the opportunity to beat me. I wouldn't live that down" said King G. "Ha-Ha you got it King G, because I was just warming up. It was bout to get real." As they returned the balls and were walking out, 3 Italians stepped out behind them. "Hey, what the fuck you doing with this fucking eggplant? Your own kind isn't good enough?" The first Italian said, as he grabbed Butterfly's arm. In a flash, Butterfly whipped a Butterfly knife out and sliced his forearm open and he screamed, "Aargh Bitch! you cut me!"

King G hit the second one with a left hook, side stepped to the right, kicked him with a left high kick. He pivoted and hit the third one with a right uppercut. They both hit the ground at the same time. He spun to deal with the first one when he saw Butterfly kick him in the knee breaking it. She got ready to stab him in the face with the knife.

"Butterfly stop!!!" King G screamed as he grabbed her arm. "Fucker, don't ever touch me again in your life! You fucking cock sucker. This ain't no eggplant this is fucking King "motherfuckin" G, you pasta eating pussy!" King G pulled Butterfly away "Are you okay, Butterfly?" With a calm face and gorgeous smile, she said, "Yes King G. I'm just fine. I will let you know in a week how things go." King G just shook his head, "You never cease to amaze me! Guess I know why they call you Butterfly. Quick question, aren't you Italian?" "Yes, 100% Sicilian King G, why?" "Nothing, just the way you cursed that guy out was crazy." "Oh, that was just something he needed to hear. See you King G" she said and gave him a hug and kiss on the cheek.

She pressed against him, and they hugged tightly with a new feeling of camaraderie having put working together. King G got home and told his wives exactly how things went, he also decided to tell him his plans for Butterfly.

"You should have seen Butterfly move. She was like a trained killer! I'm pulling her into work closer with our inner circle. I also wanna make her y'all security. I know, y'all can hold your own but I'm telling you, It's something different with her! Then she just turned back into her regular self, like nothing happened. That shit had me shocked for real." "Well, my King, if that's what you wanna to do, that's fine with us. We told you we fuck with her." said LUV. "I don't even think Jungle knows what she's capable of cause he would have told me," said King G. "Daddy, I think after this move, you should move Butterfly up here because she needs to get herself off the scene in the city." Brandy said. "You're right Babe.

Everyone else agree?" "Yes, my King" "Yes Boo," LUV and Empress said.

A week later Butterfly said, it was easy to get them to agree to come through. She had told them; it was a pajama and lingerie get together. Butterfly had a home that was tucked away in Long Beach, Long Island. The basement was soundproofed and had thick cement walls. It was made to serve as a storm shelter and living quarters.

King G hadn't laid eyes on Mama LUV, Mama Judy or Crazy Joe in a while, so he drove to the city to check on them. He pulled up on Mama LUV at the Diner. She was so happy to see him.

"Oh my God King it feels like I haven't seen you, Royal and the ladies in forever." "Sorry Mama LUV they haven't been coming down to the city much, you're more than welcome to come up." "I know honey, but the diner be so busy. I'm trying to make as much as I can. At this rate, in a year, I can hire someone else to do all this and live well. Thanks to you!" "You do all the work Mama LUV, no need to thank me" Mama LUV gave him some food to eat to take home to his family. He thanked her and went to Mama Judy apartment. When he reached the building and knocked on her door, nobody answered. He saw the Super coming in the building. "Hey King G what's up? Why you knocking on that door?" "I'm looking for Mama Judy, Super" "Boy, Mama Judy don't live here no more! I thought you knew that" "What you mean she don't live here?" "She moved out King G" "Ok Super later."

King G was confused so he went to the warehouse to check on Crazy Joe.

"Yo Joe, you in here!" "Upstairs in the kitchen King" King makes his way upstairs. Lo and behold, Mama Judy and Crazy Joe were sitting there enjoying a cup of coffee.

"Mama Judy I just came from your apartment. Why didn't you tell me you moved?" "Well son, I just moved last week and since we haven't heard from you, we figured you were busy. Might as well tell him, Joe." "King G, me and Mama Judy are engaged, and she moved in with me."

King G stood there with his mouth open.

"Close your mouth son, before you start catching flies," said Mama Judy. "I just can't believe it. You and Joe engaged, and we didn't even know y'all were dating" "Well grown folks keep their business, to themselves," said Crazy Joe. "I guess so Joe. Well, congrats to you two. Does Brandy know?" "No King and I will tell her this weekend, when we come up to the Poconos," said Mama Judy. "Yes ma'am. Well, when is the wedding?" King G asked. "After my grandbaby drop that baby of course. So, we are planning for summer wedding next year." "By the way King G, I want you to be my best man," said Joe. "Of course, Joe, I gotta get y'all a good wedding gift." "Now don't go to hard King. We are older and don't need much," said Mama Judy. "I got y'all;

Well let me let you two love birds alone. I'm happy for y'all. See y'all later."

Chapter 18

The day came for King G to deal with the SouthSide Mafia niggas. He would do this solo! He didn't want anyone in the house with him. This was personal! Nutso was his brother from another and he felt he failed him. So now it was time to clean this up properly. King G thought like the enemy, so he figured they would arrive earlier than planned. He knew they would bring extra men to scope out the outside, while they were inside. He arrived at Butterfly's crib around noon, in a taxi. She had an electric privacy fence; so, when the cab drove in the gate to drop him off, nobody could see who exited the cab. Butterfly answered the door in a pair of leggings, a sports bra, and barefoot.

"What's up King G? Welcome to my humble abode."
"Thank you for having me. This is nice!"
As King G walked in; he couldn't help but notice Butterfly's ass and the way it bounced and swayed with every step. Butterfly looked back and caught him staring and smiled to herself.

"You want something to eat King G?" "What you got?" "I made some Baked Ziti, Fried Eggplant Parmesan, and some Zeppoli's, as a snack." "Damn Butterfly you did all that?" "Yeah, I do this all the time. A girl gotta eat and feed this figure," she said with her hand on her hip. They sat down and ate, then drank some homemade lemonade. "Damn

Butterfly that shit was banging. I'm glad you didn't make no swine, or I wouldn't have been able to taste that top-notch cooking!" "Thanks, King G. I'm glad you enjoyed it, and I don't eat nor cook pork. You will definitely never find pork on my fork!" "I like that," said King G.

They went over the plan, one more time. Butterfly assured him, she had it all memorized and would hold him down. Since they had time to kill, they chopped it up about their lives. They were both enlightened by the convo, especially King G.

"King G I don't know if you know this or not, but I was never a hoe for Jungle. I would just bring the girls to him to work, and he would pay me 10% of what they made. I would see anywhere from $3k to $5K a week. He was cool, so I just hung around him. It helped make his pimpin look better! I didn't mind cause I was getting paid." "I didn't know that Butterfly. I just figured you were one of the girls that worked, but just had more to offer. "Well, I did have more to offer. You peeped that and gave me the opportunity. Now I'm one of the best talent scouts for adult films. You see how good we are doing with the porn company?" "Yeah, I do Butterfly and you're right" "You also believed in my loyalty, when you trusted me to handle the situation with them dudes" "Well you showed and proved. So, it was a pleasure to work with you." "You ain't seen nothing yet King G."

Butterfly had told 911P to come around 8pm. This made King G. believe they would show up between 6pm and 7pm. Butterfly went to get dressed and King G sat waiting in the kitchen. Butterfly yelled downstairs,

"Go checkout the set up in the basement."
King G went to the basement where there were two stripper poles, a mini stage and a long couch covered in latex, the floor was also covered in latex too. There were whips on the walls and handcuffs. While looking around Butterfly came downstairs in her robe and stripper heels.

"You like King G?" "Yeah, this set up is nice Butterfly" "Ok good. This mirror right here on the wall is a two-way mirror, behind it is a safe room. Once you lock it from inside, no one can get in without a key. Plus, it's undetectable, if you don't know what it is. You will be good in there til you're ready to come out," said Butterfly.

King G called Alvino to make sure his shooters were ready at the end of the block. Alvino confirmed they were. Butterfly got a call at 6:45pm from 911P, saying they were outside.

"Damn y'all are early, my girls ain't here yet... Nah, it's not no problem, I'm just letting you know. Let me open the gate for you... Ok see you in a bit."

She dropped her robe and King G felt his dick instantly brick up. She had on a fully see-through baby doll lingerie with a see-through thong on. Her breasts were perfect, and her ass was too! Her pussy looked fat and juicy and was bald; not to mention pretty.

"Ok King G, it's showtime! Go in the room and once I have them entertained and well distracted, you come out and do your thing."

With that she walked off…

"Man, this is a nice house, Butter!" 911P said "Word!" Sheisty and the four other dudes said. "Damn I knew you was sexy Butter, but you look like the Goddess of sexy right now." said 911P "Thank you 911P; That's sweet of you. It's just a little something I threw on."

They were all standing there grabbing their dicks! Butterfly turned and walked towards the kitchen, with her sexy walk hypnotizing them.

"Would you guys like something to drink, while we wait for my girls?" "Sure, that will work. I like that you got an electric gate. That's real good security!" said 911P. "Never can be too safe," replied Butterfly with a smile. "Where are y'all pajamas?" she asked as she handed them all double shots of Hennessey." "Oh, there on, under our clothes!" said 911P. "Well get out those regular clothes and let's see them. I'm not gonna be the only one dressed for the theme. By the way what are your friends' names?" "My bad this is Gee, Pistol, Dollar and Lambo" 911P said coming out of his clothes and putting his gun in his pants pocket. "Hello Gee, Pistol, Dollar and Lambo, Butterfly said. They disrobed like 911P. "You guys didn't need them guns. I know y'all not scared of some ass and titties" "Ha-Ha Nah never that, like you said never can be too safe." They were all standing there in silk pajama shorts and shirts. "Oh, I like those pajamas and y'all all match" Butterfly said sexily. "So, what do you wanna do til your girls get here? asked 911P. "I guess I could entertain y'all downstairs in the party room" "Party Room?" Sheisty said. "Yeah, my basement is for the entertaining. You will love it, c'mon."

She walked ahead swinging her hips and had them all stuck behind her following like little puppies. Down in the basement, they all smiled at the site of the poles.

"I take it you like" Butterfly said, twirling around one of the poles. "Hell yeah," they all said.

"Well, y'all have a seat and break out some money. That's gonna help motivate my show." "You ain't said nothing Butter."

The SouthSide Mafia all pulled out knots of money. "Ooh I think we gonna have lots of fun." Butterfly said.

She put on some music and began dancing. As soon as she grabbed a pole and held herself up and spread her legs wide open the room went completely silent and then it exploded in cheer!

"Damn Butter! Do your shit! Show us what this money make you do!" 911P said.

… as he and his boys threw money at her. She got on the mini stage and eased her panties down, around and off her ankle. Got on her knees, arched her back and began making her ass cheeks shake. These southside niggas were losing their minds. She laid on her back, spread her legs and put them behind her head. It was so much money flying through the air.

"We don't need your friends for real Butter," said Sheisty, "Who wants a lap dance?" she asked as she noticed all of them with hard-ons.

911P jumped up. She sat him back down on the couch and mounted him. She squeezed his dick between her ass cheeks and slid along his length. He was gripping her ass, spreading her cheeks as his boys looked on. She reached behind the back of the chair, so she could get a better grip, and started rocking on him. Slamming down every time she moved back. 911P had his eyes clothes and his boys were behind her watching her ass move. They were so mesmerized; they didn't even hear the safe room door open! King G came out with a 9mm Beretta with a silencer.

"GGC motherfuckers!!!"

The whole SouthSide Mafia turnt around. Butterfly came from gripping the back of the couch to holding her butterfly knife in hand, which was taped to the couch. She stabbed 911P in both shoulder joints which immobilized his arms. The rest of the Southside crew went for their guns, and King G unloaded on them! Shooting all of them multiple times in the face, killing them instantly! 911P tried to use his hips to push Butterfly off, but she locked her legs around his and pushed her weight down. She rained down elbows to his face till he was unconscious.

"Don't worry King G, I didn't kill him. I just needed to make him pay for touching my ass" she said this with the loveliest smile on her face then jumped up and said, "I'll get the duct tape so we can start the questioning."
She walked off and again King G couldn't help but look. This woman was a cold-blooded gangster and it turnt him on completely! His mind couldn't comprehend why he was so enticed. He called Alvino,

"Yeah, the food is finished. You got any guests for dinner?" King G said "Yeah there were two, I was thinking of bringing," said Alvino.
Meaning 911P had 2 cars sitting on the block watching out.

"Please invite them to the party." King G said.
The word was sent. Those in the two cars met the same fate, from a silenced weapon, like their Homies. After taping up 911P's hands and feet and stripping him naked, Butterfly slapped him to wake up. SLAPPP!

"Wake up Mr. 911P, I'd like to ask you a few questions" Butterfly said. "Ahhh, what the fuck? Please don't kill me, I got money you can have it just don't kill me." "How much money you talking?" King G asked" "I just collected $180K before I came here. It's in the back of the Yukon we pulled up in" "Ok, but what we want to know is how can we find the rest of your boys? Oh yeah, by the way, the 2 cars you brought with you are dearly departed." King G stated. 911P hung his head then said "Look man it ain't gotta be like this. It was all a misunderstanding. We can work this out." "Wrong answer," Butterfly said and then stabbed him through his foot. "Ahh ok, ok please" "Now where is the rest of your crew?" "They are all going to the car races out Hunts Point tonight. There was only 20 official members left." "Where is the bitch Pinata?" "She will be there with them. Please just let me go." "Sorry no can do. But I promise I won't shoot you. Butterfly wants you all to herself" "It's time you bow down to the King," Butterfly told 911P. "Motherfucker, I said bow to the King."

When 911P bowed his head to King G; Butterfly stabbed him through the back of his neck into his brain killing him instantly!

"C'mon on King G let's go upstairs. I will have this all cleaned up."

They went upstairs King G went to the Yukon and found the money in a duffle bag. He came back inside and tossed the bag on the counter. 20 minutes later; Butterfly came down, hair wet in a short silk robe that clung to her naked body underneath and some slippers.

"That money is yours Butterfly you more than earned it." "Thanks King G my cleanup crew is on the way." She said as she grabbed a garbage bag. "Step out those clothes and those sneakers. All of that has to go!" she said while holding the bag open. "Don't worry I have a change of clothes for you. Hurry up, they are almost here and do not wish to be seen. We will wait in my room while they provide their service."

As King G did as he was told; he wondered how safe it would be for him to be in Butterfly's room alone with her. He turned his back to her while taking his pants off. Being around her, had his dick on brick and he couldn't control it. No other woman besides his wives did this to him,

"It's ok King G. I have seen that your dick has been hard all evening around me. If I may be honest, you have had my pussy dripping. But I respect you and your wives too much to violate! Just know that in five years, you are the first and only man that I would and want to let inside of me. I will be sure to be honest with your wives and let them know nothing happened. Now let's get your ass in the shower and get you cleaned up!"

In Butterfly's bathroom, King G stepped into the shower and washed up. As he was rinsing off, he heard the door open. Butterfly stepped in.

"Your clothes are right here on the toilet seat King G." "Here use this soap. It's from the hospital and I put bleach in it to help get rid of all the gunshot residue. Make sure you hit under your nails." "Thanks Butterfly. I really appreciate your thoroughness." "No problem, King G."

Once King G heard the door close, he grabbed the soap and began to re-clean. He still couldn't understand why his dick would not go down. Especially since he needed to be ready and focused for the rest of the mission tonight at Hunts Point. Meanwhile in the bedroom, Butterfly was laid on her bed on her back, feet flat on the bed with her legs open completely naked playing in her pussy.

"Damn you got me so fuckin wet King G. Mmm, Yesss make me cum Papa Bear! Damn I want you to own this pussy. Fuuuuck! Please Papa Bear, take this pussy. Pleeease. I'm gonna cum King G. I'm gonna cum. Oooh, I'm cummin Papa Bear! I'm cumin ssss ahhh."

Butterfly opens her eyes after cumming down off of her orgasm, to find King G at the bathroom door staring at her.

"I'm sorry King G I didn't think you would be done before me. Please don't be mad at me." "It's cool Butterfly. This your crib and there is obviously some energy in here tonight that needs to be released!" "How long were you standing there?" "Long enough to know I should be calling you Goldilocks!" King G said with a chuckle. Butterfly giggled and said, "Good one King G! I think we should call the Lady G's and explain what happened." I think you're right. I don't want to lie to them or keep no secrets." "You are the perfect man King G."

Butterfly got up, completely naked and walked to King G and hugged him. When she felt his hard dick through his pants, she had another mini orgasm. Especially when she felt his dick jump!

"Damn Butterfly, you making it hard for me!" "I can see that!" she said with a smile.

King G called his wives and explained that part one of movie was done; and he would be getting ready for the sequel later after he took a nap. Then he explains the Butterfly situation. Butterfly then got on the phone and also explained and sincerely apologized. The Lady Gs's didn't flip out though. When King G got back on the phone all they said was,

"Bring her home with you when you done tonight, so we can all talk face-to-face."

King G felt like this would be bad; especially with them being pregnant, but he would do as requested.

"Listen Butterfly we need to get some rest before we head out" "ok King G."

King G called LT and told him what they needed and where to meet up. Then he and Butterfly crashed out for two hours. After their nap, they were up and dressed. King G had on a black tee, black cargoes, black socks and all black Chuck Taylors, all courtesy of Butterfly. He wondered how she knew his sizes. Butterfly was dressed in a tight black tee, black biker shorts, black socks and all black Chuck Taylors. King G still thought she looked sexy in plain clothing.

"Pack a bag, Butterfly. After we complete this mission, you're coming to my house." Butterfly looked shocked but said. "Only bag I need, is my bag of money. I'm sure $180K will get me through."

They checked the basement, and everything was gone stripper poles and all! It smelled really clean with a hint of Pine-Sol and bleach, to cover whatever else they used to remove any evidence.

"Your cleanup crew is top notch I see. How much do they cost? asked King G.

"Usually, $10K but I'll let them keep all the money that they found on the bodies and the floor. Said Butterfly. Them dudes had to have at least $50K on them. So, I should be due a couple of clean ups on the house. They even took the truck which they will probably take to a chop shop."

King G was amazed by Butterfly.

"Before we go Butterfly, let me offer prayer."

"Ok King G, do you mind if I pray with you? Can you teach me how to pray like you?

"You seriously wanna pray with me Butterfly?

"Yes, King G, I mean I'm interested in learning."

"C'mon, just follow my lead and move how I move and stay silent."

After they prayed, King G really was blown away. Butterfly was the first woman and non-Muslim to show any interest in his religion, in this way. His wives definitely knew about it, but they never prayed with him.

"Thank you for the prayer, King G. I feel at ease."

"You're welcome, Butterfly, now let's get this night over with."

King G grabbed his silenced Beretta, which he noticed was cleaned and oiled. Butterfly came out with a compressed Mac 11 and two butterfly knives.

"Damn Butterfly that's a hell of a gun you got. Where the fuck you get that?"

"Oh, this Lil thing? It was a gift from my grandfather."

"I swear Butterfly you full of surprises. Why the two knives tho?"

"Oh, these are for that Lil bitch Pinata. When I catch her, she gettin the special treatment!"

All King G could do was laugh. They went to Butterfly's garage. She had her 2000 S430 parked and another car with a car cover over it. She pulled the cover off to expose a 1986 Buick Grand National in showroom condition.

"You got a Grand National Butterfly!" King G exclaimed.

"Yeah, just another gift from my grandfather. I love American Muscle." King G couldn't believe his ears.

"We got a lot to talk about later Butterfly."

Leaving off her block, they didn't notice any dead bodies in cars. Alvino's men had gotten rid of them. They met up with LT at Hunts Point, down the street from the races.

"Yo Bro, everyone's down there getting ready for the races." stated LT. "Aight Bro. We gonna send Butterfly down there to scope the scene, to see what's our plan of attack" King G replied. "Man, all of them dumb. Southside niggas got T-shirts on that say SouthSide Mafia. They gonna be easy to spot." LT said. "I wanna know where that bitch Pinata is," was all Butterfly said. "Aight Butterfly, go down there and see what you see. I'm gonna hop in with Bro." "Ok King G, see ya when I get back." "Yo King G what Butterfly meant by she wanna know where Pinata at? She does know we ain't come down here to catfight, right?"

King G thought to tell LT, but decided he would see for himself.

"Yeah, she knows that Bro." Butterfly
pulled back up.

"Yo, they all are standing in their own lil section huddled up, King G. The bitch Pinata sitting in a little Mazda Miata convertible; about 3 cars lengths away from them; off to the side like. She by herself!"

"Aight! We gonna come from the direction closest to Pinata. So, Butterfly, you can have your fun, then we are rushing those fools. Deal with them and we out! We will park our whips on the street behind them, so everything is done in one a swift move." King G said. "This MVP belongs to a crackhead King G. We can just pull up, hop out and do our thing and drive off. I will leave this shit, set it on fire and jump in with y'all." LT stated.

"It leaves us less expose King G. Just means I will have to deal with that bitch faster than I intended." said Butterfly.

""Ok, then we still come in from the same direction Butterfly. You will jump out before we reach Pinata and start the party. Then we hit the crew and mash out!" said King G.

They waited til the police had shift change, then made their move. Butterfly hopped out and saw Pinata leaning on her car, with her back to Butterfly's direction. Butterfly took out her two knives, ran up on her and stabbed her through her throat on both sides.

"That's for Nutso bitch!!"

Butterfly took off running towards the rest of the intended target; after the screams of the crowd filled the air after seeing what just happened to the spanish chica. LT and King G were approaching, driving slowly; while the SouthSide Mafia were trying to see what the commotion was. As they got closer, they noticed a woman with a cane walking towards the mafia crew and then gunshots erupted. Boom, Boom, Boom! The mafia was getting moved on King G. slid the door open and started letting his Beretta work. Tat, Tat, Tat. LT came out the driver side window with his P89 letting it rain. Boom, Boom, Boom, Boom! Some of the mafia crew tried to run down the block only to be chopped down by Butterfly's Mac! Tu, Tu, Tu, Tu. The woman with the cane stood over one of them and dumped a clip. From the flares in the gun, King G could see that wasn't no women, it was Nutso! He was bending the corner, moving fast as he could with the cane. LT bent the corner and King G yelled out the window.

"Follow us Bro" as Nutso jumped in his car.

They met up by Butterfly's whip. LT was already setting the MPV on fire, then he hopped in the car with Nutso.

"Go to the warehouse" King G screamed.

Chapter 19

Back in Brooklyn at the warehouse, King G let Crazy Joe know they were downstairs in the office.

"Yo, what the fuck you were doing there, Nutso?" asking King G. "I've been on them niggas heels for a week, following them around. I told y'all I wanted in on a move against them. "Why ain't nobody try and come get me?" "Listen Bro, it was a random thing. We happened to get the drop on them, through some info. I just chose to make the move. I wasn't trying to leave you out." King G said.

"It's cool bro. I know it's all love, but I had to get my hit back." replied Nutso. "Man, I aint' know what that crazy lady was doing out there. Then when I noticed it was you it really fucked me up Bro." stated King G.

"Yeah, y'all like that one huh? Ha-ha, but what's up with the Italian version of "Rock-a-bye baby" from New Jack City over here?" Nutso said, eyeing Butterfly.

Everyone laughed.

"She is something, ain't she?" King G stated.

"Surprised the fuck out of me." LT said. "Don't sleep on Butterfly, I don't need a cocoon to transform, Butterfly said. I know I don't need to say it, but business is only for those who do it! We gonna keep this between us and only us." King G said.

"You already know, Bro" LT and Nutso said together. "Leave the hammers here. Joe will deal with them. Y'all lay low from out of the streets. Just handle normal business. Princess G will be handling the trucking contacts and schedules, so get with her. I will be in the Poconos, King G told them. Aight Bro, I'm going to drop LT to the crib." Nutso said.

"Burn all of them clothes y'all and shoes" Butterfly said. "Crash or Get cash" stated King G. "Crash or Get cash" replied LT and Nutso.

King G and Butterfly finally made it to the Poconos tired and ready for bed. First, Butterfly bags all the clothing they had on she tosses it on the grill in the backyard and burns them. They both take showers and King G shows her to her room. He kisses his sleeping wives, then gets in bed and falls out. The next morning, he is awakened by the smell of food and female chatter. King G came into the kitchen, kissing each of his wives. "

"Good morning my beautiful wives, I'm so happy to be home." "We're happy to have you home my King," said LUV. "Yeah Daddy, we missed you" said Brandy "For real Boo we couldn't wait for you to get here." said Empress. "We made pancakes, scrambled eggs and beef bacon. You take a seat so we can eat," said LUV. "Now y'all sit down so I can make y'all plates" said King G. "Daddy just cause we're pregnant don't mean we can't do stuff" said Brandy. "Man, you might as well stop. That man ain't trying to hear that.

Take it from me, this is my second child with him," said LUV. "Aight LUV, I guess you know best when it comes to that!" "Good morning, everybody," Butterfly said walking into the room in a big T-shirt and basketball shorts, she got from King G.

"Morning Butterfly." The ladies and King G said together. "Sit down and eat so we can all get to talk," said *LUV.*

They all ate, and Butterfly cleared the table, washed the dishes, then excused herself. She came back with her duffel bag and gave each of the ladies $45K.

"This is for y'all it's just a token of my appreciation and my apologies again for yesterday." Butterfly stated. "First of all, Butterfly, stop apologizing. So, what you was masturbating and King G saw you. Y'all ain't do nothing. Plus, you kept it real. We really fuck with you," said LUV. Empress and Brandy shook their heads in agreement.

"Well, I still want y'all to have it out of appreciation because y'all really do fuck with me. I have never in my 25 years of life, had real friends." Well, we thank you very much," LUV stated.

"Ok now that we done with all the small chat. You was playin in dat pussy thinking about Daddy. Are you in love with our husband?" "Brandy asked.

Butterfly looked them all in the eyes with no hesitation, and said:

"Yes, yes, I am. "Why?" He is a real man! He is genuine, honest, protective, a provider, non-judgmental, faithful and sexy as fuck to me. I see how he is with y'all. When I'm around him he isn't lusting after me or making me feel uncomfortable. He respects me and my mind. A man hasn't seen me naked in five years. Having King G see me that way felt normal to me, like it was supposed to be. I'm not gonna lie, I wanna be a part of this family. I'm also in love with y'all. Not on no lesbian stuff, but in love with who y'all are and what y'all are to him and each other." "That was deep! You got me over here, misty eyed. I don't know if it's the hormones or what." LUV said. "Well, I understand all that and you definitely make valid points bout my Boo. We knew you were in love because we see the look in your eyes and that was so familiar to all of us. You have done a lot for him and held him down in ways, we have never. Like LUV said, we really fuck with you. We definitely think you are a sexy bitch! The funny thing, none of us has wanted to beat your ass. Not even once. Which is weird to us, since we don't play bout our husband" stated Empress. "Ok Butterfly spoke her piece here, but I want to know, why my King had a hard dick for her?" "Listen, my LUV, I can't explain that! I have never been turned on by another woman before, besides y'all three. I'm happy with y'all completely. It's just something about Butterfly. It's not just her being sexy because I've seen and been around sexy women in the club and have never wanted them." Said King G. "There is something here my King. You haven't even looked at her once since she came in the kitchen. I want you to look at her and you look at him Butterfly." King G and Butterfly locked eyes and she smiles instantly. Instantly he can feel his dick bricking up! "How do you feel about what she said Daddy?" said Brandy. "I'm very appreciative of her honesty and respect for me and y'all."

Brandy walks over to King G and grabs his dick.

"Daddy, you hard as fuck right now! Empress and LUV come feel this shit," said Brandy.

They walk over and feel it too,

"Yeah Boo, you definitely bricked up," said.

Empress. "Yeah, my King, and y'all just sitting here across the table. You be fantasizing bout her or something?" asked LUV. "No, my LUV, I promise. My body just reacts to her. I think she is very sexy and alluring and I feel a strong emotion for her but my love and dedication to y'all won't let it break through." Said King G. "So, if we told you, it was ok to act on it, would you?" asked LUV. "No, I wouldn't my LUV, because she isn't my wife. If I did that, what would my discipline be like around anyone else? Not that I want anyone else, but I didn't think I would want or be attracted to anyone besides y'all." said King G. "So, you do want her?" asked Brandy "cause that's what you just said." "I guess in a way I do," said King G. "See this is why I'm in love with him. He respects y'all and his marriages and believes so much, he won't even go for a want he has. I don't know any man like that! It really touches me deep in my heart. I want that in a husband." says Butterfly. "Listen Butterfly you gonna be staying with us? I'm due to drop this baby in September, Empress and Brandy due in February. It's August now. Sell your house because we are the ones who told my King to bring you out here. It's safer for you. After six months, if my King's feelings haven't changed and you both can maintain your discipline and respect, we will agree for you to be his final wife. We can see you respect us the way we respect each other. Which is something that tips the scale in your favor. Do you agree to this?" asks LUV. "Yes, LUV I do," states Butterfly. Do you, my King?" "Looks like y'all made the decision for me. One thing I will say is my respect and discipline can pass any test" "Ok well since that's final Daddy; I just got a question for Butterfly, Girl how in the hell are you so damn stacked? And! you got a tan like you Spanish is something," said Brandy. "My grandma on my mother's side was black. She was a French Italian. Plus, you know they say all Sicilian's got a little black in them ever since Hannibal invaded Italy." "See y'all I told you she wasn't all white is, she too damn sexy and cool." Brandy said, making everyone laugh. "Would y'all like to take me to get some clothes?" Asked Butterfly. "Sure, we will all go with you and leave my King here to gather his thoughts. I ain't never seen him this quiet. You can borrow some leggings and a T-shirt from me to go to the mall. Matter fact we will go to Reading to the Outlets." Said LUV.

Chapter 20

While they were gone, King G sat and planned. News of the SouthSide Mafia being wiped out, spread through New York City like wildfire! It was said two men with bandannas on their face in a minivan, and one woman with a cane and another Hispanic woman with a black bandanna over her face; were responsible for the killings. K9 was in the hood saying that he was the one who crushed the entire SouthSide Mafia. Well, him and a few of his militant soldiers. When Nutso and LT got word of this all they could think was why Bro be faking like that! It wasn't like he didn't put in work, but taking credit for work you didn't do, was phoney as fuck! Not to mention stupid, because who talks about shit like that.

"Yo, this nigga K9 is bugging Bro." said Nutso.

"Yeah I know, but if he wanna do that I ain't gonna correct him. I just never thought Bro would go that far with his lies." stated LT. On the other side of Flatbush, K9 is chilling with Gauge and Chip. "Yeah Bro, I had to go out to the Bronx and show them fools how Brooklyn gets down," K9 stated. "Why you ain't take us?" asked Chip. "Nah, y'all was getting to the money I had to try out some new soldiers. Feel me, Bro?" "Yeah, I feel you K9. Somebody gotta get bread while a sucker catches lead." Gauge said.

They were still eating good off the work, King G put K9 on too. They had a mean flow upstate and in the hood.

"We gonna have to find a connect for the re-up K9." Chip said. "Yeah, I know Bro, but we still got 50 pounds of haze left. Since we stretched the 10 keys of boy to 20, we got 10 left. We all up. Money talks! So, the connect game will come to us. Trust me." stated K9.

He had no idea what he was gonna do, when it came time to re-up. He just knew, he didn't wanna have to ask King G.

It was now September 26, 2000, and LUV was having her and King G second son. Mama LUV, Empress, Brandy, Butterfly, Mama Judy, Princess G and Mama G were all there. Crown G was born 7lbs. 12oz. Three days later, everyone was back in the Poconos. Royal was with Mama G, so everyone could focus on Crown. Everything was going well with Butterfly in the crib. She helped out tremendously! She even had Empress and Brandy doing light exercises to get ready for their babies. Empress and Brandy were always horny; so, King G spent the night or early morning making love to one of the two. He took it easy on them because of the babies. But he really wanted to beat something up! He got to work out a lot and spend time with the family. King and Butterfly came up with some great business ideas. LUV was moving around normally. It has been three weeks since she had Crown. Her and Butterfly were doing yoga in the basement. After 30 minutes she was through. Butterfly wanted to keep going. Butterfly was wearing some yoga pants and a sports bra. LUV decided to apply the first test as she went upstairs.

"Hey, my King can you go downstairs and take Butterfly this towel?" LUV said, handing him the towel. King G went to deliver the towel and saw Butterfly in the downward dog position. Her back was arched perfectly, and it looked like her pussy was busting through the leggings. Instantly King G felt his dick. She switched positions and noticed him standing there.

"Oh, hey King G, I didn't know you were standing. there" "Uh-Uh, I came to bring you a towel." "Looks like you brought the rod for me to hang it up on too." she said looking at his hard dick, pressing to his basketball shorts and smiling. "My bad" he said and left back upstairs. He passed LUV and went straight to his room. LUV laughed when she noticed his hard on and said to herself this might be fun.

Empress 19th birthday came, and due to the pregnancy, King G kept it simple. He had a beautician come and do her hair and nails. Everyone in the house bought her one outfit a piece. She took professional pics in every one of them. Then everyone gave her a gift. For Brandy's birthday, King G rented a circus tent for the backyard with mobile heaters. He got a DJ and flew in her family. There were 3 thrones set up for her and her siblings since they were all turning 18. Cousins, Uncles and Aunts, she hadn't seen in a while, were all there. King G bought her, Candy, and Andy all Gucci outfits and shoes. There was a caterer and all. Brandy cried happy tears because she was overwhelmed by the love and her husband's efforts.

King G and the Ladies decided to start his wives and Butterfly, a management company. They named it "Gorgeous Girls Can Management." Butterfly taught them all that they would need to scout talent and sign them. At the turn of the year, they would get started. Princess G would be left to run the trucking business' day-to-day activities. Both King G and Butterfly's birthdays were coming up on January 3rd and January 5th. December 29, Butterfly closed on the sale of her house for $350K. The bank took $100K she owed, and she was left with $250K.

Jan 3rd arrived; it was Kings G.'s 21st birthday. He had been telling his wives for a while that for his 21st birthday he wanted to have a naked day. Where they all catered to him naked, and they could have sex all day and play sexy games. He just wanted it to be a sexy day, filled with lap dances, sexy cooking and serving. Basically, he wanted the King treatment. The morning of his birthday LUV, Empress & Brandy woke him up, butt ass naked!!

"Happy Birthday Hubby!" They all screamed.
They escorted him to the bathroom where they brushed his teeth, washed his face for him and held his dick while he peed

and wiped it clean. Then they showered him and lotion his skin.

"Come on Daddy it's time to eat," said Brandy.
All this naked flesh had King G dick sticking straight out! His wives all took turns playing with it, on the way downstairs to the kitchen.

"Damn y'all cooked already? The whole house smelling right" King G said. "Yeah, something like that Boo." Empress said.
When they entered the kitchen, King G's jaw dropped! There was Butterfly butt naked, bent over. Pulling honey biscuits out of the oven, in some stripper heels. He looked at his wives.

"Well, she lives here now, so she got to play along for your birthday." LUV said with a smile "Happy Birthday King G" Butterfly said, while setting up the table.

They all took turns feeding him. When they were done, they all cleared the table. Then they all had hot chocolate and sat around talking.

"Where is Crown?" King G asked. "He is at Princess G house with your twin nieces Queen and Dutchess. Ya sister said enjoy your day." LUV said as she spilled a lil hot chocolate on the floor. She bent down to clean it up. "So, what y'all got planned for me today?" asked King G. "Daddy just sit back and enjoy. We got this" Brandy stated.

Just then King G felt a familiar set of lips on his dick. LUV was literally making love to it with her mouth.

"Oh Shit, my LUV! Your mouth feels so good." "So, King G are you enjoying the services of the women of the house so far?" asked Butterfly. "Mmmmm, yes absolutely! The breakfast and hot chocolate was delicious and this after breakfast treat is amazing. "

All you could hear is the slurping coming from under the table. Brandy and Empress were laughing. Butterfly was smiling. Then LUV stopped and got up.

"We better find something to do before, it be puddles all in the seats and on this floor." They had King G dizzy. "Let's give my Boo his first gift of the day," Empress said, as they all went to the living room.

Butterfly couldn't take her eyes off King G's pole. Her pussy was dripping down her leg. The Lady G's gave him a Rolex, Presidential Edition, and an Iced out chain with a pendant of a "G" with a Rolex crown over it.

"Thanks, y'all I really like it."

As King G tried on his jewelry, all the girls could look at was his dick, standing at attention! King G was sitting in his recliner. Brandy said,

"Let's play musical chairs. When the music stops whoever is in front of Daddy gets to sit on his lap for 60 seconds. Butterfly you DJ."

The music started and they circled King G. The first time it stopped; Brandy was in Front. She opened his legs and sat right on his dick, bouncing on it.

"Oooh Daddy that feels so good. Mmm fuck me, this your pussy!" She was so turned on and she started cumming. "I'm cumin, I'm cumin."

60 seconds was up she got up wobbly. When the music started back, it was LUV and Empress playing. The music stopped, and Empress was in front of King G. She did the same as Brandy and sat on him with her back to him and bounced and grind on him.

"Fuck, Fuck ahhh, yes fuck aah shit. Slap my ass Boo. Harder Harder!!"

As soon as the music started back; she started to cum but had to get off. Butterfly was unconsciously rubbing her clit.

"Hey Butterfly, leave the music on for my 60 seconds, LUV said. She mounted him, facing him and bounced her 48" ass up and down fast on her husband. "Ooh shit, fuck yeah, I need this dick my King. Give it to me! Damn you in my stomach. Motherfucker ooh yesss! I'm bout to cum. Cum with me my King, cum with me."

As they were preparing to cum together; King G looked around at his other two wives playing with themselves. Butterfly had her finger, thrusting in and out of herself. It was too much for him, and he came with LUV.

"We need to go in the pool to cool off," said Brandy.

The pool was enclosed and heated, so they walked out there. King G was still semi hard as he watched the ladies walk in front of him. Damn! He was enjoying his birthday! After the swim, they all got in the six-person shower. There were eight showerheads. It was nice and steamy. They all washed King G, taking different body parts. After he was cleaned, they cleaned themselves. Brandy bent over, with her hand on the bench, and guided King G into her. He fucked her into another orgasm. Then it was Empress turn. After she got hers; He laid LUV on her back and fucked her long and deep, while Butterfly just looked on. When LUV climaxed; Butterfly was on the wall finger poppin herself into an orgasm!

"Yes, Papa Bear make me cum" she said.
While eyeing King G's body. They played naked twister, which led to more sex. Empress and Brandy tapped out, the pregnancy taking a toll on them. Finally, it was gift giving time again. The Lady G's got him a mink bomber with matching headband, and a butter soft leather snorkel, and a bubble north face with the bubble hood.

"I have something I wanna give you King G," Butterfly said. "What is it" asked King G. "Let's go to the garage."
They went through the house into the garage, which was also heated. There was a car with a cover over it. Butterfly went to the car and removed the cover. There in all its glory, was a

1986 Buick Grand National! Custom all black crushed velvet interior.

"You got me a Grand National?" "I saw how much you liked mine, so I thought you would like to have one of your own. It has a completely new frame, new suspension, new tires and rims, custom interior, new lights, gas tank, muffler system, and the whole engine is new. It's an upgraded turbo V6 with larger turbo on it." Butterfly said.

Without thinking, King G hugged her tightly, which made their naked bodies touch and sent a shockwave through both of them. They both backed up quickly!

"How much did this run you?" King G asked "About $50K and to see the expression on your face, it was all worth it."

The Lady G's didn't know anything about old cars, but they knew their husband loved it. This was a perfect birthday for King G.

Chapter 21

The next day King G called his wives into the garage to talk privately.

"What should we do for Butterfly for her birthday?" King G asked. "Well, we know what we wanna give her "LUV said. "Are you gonna tell me?" asked King G. "Yeah we wanna give her the opportunity to become your wife; if you will have her." LUV said. King G was silent for a while, "Well do you, my King." "Just one quick question my LUV. What brought this on?" "Well for 5 months, y'all haven't crossed any lines, even with some moments of pressure. Then after yesterday, y'all showed extreme control, discipline and respect! We see she wants to be with this family, not just you. One more month wouldn't have made a difference. So, what do you say?" LUV asked "Firstly, I love all y'all and I'm lucky to have such beautiful, caring, loyal and understanding women. Yes, I accept" "Good Daddy and just know; if she ain't have a black grandma, I was saying no! She is a sister just like us, but with blue eyes and straighter hair." Brandy stated. "Babe your crazy! King G laughed. "We already scheduled it, at the nearest mosque up here," said LUV. "Ok my LUV that's a bet! So, I need to go see the jeweler, and get a matching ring to the one y'all got. Then her birthday present, which I haven't decided on. I'm gonna head out, to register the car and get the ring and present. See y'all later."

After running around in the city getting everything together King G didn't make it back home til about 10pm. The next morning everyone knocked on Butterfly's door and came in yelling,

"Happy Birthday!" "Thanks, y'all" she said rising out of her sleep. "Get up and get ready. We are having breakfast downstairs." Brandy said.

Butterfly made it downstairs after getting herself together. She was rocking a high ponytail, a long tank top with nothing on underneath and slippers. There was Blueberry Belgian waffles, turkey sausage, and stewed apples.

"Aww thanks, y'all this is so nice. I'm starving too." said Butterfly. They all ate together, then LUV said, "It's time for your present from us. Now we thought long and hard about this and tried our best to come up with the perfect gift" "Y'all ain't have to go through all that trouble. I'm just happy being here with the people I love." replied Butterfly. Girl, we done worked on this. Are you gonna take this gift?" said Brandy. "Boo, bring Butterfly gift out for us. You know we can't carry it." stated Empress.

King G went and got a big box wrapped in gift wrapping paper and sat it on the table. Butterfly tore into it wondering what could be so big. She opened the box and there was another gift-wrapped box. She got through that one and there was a little gift-wrapped box. She looked around confused. She opened the small saw a ring box and opened it. When she looked up, King G. was on one knee.

"Butterfly today is your day, and my wives would like to give you the gift of love; and I would like to give you, my heart. Will you marry me?" "Yes, yes, yes," Butterfly blurted out, while crying as everyone hugged her. "This is the best birthday ever!" she said. "We are glad you're happy. We wanna welcome you into this family officially. You ready to do this today?" asked LUV. "Hell yeah." But what am I gonna wear." asked Butterfly. King G pulled out a DKNY maxi skirt with the matching long sleeve shirt and a DKNY 3" scarf. LUV fixed the scarf like a hijab by pinning it to Butterfly's hair. Everyone got dressed and proceeded to the mosque. Even baby Crown was there. With the marriage complete they went back home. LUV explained they Booked them a honeymoon suite at a Pocono Mountain Resort. "Now y'all get outta here and enjoy y'all honeymoon. Don't come back til tomorrow either." Brandy said with tears in her eyes. Butterfly ran over, "What's wrong Brandy? We won't go if it upsets you." She said hugging her "No, I'm fine, I'm just happy for you and happy to have a new sis. "Now gone, get!" They rode in Brandy's Benz truck. Butterfly had changed into some thick polo sport leggings and a polo sport hoody that stopped at her waist, and the polo sport 2 in 1 ski jacket with fleece liner. King G was in a cream polo invisible P knit, Polo khakis and some Polo shoe Boots and his North Face coat. As soon as they got in their suite, Butterfly started stripping King G out of his clothes. Once he was naked, she stripped, and they were all over each other. Kissing heavily and caressing each other's bodies. King G pushed her on the bed and spread her legs and pushed them back. Butterfly took it a step further and put her legs behind her head! King G dove in; eating her pussy like it was his last meal. Her pussy was so soft and wet. She tasted sweet. He sucked and licked her pussy as she cried out. "Yes, eat this pussy. It's yours Papa Bear, it's all yours! Oh, my fucking God, what are you doing to me, Yes, yes mmm mmm." When he felt her body tense up, he went harder, and she came hard squirting all over his face. "My turn Papa Bear." King G laid down and she said, lets 69." She got on top and they attacked each other like it was a competition. Butterfly was slurping dat dick up and gaggin. "Ack Ack Ack!" There was spit everywhere. King G grabbed her by the waist, then stood up with her. Standing 69, was too much for her! She had her hands on his thighs, and she was meeting his thrusts as he fucked her face! At the same time, he was tongue fucking her, then sucking her clit. She exploded in another orgasm. "Aah you're making me cum agaaaainn." He eased her onto the bed and slid into his wife, long stroked her looking in her eyes, watching her eyes roll in the back of her head. He felt her tighten around his pole. He knew she would cum again! As she started cumming, he stayed in her, flipped her over. She arched her back and he started pounding her pussy rapidly! "Oh, shit Papa Bear! This your pussy! Ahhh, Ahhh, Ahhh, beat that shit up! Aah Aah-fuuuck! You in my stomach" "Whose pussy is this?" "Yours Papa Bear." "I can't hear you, whose pussy is this?" "Your's Papa Bear! Smack, my ass please Papa Bear." King G slapped her ass and watched it shake over and over. "Cum with me Papa Bear I'm gonna cum again" King G went full jack hammer, and they came together. This is how the whole day and night basically went with them.

Chapter 22

February 14, '01, Empress had King G's first daughter. They named her Majesty. She weighed 7lbs. 8oz. 3 days later February 17 of '01; Brandy had their son Prince. He weighed 8 lbs. 4 oz. King G was extremely happy!! All he could think about was making more money for his family. Princess G was pregnant again, so he had to make sure everyone was good. Alvino called with another heist for the crew. This time it, was a location that held all the drug money, before it made its way to Cuba.

"Listen hermano, it should be anywhere from $100 mil to $200 mil in there. If you and your hombres can make this happen, it's a split of 50-50 hermano. This will cripple another one of our competitors." "Vino, you already know, if I put my mind to it, it's going to happen. Just give me the rundown so I can plan how to go about it." King G stated. "Ok, hermano, check it out." "There is a house in Sarasota, Fl. It's small. It's the only house with an orange door on the street. An old lady lives there, but she is no normal old lady. Her sons are the drug lords now, only because she got too old. Her name is Marisol, even at her old age, she is known to still pose a real threat with a gun in her hand! Don't underestimate her! Now the money is in that house, under the floor in her bedroom. The whole floor is basically one big stash spot. The house behind it, and across the street from it, has 24-hour security waiting around, right before the money is to be picked up. You must either hit these houses first or be so sneaky getting into the stash house, that you go unnoticed. Both those houses have four men a piece in them. They are fully equipped with high powered firearms. I can't send anyone who is Spanish because this will automatically cause a war, with a different cartel. This would be bad for business. By sending black people at them, the deniability will go over well. That's basically it." "Ok Bro, well firstly, I need all silenced weapons. Preferably the 9mm Beretta 's and some compressed Mac 11's. We will need six bulletproof vests, matter of fact make it seven just in case. We need a 2001 Chevy suburban; all black with tinted windows, some night vision goggles and beams for the guns. Also, when does this have to be done by?" King G asked. "Usually on the 25th of every month they ship the money out." Alvino stated. "How do they get it out?" "It's loaded into a Goodwill donation truck." "Ok Bro, we got it. Let me know when you have everything ready." King said before he departed.

King G made a phone call to Lauryn, checking on her and asking for a favor. Then it was off to holla at the crew that would go on this mission with him. He chose LT, Illy, Nutso, TEC and K9.

"Listen y'all, we can hit the truck when it leaves. That means we will be exposed to witnesses and possibly cameras. The other option is to cause a diversion to distract the security and then get in the stash house and take control of the old woman. Or we can take out security and then overpower the old woman and get the money." King G said to the crew. "Man, I don't care how we do it, let's get this bread" stated K9." I feel you Bro, but we gotta plan this out. This ain't no corner boys we robbing." LT stated. They went through multiple ways of executing til they felt they had a solid A, B &C plan. "Check it y'all everyone stays out the streets and just handle business. Just spend time with your family or your women. I need everyone relaxed and ready to move when the time comes. I'm headed home, so I will call y'all when I know the time's right," said King G. "Crash or get Cash y'all." said King G "Crash or get Cash!" The crew said.

Back in the Poconos, King G took Butterfly to get her tattoo that matched the rest of his wives. He added Butterfly's face to his tat of all his wives, and his new kids. He told the move to her, and said she wanted in. She also had an idea to make the move smoother.

"Papa Bear, I gotta connect on a sleeping agent. We can put it through the central air in the house. It will put everyone to sleep. Then we walk in and do us." "Sounds good babe. Find out how much it's gonna cost us. We will go that route!"

Alvino called, letting King G know he had all the things he had requested. After picking everything up and putting it in the warehouse, King G executed the first part of his plan. It was now April 20th; Butterfly had secured the sleeping agent they needed. They were on their way to Florida in a private jet. All the tools needed for the robbery had been transported in a trailer a week before. It was stashed in the Suburban, that would be waiting on them. Once in Sarasota, King G let them know how things would go.

"Aight, y'all we gonna split up and go to different hotels. Illy and Nutso, y'all will stay in the same hotel. TEC and K9, y'all will stay in the same hotel, but far enough away from Illy and Nutso that nobody can put y'all together. Me, Butterfly and LT will stay in the same hotel. We all will get rentals from different companies. I will be sending out Butterfly to scope the scene out for us. A woman in a car by herself or just walking shouldn't arouse any suspicions. Everyone got that?"

Everyone nodded their heads in agreement. After getting the rentals everyone headed to their separate hotels. After settling in, King G was ready to get the homework done.

"Listen babe, take the rental and go peep the layout of the street and the houses on the surrounding blocks too. We need the best entry and exit points we can get. Also, you need to figure out where the central air is set up at, so we can let the sleeping agent work its magic." "Ok, Papa Bear I got it. I'll go take care of that now."

Once Butterfly left, King G sat back and ran through all the thoughts in his head. Back at the hotel with TEC and K9, after getting settled in, TEC noticed K9 looking upset.

"What's up with you Bro?" asked TEC. "A nigga just ain't feeling how this nigga King G gets to bring his bitch on a move! Like he the only one who can get some pussy or something." "K9, you know King G ain't on that. You know you can't be disrespecting sis, calling her no bitch! Bro, would you feel some type of way, if he heard that. She is here to help us. You know King G is only focused on the mission and that's it!" "Whatever Bro. All I know is this shit better go right or King G gonna have a serious problem!" stated K9.

TEC couldn't believe how this nigga K9 was walking. He was definitely gonna have to holla at King G bout this! In his mind, he knew if push came to shove, K9's ass would be the one to have a problem, if he crossed King G.

"Look Bro ain't nothing gonna go wrong. Bro ain't never led us wrong and always has looked out. He is the reason why we got money since day one and still got money coming in." TEC stated seriously.

After two hours, Butterfly made it back to the hotel room with King G "What's up babe? Tell me some good news" King G said. "Sorry it took so long Papa Bear. I decided to stop and look around like a tourist would and casually made it to a destination. It will be easy to access the house with the cash and the house directly behind it. They have connecting backyards. The central air units are on the sides of the house. I didn't see any cameras; so, we just wait til it's pitch black and pull up and do our thing. The house across the street is basically the same set up. We have to hit the two security houses for the best results." "Ok babe, you did good. We gonna get on it around midnight. They shouldn't be too aware since the pick-up ain't until the 25th. We will all meet up at the truck and get to work."

After calling the rest of the crew and telling them the meeting spot. King G decided to rest and have his mind cleared for the job that lay ahead. At 11pm, King G and Butterfly were getting dressed. Butterfly wore a long-sleeved black catsuit and Gore-Tex Boots. She had her hair pulled up in a black scarf which she put a rolled up black ski mask over. King G had black cargo pants on, a black long sleeve T-shirt, and a black rolled up black ski mask. The rest of the crew would have the same outfit as King G. At midnight, they all met up at a storage facility, where the suburban was parked.

"Aight y'all, after this is done, we drop the truck back off here. Alvino's people will take care of it. Then we drop the rentals off. Alvino rented us a Charter bus that will drive us all the way back home." King G stated. "Let's just go get this money" K9 said.
Butterfly went into the truck, separating all the night vision goggles, firearms, and bulletproof vests. She explained to Illy and TEC, how to release the tanks of the sleeping agent into

the central air. Once they understood, it was time to work. The street the stash house was on was completely silent. King G dropped Illy off at the street behind the first security house across the street from the stash house. He then drove to the security house behind the stash house and dropped off TEC and Butterfly. Butterfly went to the stash house once TEC started to hook up the tank. Once they were all done, King G picked them all up and they waited in the truck for thirty minutes.

"Game time y'all let's go." King G said.

King G, Butterfly, and Illy went to the 2nd security house, while the rest of the crew hit the 1st one. They killed the electricity to both homes, then donned their night vision goggles. After picking the locks, they were in. King G was the first to enter the house followed by Butterfly and then Illy. He swept his gun from right to left while looking for the occupants. He found two in the kitchen, on the floor asleep. He proceeded to the bedrooms and found the other two. At the same time, K9 entered the other house followed, by LT and TEC. As soon as they hit the living room; all four security men were found on the couch and floor asleep. The crew secured both security teams with zip ties. Then put a bullet in each one of their heads. Eight down and one old lady to go! At the stash house they all met up and cut the power. They all filed in and spread out through the house, then went straight to Marisol's bedroom. There was nobody in there, King G held his finger to his lips, signaling for everyone to stay quiet. He pointed towards another bedroom and then a bathroom door. They went in and found no one. Just as they were coming out, King G seen a hand coming out of the closet door. The hand was going straight for the back of K9's head! Without hesitation, King G let off one shot to the head of the person coming out of the closet and the body fell.

"What the fuck yo!" K9 shouted." Shhh" King said. Shining a flashlight at the body, King G said "Man that fucking old lady was gonna kill you Bro. She had the drop on you. And look at this big ass .50 Desert Eagle she had." "Why wasn't that bitch knocked out?" K9 asked visibly upset and staring at Butterfly.

Butterfly shined her flashlight at the vents in Marisol's bedroom and saw they were closed. She then went through the house, looking at the vents, only the living room vents were open.

"She must have been in her room the whole time! That's why she wasn't sleeping. She probably came out when we cut the electricity." stated Butterfly. "Fuck all this talking y'all! Let's get this money and get the fuck outta here!!" LT said.

They removed all the furniture out of the bedroom. They began pulling on the floor, til they found a lever that opened the floor.

"Oh shit, my nigga! That's a lot of fucking money."

K9 said. "Yeah, everybody take their duffels and start filling it up" said King G.

After clearing out the money, they exited the back of the house and went passed the security house and hopped in the truck. Later that day the driver stopped in Savannah at a Walmart. Butterfly went in and got everyone T-shirts, sweatpants and toothbrushes. She got some food. She changed in the bathroom and threw away her catsuit. Back on the bus, everyone changed, and they threw their clothes in the dumpster. It was time to go back home. Back in New York, they had the driver pull up at the trucking company lot. They loaded the bags into the cab of the truck. King G and Butterfly drove in the truck, while the rest of the crew hopped in King G's van. At the warehouse, they began counting out the money in five money counters. When they finally finished Butterfly said,

"That's $112,500,000" "That leaves us $56,250,000 to split," King G stated, while texting Alvino to come get his. "Yo that's $8 mil apiece Bro" said K9. "Yeah Bro, I know," King G said with a smile. "I think we should give the $250K to Mama Judy and Crazy Joe as a wedding gift, from all of us." said King G. Everyone nodded in agreement. Butterfly started separating the money, so everyone could take their $8 mil. "We gonna chill for a while with the illegal shit. We got enough money and legal funds coming in, to live good. If Alvino got any deliveries or money for us to take; cool! But we ain't touching no more drugs or hitting trucks or shipyard shipments. I don't know about y'all, but I'm going away for a while to establish some new business," stated King G. "Yo Bro, I feel you. I got homies to feed, I ain't turning no dollar down, the streets can give me." K9 said. "Aight Bro, you are a grown man. I don't agree with you, but hey! Just think about this, if I didn't save your life, you would be dead! So, this chance shouldn't be taken for granted. I wish you luck, tho." K9 had a scowl on his face, that let everyone know what he was feeling.

"Yo, LT take me to my car Bro. I'm out!" was all K9 said.

The rest of the crew decided to leave too and go home. They all looked at King G and said, "Crash or get Cash Bro," "Crash or get Cash." King G replied.

Twenty minutes later, Alvino pulled up. He collected his cut and didn't bother asking King G what happened.

"Hermano, it's always a pleasure doing business with You." "Likewise, Bro," replied King G. "Vino, listen Bro, I'm bout to get out of town for a while. Probably move south or something; but if you need me for any moves, I'm available. Me and my team." "I understand hermano, but it should be a while before I would need your services. See those that I had you take care of for me, were snakes and snakes always die alone. Other snakes do not come to help them or anything. Those men were trying to steal from me and my family. They were even trying to inform on us to the authorities, to stop our business. Now I can respect, if we are at war or odds, that they come at mi familia like real gangstas. But a snake is something I can't stand, hermano! Be sure to never let them amongst you." "I dig what you are saying Bro. We call them "Phoney Homies," when they are in your circle." "Ha-ha. I like that one, "Phony Homies," has a nice ring to it! Well stay in touch hermano." Alvino said before leaving out.

On the way home, King G let Butterfly drive, while he sat back thinking. His phone rang, it was TEC.

"Yo King G, I need to holla at you bout this nigga K9!"

TEC proceeded to tell King G about K9's attitude and behavior; from claiming credit for the work put in at the car race of them Southside niggas, and his obvious jealousy and envy towards King G. After the call, King G could only hear the words Alvino had spoken to him. Then and there he knew he would have to put a plan in motion.

Back at the crib, he sat his wives down and let them know his plans to move.

"I was thinking, we could go down to where Brandy is from and start a few businesses and just lay low for a while." "What about the house my King? LUV asked. "Princess G and Illy can watch the house for us, or Mama Judy and Crazy Joe." stated King G. "If you think it's best, then we all with it. Right y'all?" LUV asked. Together they all replied, "YUP!" "Now that that's over. I got something for y'all," Butterfly said to her sister wives.

Then dumped her $8 million on the table.

"It's $2 million apiece for all of us." LUV, Brandy and Empress sat there looking surprised! "You ain't have to do that Butterfly," said Brandy. "We are a family and because of y'all, I'm a part of this family. So just take it," stated Butterfly.

All King G could do was smile.

King G sat his wives down. He filled them in on his feelings about K9. They all agreed he was phoney as fuck. So, King G told them of his plan. They all smiled, knowing their husband was a very smart man. A couple of days later, King G called up Lil Kenny and met him at Lindenwood diner.

"Yo King G what's up big Bro?" "Gettin Cash Lil Bro. Listen, I got a job for you to do. Once it's done, don't worry, I got you. It may take a while but trust me you gonna be straight." "Man, King G cause of you me and my homies are on anything you need. I got you! You don't gotta give me shit. Just let me be a part of GGC." "I'll tell you what, Lil Kenny I admire your loyalty get this done, and I'm gonna take care of your pockets and you are now GGC. Don't Broadcast it and here's why..."

King G Broke everything down to Lil Kenny and they left the diner.

After securing everything with the crew, King G got a car trailer to hitch to his tractor trailer truck. He loaded the three Benz's, his Chevelle and him and Butterfly's twin Buick Regals. They loaded the cars with whatever luggage they were taking. His wives and the kids were in the Astro van. Butterfly will be driving. Legend was helping him drive the semi. They were ready to hit the road. P-Nut was awaiting their arrival. He already had some homes for King G to look at. As soon as they hit the highway, King G felt this would be the start of something big. He also wanted his children to experience something different than what he was used to. He needed to secure his family away from all outsiders. He had cut the grass low and was on the lookout for snakes! He hoped none showed up or there would be heads to chop off!

Chapter 23

July 2001, King G had been in North Carolina for three months. He hadn't seen any homes he liked. After a couple weeks of looking, he decided to have one built. Mama Judy had a few acres of land, she let him get. It would be another month before the house would be completed. It would showcase eight bedrooms, nine bathrooms, a full basement with movie room, indoor pool, gym, back patio, sauna, six car garage and a playhouse specifically for the kids. It only cost him $300K to build. Alvino had a link with some Mexican contractors that owed him a favor. P-Nut had a lucrative bikini car wash business going in Knightdale. He had four gorgeous Dominicans working there, that he brought straight from the Dominican Republic. P-Nut was making about $14K a week. He paid the ladies $1000 a piece a week. He paid a young boy named Champ, who he took a liking to, $500 a week just to vacuum the cars and wipe down the interior. King G had the Lady G's working their management company, which was starting to pick up fast. King G sat down with P-Nut to discuss some business.

"Yo P-Nut, I was thinking about opening up a Gentleman's Membership Club called, "Genteel Gentlemen's Club." I wanna charge $500 every 6 months for a membership. I only want men with money as members. I'm trying to build a spot that holds like 1500 people. My goal is to start with 500 members. The homey Jungle got girls and his pimp partners can provide more. Then the Lady G's and their management company could get us more. I wanna provide the entertainment and take a percentage from the women; for getting them into a crowd of people with real money. We could also get some Dominican girls out here or Puerto Ricans. Really any females from poorer countries to give them an opportunity. What you think Bro?" "King G you know any idea you have, I'm gonna back it. If it's truly what you want, let's do it! We get the numbers together and go." "Aight Bro. I'm gonna bring LT and Jungle in on this." "Aight bet, Bro." King G called LT and Jungle and bought them up to speed with his idea. They agreed to go in with him. LT had a convo with King G about the happenings in the hood.

"Yo Bro, this nigga K9 out here flooding the city. He got a bunch of new niggas screaming "GGC." I ain't gonna say too much, but when you can you need to come through. Princess G. and Illy bought a strip club. They're naming it "Cash Dolls." Me and Chef can promote and Jungle gonna have his pornstars, guest host to get it jumping. Lil Kenny out here winning; but he be hanging with K9 all the time, like they buddy buddy! I don't know Bro, Shit just ain't the same without you, Bro." "I feel you Bro, but as long as everyone is eating and ok, shit will be cool. I'm gonna try and pull up this summer. Keep that on the low though." Aight Bro, Crash or Get Cash, Crash or get Cash!"

While King G is contemplating over what LT was saying, Lil Kenny is chilling with LL, Chip and Gauge.

"Man LL, this summer gonna be jumping. We are getting money crazy! The hoes loving us. We got fly whips and the city is ours," says Lil Kenny. "Yeah Lil Bro; you already know, with my vision and me leading, we bound to be at the top," replies K9 "For real big Bro, in 3 months, you got us so flooded, it don't make no sense!" says Chip. "It's like I told y'all before, dat money talk! Just like I said, the connect came to us." "Who was the connect though big Bro? Cause he really holding," Chip asks. "Mannn Bro, shit so crazy right! I don't even know our connect. Never met them and he never met me." "Wait, how that work big Bro?" asks Gauge. "Listen y'all, this connect like a magician. See, I was cruising out in Long Island City in the Jag. I was trying to find another lick and almost crashed into this bad Spanish Broad. Long story short, I apologized and asked her on a date, to make it up. I take her out and she asks me what I do. So, you know like the boss I am, I told her all I do is get cash! She comes right out and asks if I'm a hustler. I basically said yes, without saying anything when I smiled at her. She gets on her phone talking in Spanish. I catch a few words and realize she trying to plug me. She then gives me a number and tells me to call it. So, I called the number. A Spanish dude tells me if I wanna do business write a number of how much and whatever in particular I need and give it to shorty. I do that and she tells me, wait here she will be right back. Now, I'm wondering, what's going on? I'm in Long Island city and don't know anybody! Anyway, after about 30 minutes go by, she comes back to the restaurant. She has a piece of paper that has this price on it that will cover the cost of everything. I'm not knowing what's really happening, but don't wanna fuck up an opportunity! She tells me to go get the money and bring it back and she will tell me where to pick up my order. So, I'm like, you really think I'm gonna give you all that money first, shorty? Then she looks at me with a serious face and says, "if that's a lot of money to you, maybe I read you wrong. A man who drives a Jaguar; usually knows the real value of money. I tell you what, so that you feel safe this one time. I will ride with you to get your order. No business can only be done with you dropping money at one location and then picking up your order somewhere else. So, I'm like fuck it! I already had 200 grand in the truck. So, we ride out, we ride out to a dead-end block and pull up to a beat up MPV. She tells me the order is in there along with the keys to the van. I park up the Jag and she walks away with the duffel. I drive off and basically that's how I started with the connect. Since then, I haven't been out with Shorty. She just calls me from a different phone on the first and the fifteenth of the month, to see if I'm straight. I tell her the amount and then I drop the money at a location in the vehicle, I did the last pick-up in. Then I pick up the order in another hoopty!" "That's crazy Bro. You took a mean chance, but it paid off," says Gauge. "Yeah Bro, I figured that first time; if it was anything funny, shorty was gonna die and whoever else was around," stated K9. "I bet you was glad King G bought you that motherfucking Jag, huh big Bro?" said Chip. "Man King G. ain't have shit to do with my success on this. That was all me! Look what I did with GGC in 3 months. We got niggas from all over the city down with us and all, that's bringing money in cause, they got a cop from me! That nigga somewhere down south, playing happy families and chilling, while we putting work in." Lil Kenny smiles and says, "Can't argue with that big Bro. I'm gonna always be where the money and the gangstas are at! You think King G. gonna be back tho, anytime soon?" asked Lil Kenny. "Lil Bro, I don't care if he do or don't! But, if he do, he gonna have to march to the beat of my drum. Once them fine as wives of his see how a real boss play; I bet I can show them how I play in something else."

They all laughed and dapped each other up.

"Listen y'all I gotta go bust a move. I'll holla at y'all later." Lil Kenny says, "Crash or Get Cash Bro" says K9, "Crash or Get Cash," replies Lil Kenny."

Lil Kenny jumps in his 2000 Acura, TL and peels out.

Chapter 24

The new house is finally finished! The Lady G's named it The Royal Palace. The week before, they went out and got all the furnishings, kitchenware, linen and anything else the new home needed. The Lady G's had to pick their rooms; out which all had Queen size, all Mahogany canopy beds. Royal, Crown, and Prince had a California King size bed custom made to look like a big playpen. Majesty had a queen size bed, customized the same way. The Kings Quarters, which the ladies jokingly called the main bedroom had a California King size bed, a customized couch that looked like a big throne that could seat six people. There were hand paintings of the whole family. All linen in the house was Ralph Lauren.

After getting settled in King G left to go pick up Andy.

"Get off at the Capitol Boulevard exit Bro and bust a U-turn" Andy said.

As they pulled up in the dealership, they could see the salesman coming out to greet them.

"Afternoon gentlemen, can we help you find anything today?" "Yeah, I would like to look at an Excursion," stated King G.

Looking at the Astro Van they had pulled up in the salesman obviously thought King G wasn't trying to do a complete buy of the vehicle.

"Sure, I can show you our Excursions in stock. How's your credit sir?" "My credit is good." replied King G. While walking towards the Excursions on the lot.

"Are there any particular wants or needs you have for the vehicle sir?" "Yeah, I want it fully loaded." "Ok sir all the bells and whistles are gonna put a hefty mark up on the price tag."

King G stopped looking at the truck and eyed the salesman, thinking; Damn, this is a black man judging me; as if I'm a Broke joker. Just then he noticed a young white guy standing off to the side, timidly. Turning back to the salesman, he felt was judging him, he asked,

"What's your name sir? I never caught it." "Oh, I am Mr. Joe Bryant." "Ok Mr. Bryant, is this young man with you a jr salesman?" "Yes, this is Mr. Bobby Teller." "Nice to meet you, Mr. Bobby Teller. Mr. Joe Bryant, can you please go and find out what the bottom line will be for the vehicle with all the bells and whistles, as you say. Let Mr. Teller show me some of the other color options." "No problem, sir, and your name?" "King Greene," answered King G.

Once Mr. Bryant walked off, Mr. Teller assisted King G in every way possible and was polite. Through conversation, King G found out, he had just graduated college with a degree in business management and accounting. He was only working here because he was expecting a baby and needed to make money. Mr. Teller let him know the price for what King G wanted.

"Fully Loaded the Excursion will probably run you close to $65,000. I have seen cash offers reduce that number in the thousands," Mr. Teller says. King G smiled and said, "Let's go inside Mr. Teller" "Please call me, Bobby." "Ok Bobby and call me King G."

Inside Mr. Bryant came up with a paper with all the price additions for the fully loaded vehicle and then an application for a car loan.

"Excuse me Bobby, can you get the person who makes all the decisions for sales, please?" King G asked. As Bobby walked away, Mr. Bryant asked,

"Is there a problem, Mr. Greene?" None at all, Mr. Bryant I am ready to make my purchase and just wanna discuss a few things, without the back-and-forth."

After talking to the boss, King G and him agreed on a $60K price tag including Tags and Title. King G had Andy bring his duffel bag out of the Astro van. Back in the boss's office, King G counted out $60K cash and signed the papers, putting the vehicle under the porn company's name. He also made sure Bobby got the credit for the sale. On the way out he tossed Bobby 5 grand and thanked him and got his business card. Then looked at Mr. Bryant,

"Next time, don't assume a customer can't afford to buy a vehicle straight out! Have a nice day sir."

King G stopped at a car audio and rim shop. He ordered 22 inches" Lexani Rims and Yokohama Tires, in dash 7" screen TV, CD/DVD player, 2 7" headrest TV's, a complete Rockford Fosgate speaker and amp system for his doors, a separate Rockford Fosgate amp and 2 12" Rockford Fosgate subwoofers to be housed in the side panel of the truck's cabin and a new suspension system that lowered the truck so that the rims looked almost tucked. Andy also made him buy an Optima battery.

"Big Bro this gone last long and keep you from draining your main battery. You should let me hook up your electronics tho. I'm nice with it. Anything to deal with cars I'm good at." "That's a bet Bro," said King G.
After getting his suspension and rims and tires put on, they pulled out.
Back at the Royal Palace King G gave the Astro van to Andy.

"Check it Lil Bro this yours now. Use it however you want. I'm thinking, use it as a work van for you to work on cars and build your clientele, so we can open you up a shop." "I got a lot of customers King G. I was saving up to open up a shop in the country or Knightdale. Thanks a lot for the van!" replied Andy. "Check it Bro, can you paint cars?" asked King G. "Hell yeah! I've been painting cars since I was 13, with my Daddy and uncle out in the country." "Aight Bro, I wanna paint the Excursion gunmetal gray and I want the grill all black. I don't want no chrome trimmings either." "Yo King G that's gonna to have it look sick and you can put some blacked out Altezza lights to replace your stock tail lights, Aww, man just leave it to me and I'm gonna pimp dat motherfucker out!" "Aight here take this $5000 and get all the stuff you need I will pay you when it's done." "Nah Bro, 5 grand is cool. All I gotta get is the paint and the lights. That ain't gonna run me nothing but bout $1500 to $2000." "Aight, well keep whatever is left over. How soon can you get started?" "Shiit I can go get the paint and the lights now and get started. If you give me 3 days, I will have everything done." "Ok Bro, take the truck and I will see you in 3 days."

P-Nut called King G and let him know that he had put a down payment on a property that used to be a Piggly Wiggly.

"Yo Bro, it's the perfect location for the Gentleman's Club. It's got its own parking lot and everything!!" said P-Nut. "Aight Bro, I'm gonna meet you to check it out." Indeed, it was a perfect location.

"Yeah, Bro this is right!" "Listen the guy who owns this property is retiring. He said for a mil, we can buy it. I gave him $100K to let him know we serious. He will draw up the paperwork for $900K. I figured we get a loan from the bank, using the car wash and your new crib as collateral. This way we cover our asses on paper. I got this chick that's a loan officer at the bank. She already said she would approve the loan and because we are using property as collateral; we won't need a down payment. She guarantees our monthly payments will be around $5000 a month for a 25-year loan." "Aight bet. With me, you, LT and Jungle name on the business, we can each pay dat 5 grand a month, so that they get 20 grand every month from us. Plus, with the membership fees we could pay it off in 2 years, if we want. Let's do it!"

King G invites LT and Jungle down to see the property and to invest in fixing the place up.

Four days later, King G and P-Nut pick up LT and Jungle from RDU Airport.

"Yo, King G, P-Nut what's getting?" says LT and Jungle. "That Cash!!!" King G and P-Nut say at the same time. "This Excursion is sick, Bro. You got this system thumping. This gray on gray is nice and the blacked-out grill and no chrome molding on nothing looks sick! Would you look at the wheeeeels!" shouted LT" "Yeah Bro good looking, Brandy Brother did the system and paint job. I can't lie he got this bitch shining like the showroom floor. This lil nigga put 20 coats of gloss on my shit." King G says laughing. Everyone laughs along with him.

"Aight so check it, we headed to check out this property. The contractors are there already looking over the place. I used the same people who built my crib. Me and P-Nut gave them an idea of what we want done and the layout.

We want a full basement which will have lockers, showers and private rooms. The main floor will have Booths, bar, kitchen and the back storage areas will have more rooms, including where the loading dock is." "Sounds good to me, let's just get there," "Jungle says.

At the club site the contractor greets the crew, "Hola Seniors" "Y'all this Mario, he is the head contractor." King G says. "What's up Mario!" Everyone says together. "Señor King, we have figured out it will probably cost you $500K to get everything you want done. That is the best we can do. That is without the elevator tho, we know someone who can install one for $50K." "Ok Mario, also I wanna utilize all space. So, I would like you to build some rooms on the roof too. Enclose them but keep the HVAC system outside of the enclosure. We want all the rooms soundproofed too." "Ok Senor King, for the roof that will be another $50k." "Ok Mario we will be back with half the money. Get your elevator guy ready. We also are gonna throw in another 50 grand for all new lighting."
After giving Mario $325K, the crew went to The Royal Palace. The Lady G's were happy to see LT and Jungle.

"Hey LT. Hey Jungle," the ladies all said while kissing their husband. "What's up Lady G's?" LT and Jungle said, giving them all hugs. "Hey P-Nut," the ladies said. "What's up y'all. Thought y'all forgot about me" he said laughing. "Ha-Ha, never that P-Nut," said LUV. "Daddy, you got mail on the counter in the kitchen." Brandy said. "Pardon me y'all I will be back," said King G.

King G went through the mail and noticed a letter from Lil Kenny. It was telling him bout all that was going on. It also let him know about his new way of getting money, which was credit card and check scamming. King G would have to learn more about this face to face.

The club would be done by December. He let his wives and P-Nut know it was time to go out and grab members for the grand opening. "Use every resource y'all got to get us members. Jungle hit every pimp you know and get us pics of their best girls. We need to be able to showcase what kind of women we will be in place for our members. Make sure the pics are classy but alluring at the same time." stated King G. It was time for him to head to New York.

Chapter 25

King G landed at John F. Kennedy Airport on Aug 15th. Crazy Joe was there to pick him up.

"What's up Joe?" "Ain't nothing much son. Happy to see you. I missed you. Been out here holding it down and waiting for this wedding. Everything at the warehouse and the vending machines are doing well." "That's what's up Joe. Hey check it. I need to go get a rental." "Aight, I got you."
As they pull up at Avis Rent-A-Car. King G says,

"Listen Joe, I think it's time you find someone to run the warehouse and to take care of the vending machines. You have even been collecting the money from the laundromat and making sure plenty quarters are available. I want you to have the vending machine business. After you and Mama Judy are married, y'all should have time to spend with each other." "Thanks Son. I guess I could go down to the Veteran's Hospital and find a disabled vet to take over my duties. Listen King I been thinking of moving the wedding to North Carolina. All Judy family is there, and I don't have none here. You're down there with the girls and the kids." "If that's what you want, I will tell Brandy to get a location for you." Crazy Joe agreed.
After King G got his rented Impala, he headed straight to the hood, to his old crib. He called Lil Kenny and told him come

through. King G answered the back door and Lil Kenny stepped in.

"What's getting Lil Bro?" asked King G. "Dat Cash Big Bro," replied Lil Kenny. "So, what's the word with this scamming, Lil Kenny?" "Listen King G this shit sweet. I'm busting checks for like 10 grand. Then the credit cards, I really just use to shop for me and my homies. They are busting checks too, so we are straight!" "How are you getting the cards and the checks?" "Well, the checks I make with special paper. I use real live account; and routing numbers. They come from companies and all types of places. The cards cost me $100 apiece because they from overseas. I be hitting like $1000 to $5000 off each card. I got a cool ass African Nigga, that be showing me the game. Don't nobody really know what I be up to. Me and my Homies go out of town with all the scamming. We got bitches that go out for us too!" "That shit sound right, Lil Bro; so how the cards come in?" "Oh, my African son, be making them shits once we get the info!" "Aight check it, I need some of them cards. I'm gonna drop $100K on you to get me 10,000 cards. I have got a club I'm trying to open up. I'm gonna charge all the liquor. Then I'm gonna buy all fly shit and probably sell clothes too, later on." "Damn Big Bro, I ain't never spent a 100 grand at one time! That will probably get me more info than usual." "Well, whatever you get over the 10,000 cards I want: that's all for you. Tell you what, get some of them broads you got to go out for me too. They can keep the cards once they get me a $1000 worth of merchandise." "Fuck dat big Bro! They ain't keeping shit! I will bust them down half of whatever's left. I gotta get cash too!!" "Ha Ha, I hear you Bro. Now what's up with these niggas K9, Chip and Gauge?" "Man, dat nigga K9, fake as fuck! He be playing like he run GGC and how you gonna have to fall in line. Gauge and Chip just be dick-riding and saying reckless shit. Oh yeah. Dat nigga K9 made some slick comment like when your wives see how he is bossing they gonna wanna give him some pussy, basically."

King G can feel his blood boiling.

"Oh, yeah Bro, that's what this nigga on!" "What you want me to do King G?" "Nothing Bro. I got it just keep gaining his trust and hanging round them. Keep me updated." "I got you Bro" "I'm gonna have Princess G bring you the 100 grand. How fast can you get what I need?" "I will be ready for you in two days Bro."

After that Lil Kenny left. King G called to check on his family. After seeing all was well, he hit the streets. He stopped by the diner to holla at Mama LUV and get some food. Then he called TEC and linked up with him. They decided to swing through and pull up on K9. TEC called him and he told him he was on Foster Ave, chillin with Chip. TEC and King G pulled up on Foster. They hopped out and walked into the park, where K9 and Chip were.

"What's gettin Bro?" shouted K9 enthusiastically

"Dat Cash" replied TEC and King G.

Everyone dapped each other up.

"So, what is the great King G doing back here in the city? I thought you was on vacation?" asked LL, a little sarcastically. "First off Bro, I could never be on vacation when there is cash to get! Secondly, chill with all that great King G shit! I ain't bigger or better than no man in this crew. What's up with y'all tho?" "Damn Bro, I was just fucking with you. We out here eating. Chip got this weed shit sewn up and Gauge killing dem upstate, right now! I got a certified connect that keeps us heavy." "Ok Bro, I hear you, I see you still fucking with them drugs. That's on you! You need to find something legit to invest into too tho Bro. You can't hustle forever." said King G. "I hear you Bro," replied K9 "Damn King G why you gotta come over here trying to downplay our success. You a hater or something?" asked Chip.

K9 knew shit was about to go wrong. He tried to intervene.

"Chill Chip Bro, just giving me some good advice." "Nah K9, don't tell him nothing. Check this out Chip; when I'm talking to my Bro, do me a favor and mind your business! Before we have a problem" stated King G.

Chip jumped off the park bench. All K9 could do was hang his head and shake it! He stepped at Chip and pushed him back.

"Chill Lil Bro. You buggin right now!"

But Chip wasn't trying to hear that; He was amped and wanted to show K9; he was a gangster and straight "Team K9."

"Fuck dat, what you mean a problem? You came out here trying to tell the big homie what to do. Like you giving orders. The rest of these niggas might bite their tongue for you, but I ain't one of them! Just watch how you approach K9." "And if I don't then what?", King G asked asked while walking toward Chip. "Man, y'all Chill," K9 said turning around to face King G. "Listen K9, y'all homie talking big shit. You know where we from that's a call out and all call outs is mando. So, Bro, please slide to the left, so we can handle this like men." Hey big homie go ahead and slide. I got this." said Chip.

Once K9 moved; King G closed the gap between him and Chip. He struck Chip with an overhand left, right on the nose, then broke it. Then he side stepped to the left, while ducking, and hit him with a right hook on the hip. As he was stepping back, he pivoted and kicked him in the jaw. Chip's, whole body folded up. As he was writhing in pain, King G stood over him and said,

"Next time you want to talk big shit, make sure you can back it up! I took it easy on you, this time because you GGC. But if you ever disrespect me again; we gonna do it the hard way!" "Man, K9 you should teach these dudes bout respect. You know we don't come at each other with no disrespect," stated TEC. "Damn Bro" was all K9 could say,

"Hey Yo, K9, get homie some help with that nose. I know it's Broken. I'll holla at you another time big homie," stated King G as he walked off.

K9 could swear he sensed something underlying in what King G said but shrugged it off.

"Come on Chip I gotta get you to the hospital."

Chapter 26

Lil Kenny linked up with King G with the cards

"What's getting King G?" "You already know that cash Bro." "I got them cards for you. They threw in an extra ten cards just for spending that much." "Aight Bro that's what's up." "That's all you!" "Listen though take 5,000 cards and get ya peeps to work them. I want all liquor. Only top shelf shit. Bottles of champagne too. We gonna have the Grand Opening for New Year's, so you've got till then" "I'm getting on this ASAP." "You can't sit around on this!" "I got you King G. What's up with you whooping Chip?" "Oh, you heard about that, huh. Well, he asked for it, that's all I can say. Let's just worry about getting this cash."

After departing Lil Kenny, King G was cruising through Flatbush trying to clear his head. He decided to stop by Get Sets on the Junction to buy him and his family some kicks. While at Get Set he was approached by a thick ass female.

"Excuse me, you King G ain't you?" "Who are you shorty?" My bad, I'm Keisha. I know you don't know me, but I just saw you beat Chip ass the other day. I just wanted to tell you be careful" "I don't know what you're talking about shorty. You got me mistaken." "Ok. Whatever, I'm just trying to look out. I used to mess with Chip lame ass, and I know how he get down. He's the one that told them Southside dudes, where y'all party was at."

King G instantly felt his rage building and had to calm himself.

"Hey Keisha, let me finish buying these Jordans and I'm gonna holla at you. Throw whatever you getting on the counter. I got you.

King G and Keisha jumped in the Impala and chopped it up. She was full of info and King G just sat back and let her tell it all. Now he wished he would have dealt with Chip in a more permanent way.

"Hey Keisha, I need you to do me a favor. Play Chip close for me when he isn't around none of his homies, in case he does or say something crazy. Here is $1000 and I will have more for you, if the info is valuable." "I got you King G and thank you. Put my number in your phone and call me so I can lock you in." "Aight"

King G dropped Keisha off at Kings Plaza Mall. Before she got out, he said,

"Keisha keep this between me and you." "I got you King G."

King G knew he would have to implement a new plan to take care of Chip.

He called his wives to let them know he would be flying back soon; and to see the progress they made on memberships, and a location for Mama Judy and Crazy Joe's wedding. King G let the crew know about the wedding. They all agreed to come. Only day one GGC members were invited.

He let them know to be there by 25th August. He would have their hotels, and everything situated. He paid for Mama Judy and Crazy Joe's flight. They all flew out on the 20^{th,} together. Back in North Carolina, LT and Jungle decided to stay until after the wedding. They let King G know, they had secured 50 members already.

"We got a few lawyers, some doctors and a few business owners. Man, them wives of yours are real gangsters." said LT. "I be knowing Bro," replied King G. Back at the house, the Lady Gs hugged and kissed their husband, then Mama Judy and Crazy Joe. King G could tell something was off with them though.

"Excuse me everyone while I go holla at my beautiful wives down in the basement." King G got right down to business, "What's going on with y'all?" They all did a shy chuckle, then Brandy stepped up, "Damn Daddy, you know us well. Listen don't get mad. While we were out trying to recruit members for the club, I saw Marc, my dad's old friend I told you about." "I know who you're speaking on. You mean your Dad's phoney friend." "Yes, Daddy that's him." "And what happened" "He smiled at me and tried to say hello." "Papa Bear, I never seen Brandy so upset she was shaking and everything we all knew something was wrong, so we stood in front of her. I pulled out my knife and told him to keep it moving." said Butterfly. "Why didn't y'all call me?" "My King, we knew you were handling your business and didn't want to worry you. I told everyone it would be best to let you know when you got back." LUV said. "Ok, I'm not mad at y'all. Please don't let it happen again. Now how can I find this motherfucker?" "He works at a bar in downtown Raleigh," LUV replied. "Ok, y'all go ahead back upstairs. Let me Holla at Brandy."

As soon as everyone left, Brandy broke down crying.

"I'm so sorry Daddy. I didn't know what to do. I was so mad, but at the same time scared. He looked at me the same way he did when he raped me."

Hugging his wife King G said:

"Don't worry Lil mama, I got this. You won't ever have to be scared again. Now how you want me to deal with him?"

She looked up into KING G's eyes, with the most serious face he ever seen on her and said,

"I don't want you to deal with him. I want to do it myself."

Chapter 27

For four nights King G, LT and Jungle sat downtown outside the bar in a different vehicle. They watched Marc get off around 2am and drive to a trailer out in Clayton. King G let Brandy know, after the wedding they would get with him. The day of the wedding everyone was in good spirits and dressed to impress. The whole crew rocked Gucci suits and the Lady G's and Princess G had on Gucci dresses. King G and Brandy were the only ones not in Gucci. They were apart of the wedding party, so was Andy, Candy Brenda and Chris. The wedding was beautiful. At the reception, everyone mingled. King G had put the ladies on about K9 and put them on to his plan. The Lady G's walked up to K9,

"Damn K9, you are wearing that suit. Look at you all bling blinged out!" stated Butterfly. "Oh, this ain't about nothing. Now y'all on the other hand; are wearing them dresses and are pretty blinged out yourselves." "Well, you know the King gotta have his queens looking Royal and Elegant." "As he should," stated K9.

The Lady G's all gave him hugs and walked off. K9 watched them with a smirk on his face. He just knew they wanted him. Little did he know he was falling into a trap.

Two days after the wedding everyone was gone. The crew was back in New York. Mama Judy and Crazy Joe were on their honeymoon. They were so shocked to receive a gift-wrapped box with $250K in it, from the crew. At 1:30am, King G got Brandy up and told her it was time. They drove straight out to Clayton, where King G jimmied the lock, and they went in.

"Listen Lil Mama, when he get here, you stay hidden until you hear me say, "Today's your Lucky Day." I'm not gonna kill you."

King G and Brandy were both dressed in all black. Around 2:30am, they heard Marc pulling up. Brandy hid in the back bedroom. King G was posted behind the front door. As soon as Marc opened the door, stepped in and shut it; he looked up to see King G in a ski mask. Before he could open his mouth to scream, King G punched him with all the force his body could muster and knocked him out. After tying Marcs hands behind his back and duct taping a sock in his mouth; King G hit him with a taser, to wake him up.

"Now listen up homeboy don't make a sound, or I put a bullet in your head! Nod if you understand," King G said, while holding a silenced 9mm Beretta to his forehead. Marc nodded. King G pulled the duct tape off and removed the sock. "Listen son, I don't have no money in here. You got the wrong house. Please believe me!" "No, I got the right house Marc." With hearing his name, Marc was now even more visually terrified!

"I don't know what this is about, but let's see if we

can work this out. Please!" "Nah, I don't think we can work this out. You've been a naughty boy Marc and now it's time to pay."

Marc started crying and King G slapped him. SMACCCK!

"Shut your bitch ass up! Today's your lucky day, I'm not gonna kill you. Someone wants to talk to you."

Brandy came out of the back room and walked around the chair Marc was sitting in, while pointing another silenced Beretta at him.

"Oh my God, Brandy please don't do this. I'm so very sorry for what I did. I was drunk, please forgive me." "Fuck you! You piece of shit! You weren't drunk! You knew exactly what you were doing! Daddy cut this niggers pants off him. I want him to know what it feels like to be exposed against his will."

After cutting his pants and boxers off, King G stepped back and said,

"You're a fucking low life! If it wasn't for my wife here, I would torture you for hours. You were supposed to be her uncle, her father's friend. But you are a snake, a phoney homie and you will die a lonely death!"

Marc began crying again.

"I don't care about those tears. You didn't care about Mine!" Brandy stated coldly. "This body is a whole lot different than when you violated me. You like how it is has filled out?"

Brandy grabbed Marc's balls and pulled them while telling King G:

"Keep him quiet Daddy."

King G stuck the sock back in his mouth and duct taped it. Brandy shot Marc through the skin, connecting his balls to his dick. The bullet caused his balls to tear completely away from his body! Marc screamed, a muffled scream and began to shake violently. Brandy just smiled and said,

"I thought you liked me to play with your balls, Uncle Marc."

Then Brandy shot him in his dick. Brandy went into the back bedroom and lit a candle. She turned all the gas aisles on, on the stove. She and King G exited out the back door and jumped into the crackhead's car. They had parked down the road. King G had got it specifically for this mission. About a half mile away they heard a loud explosion. Brandy smiled, kiss King G and said,

"Thank you, Daddy."

Chapter 28

It was now October. Lil Kenny had called and told King G he had run through all the cards. Princess G had $5 mil worth of liquor in the warehouse. King G knew that could easily turn into $20 mil in his and Princess G's strip club. He would have her stock her bar with some until the Gentleman's Club was ready. He had also successfully run through the cards he had. He went and got all clothing and footwear with his. Some for sale, some for the family. A prime location was indeed needed to get rid of some of the merchandise.

As King G sat in his home, plotting his ways to make more money, he came across Bobby Tellers card and decided to call him.

"Hello Bobby Teller speaking," "Hello Bobby this is King G" "Oh how are you, King G? Is everything good with your SUV?" "Yes, Bobby everything's fine. I wanted to speak with you. You mentioned you had a degree in business management and accounting. I'm looking for a business manager and accountant. Can you be of service to me?" "I'm sure I could King G. I'm one of the best at what I do. If it wasn't for my missus expecting, I would be interning at one of the top firms" "Not to be all in your personal business, but how is the pay at the dealership Bobby?" "I stand to make about $35K to $45K in a year." "I tell you what, I will give you $60K, if you come work for me. $10,000 right now today, and the same every other month, as long as you perform the way you have advertised. Any extra income, you help me incur, will be added to your salary as a bonus" "No problem, King G, I promise I won't disappoint." "I hope not Bobby. Now quit that job and meet me in an hour. I will text you the address to my new development."

After sending Bobby the address to the club, King G put some money together and headed out in his Buick Grand National. The club is coming along nicely and was almost done. King G had a privacy fence around the whole property. The entrance had an electric fence; that members would enter using a key card after showing their membership ID to the security guard in the booth. The entrance was also located behind the property, off the main road. King G handed Bobby his money and welcomed him aboard. He then explained his Gentlemen's club to him.

"King G this is a brilliant idea. How many members do you have so far?" "Well Bobby I have about 300 right now. I hope to have 500 by beginning of December." "Maybe I can help. My uncle is one of the top farmers in North Carolina and is connected with other farmers all over the state. I'm sure they will love this place. If you want, I could talk with him." "Sure, do that. I never even thought to target farmers." Bobby excused himself and got on the phone to his uncle and they came back.

"He said he is on his way into a meeting with about

50 farmers right now and will call me back."

King G explained all the other business ventures to Bobby, along with the clothing. He wanted to sell. "Listen King G, first thing I would advise is open an offshore account in Panama or the Grand Cayman's. Invest in aggressive growth funds so your money matures faster and accrues greater interest rates. Start an import export business in whichever country you choose. To please any prying eyes should anyone from our government come looking. You could easily turn $2,000,000 to $5,000,000 in five years." "Sounds like a plan. I need you to get on top of that today and once you have everything worked out, let me know. If you can turn $2,000,000 to $5,000,000 in that timeframe, 10% of that is yours."

Bobby couldn't contain his smile.

"Thanks King G. As far as the clothing, you can find a prime location or use an Internet service called eBay to sell your Merchandise. Of course, eBay illuminates your overhead" "Let's do the eBay thing, I'm gonna need someone to run that though." "Might I suggest my wife?" "Ok Bobby, but I don't want to put too much on her. She will split the time with my sister-in-law Candy. They will split 10% of the sales payment."

Just then Bobby's phone rang, and he stepped off to answer it. In five minutes, he came back,

"That was my uncle, he has 100 farmers on board. He

also has a check for $50K for you. Give me a name for him to make it out to."

King G smiled and knew he had made the right choice in hiring Bobby.

The next morning, after working out with his wives, King G received a call from Keisha. He put it on speaker, so his wives could listen in.

"What's up Keisha?" "What's up King G, I've been around Chip a few times and wasn't nothing really to talk about. So last night I told him; I know he wasn't gonna let some nigga come to the hood and handle him like that and get away with it. I told him if he needed me, I would ride. He started going off bout he had a trick for you. That once he gets you out the picture, he was going to get LL too, for letting you get away with what you did!" "Is that so?" Well did he say what he had planned?" "Nah, he ain't say but I ain't wanna press him on it and he gets suspicious or anything. If you want me to I will though,"

LUV whispered to King G, "ask her why she doing this?" "Keisha why are you doing this?" "Cause I hate that motherfucker, King G. I despise snake ass niggas. That nigga snakes everyone. He deserves to get what's coming to him."
"Ok I hear you, Keisha" "King G, I do need your help though. My money is low right now. Before you say anything, no I'm not asking you for money. I need a job doing something. Only thing I ever did was hustle and strip. I ain't trying to hustle no

more. I will take any kind of job, as long as I'm getting paid."
"I'll tell you what, I need someone to work at my laundromat collecting the quarters out the machines and depositing them in the bank. Also making sure my cashier has singles and fives for the customers. I will pay you $350 a week. I may have something else for you, if I find you dependable!" "Thank you, King G. That will work fine for me." "Aight Keish stay on your job with Chip tho."
King G thought about something and decided to see if Keisha was a real go-getter.

"Keisha you ever heard of a club Cashdolls?" Hell yeah, King G! That's only the best strip club in a city." "If I can get you in, would you take it?" "Hell yeah!" "Aight Keish, you got a job there as a bottle girl/server on the weekends. Friday be there at 11PM. You still got to do the laundry job tho." "No problem, King G. Thanks."
After she hung up, King G texted Princess G, letting her know what's up. LUV looked at King G and smiled:

"My love you so nice. You like the poor people's mayor!" Everyone laughed at that.

Chapter 29

Three days before Empress' birthday they had reached 500 members. Everyone was super excited! Bobby had notified King G that morning, that there was $250K in the bank for the Gentlemans club. King G decided they would all go out to celebrate for Empress birthday and for hitting their membership goal. Candy and Andy joined them that night. After having a good night, they all were driving on 440; when King G noticed they were being followed.

"Nobody turn around, but I think we are being followed. Let me call Andy and put him on point. Yo, Andy someone is following us." "You sure Bro?" "Yeah" "Ok, I'm gonna speed up and get off at Capital, you do the same. Take a right onto Louisburg rd. At the 5th light, make another right and just keep going straight that's going towards the country, if they follow you, I will be in the cut waiting." "Aight Bro." King G had Empress go in the stash spot and retrieve his Mac II with the suppressor. When she handed him the gun her eyes were wide.

"What Boo? Gotta have a big gun in this big truck." King G said with a smile.

He followed Andy's directions to a T. Once he made the right off Louisburg, there wasn't a car around, for the other car to hide behind. King G looked in his rearview and seen the car was a Crown Vic with spinning rims. They kept back trying not to be obvious, but King G knew what was up.

"Yo Andy they definitely following us Bro," "Aight, Make the first right and stay straight. I'm in the cut bout a half mile down." "Aight,"

As soon as King G passed, Andy crept out to see the oncoming vehicle. Then he opened fire at the driver, with his trusty P89 Ruger, which he now had a laser sighting on Boom Boom!! He hit the driver in the neck. The car swerved out of control. By then, King G had already stopped and pulled up. Jumping out with the Mac! The Crown Vic was flipped upside down. Its occupants trying to crawl out. With no time to waste, King G filled all of them with rounds out the Mac Tat, Tat, Tat!! King G and Andy sped up out of there on the back country roads before anyone noticed what happened. Back at the Royal Palace, Andy assured King G there was no cameras on that road.

"Listen y'all let's just chill and get back to business. We don't need to be going out right now, until we figure out what that was about. Let's focus on our cash flow," said King G.

Four days later, P-Nut had found out the dudes in the car following King G were some jack boys. They were down with a crew known as the PRJ niggas-Poole Rd Jack boys. P-Nut pulled up on King G letting him know the news.

"Yo P-Nut I ain't got time for these silly niggas. They

playing with the wrong one!" "Chill King G, I know one of the niggas the PRJ niggas are beefing with. It's some young boys off the southside called the Quarry Street gangstas. These young boys are savages. They do whatever they can to feed their families! I first got out here, I met one of the young boys from the block. I had smashed him with bout 4 ounces, just cause I liked the hunger in a lil nigga. Anyway, he the one that told me about the play with them niggas. He said their boss is the one who sent them niggas to follow you; and how they feel you had something to do with their homies getting smoked. They don't know who you are. They just know your whip and the chain you be rocking. They on the lookout for you and it's supposed to be on sight!" "These lil niggas can't be that stupid. Fuck it, let's go check ya lil man out!"

King G jumps in P-Nuts Audi S8 and they swerve to Quarry St. At Quarry St. P-Nut jumps out and hollers at a young boy posted with a bunch of other young boys; all wearing black tees, black cargos and black air force ones. King G thinks they all need a put on, but then, focuses on the matter at hand. P-Nut walks over and introduces the young boy.

"Ayo. King G this is my little homeboy, Hitman." "What's up hitman?" "Ain't shit. What's up with you King G?" P-Nut talks highly of you, so I'm gonna cut to the chase. Dem PRJ niggas need to be dealt with, and I mean fast and permanent! King G responded." "I hear you big bruh. I ain't no slave, my work cost, ya feel me?" "Oh, I feel just let's just say, I'm in a position to change all your lives, but we still start with $25K. Is that enough for you to handle that business?" "For sho big bruh." "How soon?" "Shiit. Them niggas supposed to be having a meeting tomorrow night, to go riding looking for you." "Perfect, keep this between us. Ya homies don't need to know who I am or our business. Meet us at the Laundromat on Tarboro Rd at 9am the day after tomorrow." "Say less big bruh. Business is for those that do it, I know how this shit go!"

The next night: Hitman had 3 of his homies with him, gloved and masked up, riding in a stoley through Poole Rd. They spotted the PRJ niggas walking into the backyard of the big homie's house. Hitman and his boys parked up and hopped out, all toting choppers with 50 round clips. They split up in two teams of two and went on both sides of the house. As soon as they reached the backyard, Hitman said "movie time!" Boc Boc, Boc, Boc! Boc, Boc, Boc! The first 10 people that were hit, their heads exploded and disappeared! Some tried to reach for guns and were chopped down from the 7.62 rounds. In all, it took 20 seconds, to lay everyone down! One of Hitman's boys ran to get the car and pull up. Hitman viewed the bodies and seen one twitching. It was the big Homie. Hitman walked up to him and put the chopper to his ear and pulled the trigger. BOC!!!

The next day, Hitman was in the laundry waiting. Exactly 9am, a Spanish woman walked in, wearing a hoody and leggings. Hitman was so busy admiring her ass, he didn't notice what she was doing. As she was walking out, she said, "Poppy, you leave you bag in the machine." Hitman was confused. He thought this bitch was tripping! After about ten minutes, Hitman was getting upset; but then he thought about the spanish chick. He ran to the machine and pulled out the bag. It was full of money! He threw the bag over his shoulder, smiled and made his exit.

Chapter 30

December 31, 2001, came faster than King G would've thought. It was opening night for the Genteel Gentlemen's Club. Jungle had secured about 200 top-notch females from some of his pimp partners. He also had brought 20 of his porn stars with him. He had another 50 in town, from other companies, nationally and from overseas. P-Nut had his Dominican ladies. He had round up 50 Dominican women, straight from the Dominican Republic and flew them in. The Lady G's had 25 models, that were assigned to their management company. Princess G had rounded up 50 of the best strippers she could find. King G and LT had handpicked 100 females, from all over the surrounding states. King G brought in the New Year at home with his family. They left the kids with Betty and went to the club. As they eased into the parking lot all you could see was luxury vehicles from Ferrari's to Mercedes-Benz's. It was definitely money in the building. LT and Jungle were already in the office when King G and his wives came in.

"Man, King G, this spot is jumping!" said LT. "Yeah Bro it's definitely some cash flow circulating." said Jungle. "That's what's up," said King G as he watched the screens showing every inch of the club through hidden cameras. There were strippers giving lap dances to the members, ladies on the dance floor with members, and all types of sexual acts being conducted in the private rooms and V.I.P booths. The bar was busy. There were all kinds of members in the club from politicians, farmers, business owners, bank owners, and even local guys who were well-off. The night went off without a hitch. King G asked all the members to stay back while the ladies left out.

"Thank you all for coming out tonight and being a part of this illustrious club. We will be open Monday through Saturday from 12pm until 3am. You are welcome to have meetings here during the day or just relax. There will be services offered and tantalizing eye candy for you to take a gander at."

Everyone thanked King G. He made sure to shake all their hands one by one.

After tallying up the bar and their percentage from the ladies the profit for the night totaled out to $138,000. After celebrating his and Butterfly's birthday. King G was ready to head to New York to handle Chip and to see what was going on. Once King G got to the hood, he linked up with Lil Kenny.

"Whats getting Lil Kenny?" "Dat cash King G" "Listen, I need another 10,000 cards. Asap Bro!" "No problem, King G. Cause of your last move, I pocketed a cool milly and my workers got the same! I ain't even got no card since then." "Hold up! How you turn your product into cash so fast?" "Easy King G, I got buyers that come get everything at a discounted price. They turn around and sell it and make their money." "Damn Lil Kenny I'm slipping; I should've thought of that! I'm gonna mark the clothes down to 40% off retail and still make a killing. Aight, anyway what's up with this nigga K9 and his homies?" "Ayo, this nigga K9 came back acting like your wives is feeling him or something. Something bout them hugging him and they never did that before. He has also been recruiting dudes and telling them they only listen to him, and how it's soon gonna be a takeover. It seems to me, he is plotting something slick! This nigga Chip really don't say much. I catch him looking at K9 crazy sometimes." "Aight Bro, put them cards together and pay the fee for me. When I meet you to get them, I will have the money. I need the extra cards this time though. Same deal, anything over $1000 you keep." "No problem big Bro, I got you."

King G called Keisha and told her to meet him at Cashdolls. When Keisha got there, King G was already seated at a table. Keisha walked in looking like new money! She was wearing an Abercrombie and Fitch knitted sweater, some skins tight Seven jeans and a pair of calf-high Ralph Lauren Rider Boots and a North Face snorkel. He noticed her nails were done. They were long with a perfectly done French manicure. She walked up to King G and hugged him excitingly. This surprised King G.

"What's up Keisha? I see someone is getting to some cash." "Thanks to you King G, I just want you to know I really.

appreciate you." "No problem, Keish. So, what's up?" "Well firstly, I don't be trying to be around Chip ass too much. He be trying to get with me again and I ain't going there with him. I let him know that. He tries to have an attitude. I told him we could work on being friends and if something happens later than ok. So that keeps him cool. Anyway, one day he was chilling, and I was sitting in his car listening to music. We were in Queens; he went to check with his cousin. I think he was the one who used to fuck with them Southside niggas. Anyway, I'm sitting in the car listening to music. They outside talking. I see Chip is all animated. So, I crack the sunroof and my window and turn the music down, so I can hear. I pretend I'm on my phone. I hear him say he want his cousin to kidnap some lady named Mama LUV, who works at a diner and that would get you here. Then they could kill you. That shit had me so mad King G, I swear I hate a coward and a snake to my core!"

King G just sat there looking at Keisha and thinking. He knew she wasn't lying because how could she know about Mama LUV. But what really got to him was Chip knowing about Mama LUV and the diner! This meant K9 had to tell him this Info. He just couldn't figure out if K9 did it to help with the plan, Chip had or if it was just innocent like they had stopped there to eat, and K9 mentioned who she was. He was hoping it was the latter. For now, K9 was safe; but Chip absolutely had to go!

"Thank you, Keisha, you did well."

For the first time King G really paid attention to Keisha. She had smooth milk chocolate skin with no blemishes. She didn't wear any make up and had a colgate smile.

"Keish let me see your feet." "What?" "You heard me."

Keisha paused for a few seconds, but seeing King G was serious, she did as he requested. Damn, she got some pretty feet, he thought.

"What you wear bout a 4 1/2 or five in boys?" King G asked. "Yeah, how you know that" "I know a lot of things" After she put her shoes back on, he asked her to stand up. She appeared to be 5'9. "Ok, King G, can you please tell me what's going on?" "Just thinking of a few things, there's nothing for you to be worried about. I might have some plans for you." "Oh really?" she said with a slight smirk. "Do you have a car, Keish?" "Nah, but I got a license" "Ok check it I want you to get Chip to come and pick you up tonight. I want you to take him out to dinner and a movie then go back to his place. I'll handle the rest." "I gotcha, King G. Just don't let nothing happen to me." "Don't worry about that, I told you I got plans for you."

Later that night, while King G sat in his rental down the street from Chip's crib; he contemplated all the things he had let happen by letting K9 slide with his bullshit! He couldn't help thinking it was his fault. He had to stay focused on tonight 's task! Chip lived in a small apartment building off of Liberty Avenue. There were 4 apartments, 1 on each floor, according to Keisha. The door to the building was never locked. Chip's apartment was on the 4th floor. Chip had left about 30 minutes ago. Keisha had called King G when Chip was outside to pick her up. King G saw someone approaching the car through his rearview. They knocked on the window and he rolled it down.

"Yo King G, here is the key. Sorry it took so long to make it. I had to make sure the mold was right," said the locksmith.

King G hired him to make a key to Chip's apartment.

"I ain't tripping Bro. Go ahead and get home to your fam. Forget we ever seen each other tonight!"

After the locksmith left, King G walked to Chips apartment with a duffel bag in his hand. He was patiently waiting for the guest of honor to arrive back home. Around 1am, King G heard voices and the key in the lock. He hid in Chip's room in the closet.

"Damn Keisha, you are so fucking sexy. I'm glad you came to your senses and decided to fuck with a boss again. You sure you ready to finally give me a sample of them goodies? Once I get it, I own it!"

"I hear you Chip. You're doing a lot of talking, you better be able to back it up!" Keisha said.

As she walked towards his bedroom, Chip slapped her ass. SMACK!

"Oh, I'm gonna show you I can back it up! Just make sure, you back that ass up."

They enter the room and Chip immediately pushes Keisha onto the bed playfully; but with the slightest bit of aggression and climbed on top of her, hovering over her. "Get them clothes off girl! No more games. It's time to work." Chip stood up at the foot of the bed, looking down at Keisha. She slowly started to remove her shirt, seductively. Chip smiled and then pulled his sweater over his head. When he got it off, he felt a gun to the back of his head. The last words he heard was,

"Phoney homies die Lonely! You bitch ass nigga!" TAT! As the bullet exited the front of Chip's head, his last thoughts sprayed all over Keisha. She didn't scream. She was frozen still, seemingly in shock.

"Keish, you good? Ayo Keish, you alright?"

Slowly Keisha shook her head and began to blink her eyes rapidly. She began to wipe her face frantically, while staring at Chips' body. King G knew he had to calm her down. He grabbed her and took her to the bathroom. He turned the shower on, stripped her, then put her in the shower. He stepped in with her, although he was fully clothed and began washing her. He washed her hair and cleaned her face, while holding on to her.

She finally said," I'm good King G, I'm good. I can handle the rest."

With that King G stepped out and let her finish cleaning up. He went and grabbed the duffel bag out of the closet and came back in. He handed Keisha a mixture of bleach and hospital grade antiseptic soap. She stepped out when she was done. King G couldn't help but notice her body was flawless! She had a tiny waist, flat firm stomach, shapely hips, perky full breasts and an ass, that was perfectly round and high. He handed her a towel, then stripped his boxers and washed himself with the same mixture. When he stepped out, she was standing there, drying her hair, still naked. He quickly dried off and got dressed in a tan Carhartt hoody, blue Carhartt hard denim jeans with the jean jacket to match, and a pair of construction Timberlands on. He handed her a pair of tan winter leggings, a blue carhartt sweatshirt and skully and some all-blue construction timberlands. He called up Butterfly and told her where to send the cleaning crew. He let her know, the key would be under the mat. He gathered him and Keisha's clothes and dumped it in the duffel bag, along with his silenced Beretta. After Keisha was dressed, she came out of the bathroom.

"You good Keish?" "King G sorry bout that back there, I just ain't never been through that! Thank you though for taking care of me." "No problem, Keish, I told you I got you." "I need to tell you something King G, Chip was responsible for killing my brother. That's why I stopped messing with him before. So, I really owe you for tonight."

"Consider us even. You could have told me this before, but no need to explain. You in the fam now so from now on, just keep it real!" "Ok King G. Let me ask you a question. In the bathroom when you saw me naked, do you find me attractive?" "I would have to be blind not to Keish." she smiled. "Thanks, I know your married because you always have your ring on, but it feels good to be attracted to a real man. "Don't worry Keisha, I'm gonna make sure to put a real man in your life and even more now. Now let's get out of here before the cleanup crew arrives."

At the warehouse, as Keisha and King G watched the bag with the clothes burn, she said,

"You ain't do half bad with picking out my outfit. I could have used a bra and panties tho." Hà-Ha." King G laughed along with her. He then said, "When I leave to go down south, you're coming with me. Oh yeah, here's $20,000 I found in Chips closet. That's all you. It was more but I left that for the cleanup crew."

Chapter 31

King G met up with Lil Kenny the next day and collected the cards. He scooped Keisha up and decided to charter a private jet back to North Carolina. As the P.J took off, Keisha said,

"Damn King G! I knew you was a boss, but this is some next level shit." "This ain't nothing Keish. It ain't like I own it." "Still King G, one thing I know, with you I'm going places!" "You ain't lied there Keish and just know wherever you go, you gotta get cash."

Back in NC, they hopped in his Chevelle and headed to the Royal Palace. As soon as King G came through the door, his wives greeted him with hugs and kisses. Then they all stopped to look at Keisha.

"Y'all this is Keisha. Keisha, these are my wives." "Nice to meet y'all." I knew King G was married but I didn't know he had 4 gorgeous wives. Damn King G!" "Oh, so you are the Keisha we have been hearing about," said LUV. "I guess I am, Mrs. G." "Please call me LUV, and that's Empress, Brandy and Butterfly."

King G proceeded to tell his wives everything that happened, and the part Keisha played. When he got to the part of having to wash Keisha, until the shock wore off, all the Lady G's looked at Keisha. She held her head down.

"Sorry y'all. I didn't know I would be in shock. King

G was a perfect gentleman though and never touched me inappropriately." "Oh, we know Daddy was cause he ain't trying to get nobody ass hurt or worse up in here!!" said Brandy. "I know that's right Brandy." Keisha said.

King G let the Lady G's know, he wanted them to get Keisha into modeling.

"Well, we should be able to get her some work. She is bad, Papa Bear." "Thank you, Butterfly. I appreciate that coming from you cause you bad!" said Keisha. "I don't know bout y'all, but I like Keisha. She cool as hell!!" said Empress. "Y'all are too." replied Keisha. "Well until we get you some work Keish, I got these credit cards I want you to go out and work. I need you to hit Walmart, Footlocker, Best Buy, Macy's and Victoria's Secret. Try and hit two different stores for each of them. Spend $1000 on each card. After that, you can spend what you want on yourself." "It's whatever King G but how I'm gonna get to these places?" "Let me holla at my wives and we will figure it out. Don't worry you will have a way."

After hollering at the Lady G's about Keisha's transportation issue and living arrangement; they decided to let Keisha stay in one of the guest rooms, until they found her a home. As for the car, since she would be working with the Fam, and she was GGC, they felt it was only right that King G get her a car. King G wanted Butterfly to take her out to get the car. She knew all about cars. So, Butterfly took Keisha out. LUV,

Empress and Brandy went out to try and find Keisha a home nearby. King G spent time with his kids.

P-Nut called King G to fill him in on the club's business. "Yo King G, what's getting Bro?" "Dat Cash P-Nut. What's up?" "We made about $120k since you been gone at the club." "That's what's up! So, everything good then?" "Yeah Bro" "Listen P-Nut, I Brought a GGC homegirl out here with me. I think y'all would hit it off. She a good one and a rider. She top-notch Bro. I want you to take her out. But you gotta do right by her Bro, no games." "I'll give it a try King G. I trust your word as long as she ain't crazy Bro." "Ha-Ha Nah, Bro come over in a couple hours. I'm chillin with my kids" "Aight Bro, Crash or get Cash," "Crash or get Cash."

King G called Candy and Bobby's wife, to let them know of the new strategy to sell the clothing. He told Bobby, once his wife dropped the baby, they would open the location for the clothes too, along with the eBay store. A couple of hours later Butterfly and Keisha was back,

"Papa Bear, I swear I tried to get Keisha to get a new car, but her mind was made up!" "So, what you get Keish?" "I got a '95 Honda Accord EX station wagon King G. It only cost $10,000!" Keisha said excitedly. King G looked confused. "It's like I told Butterfly, that's the same car my brother had before he died. He had it hooked up. He taught me how to drive in it."

King G nodded in understanding.

"Papa Bear what's crazy, is an older white lady was selling it. She hardly drives anywhere, except to the grocery store. We seen it in her yard, and it only got 15,000 miles on it!" "Yeah, King G and plus I can get a new car when my cash is up. In the meanwhile, I'm gonna get to the cash. Thank you, King G, for the car" "No problem, Keisha. Tomorrow we're gonna go transfer your license and get your insurance handled. Then we gonna hook the car up."

Half hour later, LUV, Empress and Brandy came in,

"That's your car out there Keisha?" LUV asked. "Yes, sis that's me" "Well I see you're happy. Stick with us and there will be more smiles to come. We found a three bedroom, 1.5 bath ranch style brick house for rent for $700 a month. It will be ready on the first" "That's what's up. If y'all think it's good, I'm with the $700? that's crazy a whole house for that! I'm glad my ass left New York."

Just then the doorbell rang, Brandy answered it.

"It's P-Nut Daddy. Hey P-Nut. "What's up Brandy? What's up everybody? When P-Nut locked eyes on Keisha, he knew he had to have her. He walked up to her, shook her hand then kissed it and they introduced themselves to each other. "Well Keisha, I know you just got here, but can I please take you to dinner tonight?" She looked over at King G, who nodded in the affirmative. "Sure P-Nut, that would be nice" "Pick you up at 8."

P-Nut turned to leave. When he got to the door, King G said,

"Thanks for stopping by Bro."

Everyone burst out laughing.

Chapter 32

The next day, King G woke up early. He called the owner of the car audio and rims shop, to see if the suspension and rims for Keisha's car was ready to be installed. Then he hit Andy, to line up a paint job for early that day. After that he called P-Nut to see how the day went.

"Yo King G, Shorty is a definite winner! I'm talking Street wifey material. I could tell out the gate, she keeps it all the way 100 and don't pull no punches!" "Yeah, I told you Bro. I'm trying to see her make it for real. Check it tho; I need you to meet me in Raleigh and then take me out to Wendell. I'm trying to get Keisha car done up for her eyes." "Aight, that's a bet Bro. Meet me at the spot at 8. "Crash or get Cash" "Crash or get Cash."

By the time they made it to Andy's spot it was bout 2pm. P-Nut had paid for Keisha 's car to get a racing brake system put on, a chip for her engine, air intake, a silenced muffler system, tint and audio system. King G opted to have all her lights changed to Altezza lights.

After dropping the car to Andy, they rode through Quarry to check on Hitman.

"Ayo Hitman, what's up Bro?" King G said from the passenger seat of P-Nuts Audi. "Ain't shit big bruh. Out here getting to it. I got shit right out here, thanks to your generous wages." Hitman said with a chuckle. "Oh, yeah well how much you got in the stash?" "Just a little 50 bands. Plus, I got a whole thang broke down. Got the fiends calling it Butter Love." "I hear that Hitman. Check it though, I got these 10 credit cards for you. Take your team shopping, til them shits stop working." King G said. "Good looking out big bruh. We're going to tear Burlington, Ross and TJ Maxx up for all their Polo and Nike shit! Then every color Dickies for the block wear." "Do whatever you want I just wanna make sure y'all good. Y'all stay safe out here. We out."

Back at the crib, King G let Keisha know he dropped her car at the shop to get checked. It will be ready tomorrow. P-Nut took her back out.

"So, P-Nut really feeling Keisha I see. Let me find out my Boo playing Cupid," said Empress. "I just want the Bro and sis to each have someone solid. If they can do that for each other, then why not." "You so sweet Boo." Empress said. Then kissed her husband.

He sat down with his wives and ran down business plans for theirs and his businesses. They all agreed on how to maximize business and excel. He said he would be staying out of New York for the next year to focus on business. The next morning, Andy dropped off Keisha's car to King G. After King G paid him, he threw on a car cover and waited for Keisha to wake up. King G and his wives were enjoying breakfast when Keisha came into the kitchen wearing a black Juicy Couture

T-shirt, purple Juicy Couture sweats and some purple patent leather Prada sneakers.

"Good morning, everybody," said Keisha. "Morning Keisha" everyone replied. "Your food is in the oven sis," said Brandy. "Aww thank y'all. That was so nice." "So how you and your new Boo doing?" asked Brandy. Keisha blushed and said, "We are doing ok, I will holla at y'all later about that when my big Bro ain't around." "Oh, so now we keepin secrets?" King G said jokingly.

Keisha sat down eating then asked.

"King G are we going to pick up my car today? I'm ready to take care of everything, so I can get on this road and start getting this cash." "It's already outside Keish."

Keisha finished eating and went outside to see her car. King G and his wives followed her. When Keisha pulled off the car cover, she screamed,

"Oh my God! Oh my God!"

She was jumping up and down with her hand, over her mouth. She ran to King G and his wives and hugged all of them with tears in her eyes. She said,

"Thank y'all so much for this. You just don't know how much this means to me." She ran back to the car admiring it.

Andy had painted it navy blue with about 10 coats of gloss, and it had silver flakes in it. It had a set of 17" Enkei Racing Rims, painted the same color as the car. The car was lowered an inch and a half, and the windows had 35% tint all the way around. All the decals had been removed as well, and the rubber molding, so the paint just flowed evenly. Even the grill was the same! The Altezza lights gave the car an even better look than King G thought. King G tossed her the keys and said.

"It's got a remote start and full security system. I will show you how everything works later. Open her up and check out everything."

With no hesitation Keisha opened her car and seen her radio had been replaced. She turned the car on, and King G came over and showed her how to turn the radio on. Out popped a 7" pioneer TV screen, which had a DVD/CD player attached to it. When she heard her system thumping, she popped the trunk to see 2 amps mounted and 2 pioneer 12" subwoofers. King G let her know P-Nut supplied her with a lot of her upgrades, which made her smile.

"Your engine and muffler system has had some work too and you'll notice it rides different too. Now let's go handle business."

Later on, that day; after Keisha got back, she had gone to Chapel Hill and done $10,000 in merchandise, P-Nut stopped by to take her out to eat. King G went through all the merchandise and thought to himself that she did well. She had electronics, handbags, shoes and clothing. Right then and there, he knew Keisha would Broaden the ability to bring in cash.

King G extended the trucking company to North Carolina. He hired Brandy's dad as a driver. He put him on salary at $100k a year. His contract was for $150k, so King G pocketed $50k a year. He hired her mom as their babysitter, for $500 a week. With everyone taken care of, him and his wives had time to really push for their goals and get to the cash.

Chapter 33

A year had passed for the GGC crew. Everyone's business ventures were profitable. King G had been feeding Hitman and the Quarry Street gangsters, 10 credit cards a month to keep the wolves well fed. The Gentleman's club was doing remarkable numbers. King G and P-Nut had made powerful contacts as well. King G and his wives hadn't spent any unnecessary money, it was part of their plan to focus on making as much as they could. Keisha and P-Nut were now living together full-time. P-Nut had just bought her a brand new 2003 Audi S6, it was black on black with a set of custom BBS 13" rims that were black and had a 3 inch chrome lip. Gorgeous Girls Can management had indeed turned Keisha into a full-fledged model. She was the "go-to" model for all urban clothing companies. She did music videos and she had just gotten a deal with Olay, a skin care company. Back home the rest of the crew was getting to the cash. K9 was still wondering whatever happened to Chip. To him his lil homie had just up and disappeared. He was still out putting random yes men down, which didn't sit right with King G. But he will deal with that later, when it came to it.

King G's kids were growing up so fast. Royal was 5, Crown was 2, Majesty was 1, and Prince was 1. Majesty and Prince had a birthday coming up in February. After that King G planned on heading to New York. King G sat in his home watching the kids run around looking happy. He already started teaching Royal how to count and save money. This was the future of his legacy and the GGC. He would make sure they were prepared for greatness! The past year, if King G wasn't getting cash or with his family, he was in the country with Andy, shooting and training with all types of firearms. He even trained with throwing knives, axes crossbows and a bow and arrow. Then he would come home and pass on the training to his wives, Keisha and P-Nut. His phone ringing shook him out of his thoughts.

"What's getting Nutso?" "Dat cash Bro, you already know. Yo check it, this nigga LL out here buggin" "What you mean he buggin?" "He got all these niggas running around doing a bunch of wild shit in the name of the Fam. It's drawing the wrong kind of attention! Then they on some fuck everybody who ain't down with K9; like they on some takeover shit!" "Check it Bro don't even trip. I will be up there next month after Majesty and Prince birthday. We will figure it out." "Listen King G, I'm gonna holla at him. If he can't control his people, you already know" "I already know Nutso. Just try to calm down. You know we gotta move militant on this! Can't let some random niggas trick us outta all our hard work." "Aight King G, I'm gone. "Crash or get Cash," "Crash or get Cash Bro."

Shit was getting out of hand King G knew it would take some reinforcements if they had to go to war with these new breeds of niggas. He knew just where to find some reliable reinforcements.

King G pulled up on Quarry Street in his Grand National and Hitman walked over to him.

"What's up King G?" "Ain't shit hit, I require some services, only you and yours can help me with." "For you big bruh, you know that ain't a problem." King G ran down the situation to Hitman. Letting him know what was in it for him and his homies. "We ready when you're ready King G." "Aight, I'm gonna have y'all come with me out to the country for the next 30 days so we can prepare for the main event. Just let me know where I need to pick y'all up. I will let you know a time." "Shiiit, you ain't gotta pick us up big bruh! We all got vehicles." King G looked around and couldn't see any cars around that even looked like they belonged to Hitman and his crew. "Well, where they at Hit?" "We got them parked. We don't need motherfuckers knowing what we in, when they are cruising through the hood. Let me ask you something though King G. This a nice old school ride you got, and all but with all the money you got, why you ain't whipping in something exclusive?" "Check it Hit, I had to make sure all my businesses and companies were in order first. The way the law could never question. Where I get the money from to ride luxury. Plus having a home is way more important, you got me? Soon though, I'm gonna hurt the game!" "Aight big bruh,

that's what I'm talking bout. Holla when you ready for us."
"Aight Hit, I'm gone."
A couple of days later King G called Hitman and had him and his homies meet him at Andy's Burger Spot in Knightdale. As King G was paying for the food, he bought for everyone; he saw 5 2001 BMW M3's, all of them Pepsi blue with the stock M series rims painted all black. The windows had 15% tint so you really couldn't tell who was inside. Hitman stepped out of his and greeted King G.

"What's up big bruh?" "Chillin Hit. I see your boys riding strong." "You already know big bruh. All gas no brakes!" Hitman said with a smile.
King G gave everyone their food and they rode out. For the next month, all they did was train, whenever they weren't getting cash. When Majesty and Prince birthday came up, King G rented out the whole Chuck E. Cheese for the kids.

On February 28th, he was ready to make his move to New York. He chartered a private jet to fly Hitman and his team to New York. As soon as they landed, King G put them up in a hotel in Queens and headed to Brooklyn. He linked with Lil Kenny who filled him in on the latest news.

"Yo King G, this nigga LL really feeling himself. He going around making sure everyone knows he built this shit on his own. He is basically telling all his recruits that anyone who says different in the crew or outside the crew is to get smashed on site!" "Oh, so he really buggin, out. Lil Bro."

"Yeah King G, his money up right now. His connect got him eating, and K9 got his people hustling hard!" "Well, that's about to stop!"

The more King G heard, he knew in his heart, K9 was definitely trying to help Chip, with that bit of information on Mama LUV and the diner.

"Lil Kenny, do you know where his so-called homies be at or where they hustle?" "Of course, big Bro." I be with this nigga every day ever since Chip disappeared. I know where all the spots are at. I even been with him on pickups." "Ok I need all that info so we can give this nigga a wakeup call." "One more thing King G, he put a bounty on your head to all his people; if they ever see you in New York!!"

King G looked at Lil Kenny with a face. He had never seen before. He knew it wasn't anything good gonna come from it. After leaving Lil Kenny, King G called a meeting with Illy, LT and TEC, Nutso, Jungle, and Princess G. After filling them in they all agreed something had to be done.

"Listen y'all, I got this! Nobody else knows I'm in town. Y'all continue doing y'all and leave the rest to me." "Man, fuck dat Bro! if you riding, we riding" said Princess G. "Yeah Bro, for real," everyone else shouted! "I never doubted y'all on riding out, but I'm asking you to trust me. I got this." "Whatever," everyone said together, all looking and sounding defeated.

After the meeting King G called Alvino,

"Que Paso Hermano?" "Coolin Vino. Listen, it's time to cut the water off. Also, I need to sit down and get a bite to eat with you" "Say no more hermano, meet me in an hour." What nobody knew was, King G orchestrated K9 meeting the Spanish shorty and getting the unknown connect. The unknown connect was Alvino and the shorty was his cousin Juanita. King G had asked Alvino to have K9 followed and when an opportunity arrived, to set up business with him. Just so happened K9 was driving through Long Island City that day, and the trail car knew what direction he was going. Since Juanita's business was in the area, he had her cross K9's path. An hour later King G was sitting down in front of Alvino.

"Hermano, it's so good to see you. It felt like forever. You're looking well." "Thank you, Vino, but look I'm gonna need your help. K9 is basically the exact kind of snake you warned me about and I need to take care of this immediately." "Ahhh, I see hermano which is why you want me to stop his supply. He is how you say a "phoney homey," Alvino says with a laugh. "Yeah Bro, I need some vehicles to put my team of savages on him and I need some tools to fix my problem too." "I got you in hermano. Meet me at my Uncle Fernando's mechanic shop in about 3 hours. I will have everything you need." "One other thing, go ahead and have K9 pick up his regular supply tomorrow. Once he dishes it out. I will hit his spots; but after that he gets nothing. I will also be introducing you to one of my savages. He will be the replacement for the currency K9 was bringing in, but he is in North Carolina with me." "No worries hermano, I can have it at his doorstep. I have familia everywhere." "See you in 3 Vino."

King G headed to the hotel and scooped Hitman. At Uncle Fernando's shop, King G introduced Alvino to Hitman. Then they got down to the current business. Alvino opened the back of a Chevrolet panel van, that was loaded with firearms. Hitman picked out 5 Mossberg pump shotguns. They were all sawed off and pistol gripped. Then they looked at the vehicles. There were 2 Jeep Grand Cherokee SRT8's, 3 Honda CBR 900's, 2 Suzuki GSX-R 900's and Toyota Supra with a Twin Turbo engine. Hitman picked the Grand Cherokee, a CBR and 2 GSX-R's. They parked the bikes outside. Alvino sent his driver to pick up the rest of Hitman's homies to bring the vehicles back to the hotel.

"King G when you are done, don't worry about the Vehicles. They are registered to people that are dead. Weapons, as you know, mean nothing so do with them as you wish. If you need me, I am only a call away hermano." "Thanks Vino but you have done enough. Hitman will leave the money for you to pick up once we are gone. He will await your call for pick up in NC." "No problem"
King G had Hitman and his crew park the vehicles at his first warehouse, then drove them back to the hotel.

The next day, K9 was scheduled to get his pickup at 12pm. He had lil Kenny driving his Jag, while he drove the beater all the work was in. Every spot that K9 dropped off to, Lil Kenny texted the info to King G. After K9's last drop off, he parked up the beater and jumped in his Jag. He had Lil Kenny take the beater back. While Lil Kenny was driving the beater back and K9 was following him. King G, Hitman and his crew was moving on the first spot. King G. was driving the SRT 8 with Hitman riding shotgun, literally! One of his homies, named Killa was in the back. His other 3 homies Web, Lukky and Point Blank, were on the motorcycles. They waited for a fiend to go in the spot and rushed it.

"Everybody get the fuck on the ground!" screamed Hitman.

The rest of his crew fanned out, gun butting anyone who didn't move fast enough! Hitman made the fiend hog tie everyone with zip ties, while the crew held them at gunpoint. Hitman stood guard while everyone else ransacked the crib, finding the work and about $50k. They bagged it all up in a duffle bag, then searched everyone's pockets and took all cell phones, money, jewelry, weapons, and all bagged up work. Hitman put all that in a Book bag, then thought about it. He took all the bagged-up work and gave it to the fiend. He whispered in the fiend's ear, while holding the pump to her head,

"Take this shit and get the fuck out of here or you can come with us and get even more."

The fiend's eyes lit up, thinking of all the work she could possibly have, not even thinking of any consequences.

"I'm gonna go with number 2."

Hitman laughed and they walked up out of there with the sawed off 's in their pants leg. When King G seen the fiend with them, he didn't know what was going on. As they got in the Jeep, he gave Hitman a look like what the fuck! Hitman said,

"Chill bruh, I Brought us a master key."

That first spot was in the Bronx, they hit 2 more in Brooklyn and 2 in Queens. When they were done King G said

"What we gonna do with her?" "You ain't got to worry bout me baby, my ass is outta New York. I ain't gonna let them kill my ass out here. Just get me to Jersey and I'm gonna be ok."

Hitman decided to give the fiend the Bookbag full of stuff they got from LL crew's pockets, minus the phones. They put her in a cab and gave the driver $1000 out of her money, to take her to Jersey. Everyone looked at Hitman and he said,

"What?! she reminded me of my crackhead aunty, so I looked out."

Everyone busted out laughing.

King G couldn't believe how easy it was to rob those dudes. LL really had a bunch of niggas who weren't cut to be GGC. After counting up everything at King G's warehouse, they had $250k and 19 bricks. King G called Alvino to meet him and give the vehicles back, along with the $200k to start Hitman and his crew off. Then he called Lil Kenny and gave lil Kenny the 19 bricks.

"Lil Kenny, I got a spot in Vermont for you to go to. You gonna make $100k off each. Don't cut it or nothing! That's 1.9 mil. I told you I would take care of you for doing this job for me. Give me 2 days, once I get back, and I will have the transpo and the spot up there waiting for you. You will probably only need to be there for about 15 days. It's gonna be someone out there to be your face, just sit back and collect."

"Say no more King G. Once you done, find a business to open up, I'm not helping you get no more drugs! You're already up and the scams are sweet. Just cruise!" "Ok big Bro, Crash or get Cash" "Crash or get Cash,"
King G and them met up with Alvino. King G told him,

"Give Hitman my price please Vino. He is GGC and I take responsibility for him" "Say no more Hermano." "And hold dat Jeep for me. I like that shit! I need it in the collection." "I will have a brand new one for you when you are ready."
Back on the PJ headed to North Carolina, Hitman asked,

"Ayo big bruh, why you ain't have us smoke them niggas if they trying you?" "Patience, Hitman. I want them to self-destruct before we hit them. I want them all at their lowest point."

King G smiled, closed his eyes and laid his head back; as Hitman looked at him smiling. He knew King G was a different breed and with him he would go far!

Chapter 34

Back in Brooklyn, K9 was going crazy!!

"Who the fuck could have knocked off all my spots? Don't they know who they fucking with?" "Calm down Bro, we gotta find out who it is first before we lose our cool," said Gauge. "Calm down? Nigga calm down! How am I gonna calm down when I just lost all my work, plus money out of my spots?" "K9 that wasn't all your money. We step up security and you just get more work from the connect and open up shop again." "You know what Gauge you're right. I gotta do that and in the meanwhile; we need to figure out where this shit came from. I gotta wait til the 15th to see if shorty calls me to get more work." "You need something now, LL or you gonna lose clientele." "I got a dude in the Bronx, he wants $30k, but I can probably get him to do $25k." "If we getting in 10 or more." Gauge stated.

K9 didn't want Gauge to know how cheap he was getting his work for. The price Gauge quoted almost made him tell Gauge that was way too much. He knew Gauge was right though; he had to get something til the 15th.

"Aight Bro, go get 10 of them and make sure they're right. I will get you the bread when you get back. I'm going to find out who did this and make them pay."

Back in NC, Hitman had already secured his 20 bricks. Him and his crew started pushing ounces for $1,000 each, nothing more or nothing less! They were flying like hotcakes! The clothing business had already netted King G $1.5 mil. Bobby's wife Lisa and Candy had made $150k apiece. There was still plenty merchandise left. The Lady G's and their Gorgeous Girls Can Management Company had over 50 females signed to them: all with different talents from strippers, singers, models and actresses. The Lady G's were making around $500k a year, and quickly becoming the most sought after managers in the country! King G was proud of them. He wanted to do something special for them for their anniversary.

It was now March 1st, K9 still hadn't received a call from anyone about the connect. He was sick, but the connect Gauge got him, kept him making money. Just nowhere near what he had before. He was putting enormous amounts of pressure on his team to find out who might've had something to do with the robberies. He pulled up at one of the two main spots, that were hit in Brooklyn, to rattle the cage.

"Yo Menace, you still ain't find out nothing for me yet? I'm starting to think this was an inside job," K9 stated. He knew it wasn't an inside job because none of his crew knew where the other spots were. Plus, everyone in the spots had been tied up.

"Check it out K9, I heard it might have been them niggas over on Gates Ave. Ever since we got hit, their flow been heavy." replied Menace." "Oh, yeah well, I'm gonna

have to see bout that! Y'all get ready. We may bust a move
on them."

As K9 drove off, another one of K9's workers, name 2quick
said,

"Now why you tell that man dat bullshit Menace?"
"Look homie, it's either we give him a target or we become
one. Fuck that! Now he got something to focus on besides us."
After watching the traffic on Gates Ave, K9 was convinced
they had to have had something to do with the robberies. He
never took into consideration anything else. He was hot-
headed and impulsive and had a need to make himself feel
bigger than what he really was. K9 hopped out of the tinted
1990 Nissan Maxima he was riding in. He walked towards
the 4 men hustling on the block, with his hand inside his
hoody. One of the men turned and noticed K9s demeanor
and upped his gun. That's when K9 pulled out his 9mm Uzi,
with a 50-shot clip, and let loose!!!!! BRRRRRRATTTT!
BRRRRRRATTTT! He cut down the four men and took off
running back to the Maxima. As he mashed, gas and
screeched off, he turned onto Nostrand Ave, immediately he
looked in his rearview, to see flashing lights! He weaved in
and out of traffic, til he got to Atlantic Avenue and then
busted a left. He was pushing 80 mph. There were now 2
cops behind him. He went to bust a hard right on Utica Ave
and lost control of the car. He tossed the gun out while trying

to gain control of the car, then crashed into a B46 bus. Next thing he heard was.

"Freeze! Put your hands where we can see them." Looking in his sideview mirror, he saw a young boy scoop the uzi up and tuck it. K9 smiled, but he knew he was going to jail. King G got the call that K9 was locked up, all he could do was shake his head. He knew K9's reckless, and snake ways would catch up to him.

"Yo LT make sure everyone drops $1,000 a piece on his Books." "Why you want us to do that King G? This the same motherfucker who wanted to go against us." "You right Bro, but just cause he's a phoney homie, don't mean that we gotta be! If he gonna pay for his actions, it will be through one of us. Not the prison system or anyone outside of our day ones." "I respect dat King G, aight bet. I'm on it."
Next King G called Lil Kenny.

"What's getting big Bro?" "Dat cash Bro. Listen K9 got himself locked up. They got him on 4 attempted murders, reckless endangerment, reckless driving and resisting arrest. I need you to hit Gauge up and make sure he put $1000 on his books. You do the same. I'm going to have a lawyer meet up with him and see what he needs done with his money. Then have the lawyer holla at you." "Ok King G whatever you say, I got it."

May 15th King G's wives flew out to Europe to do some scouting and to ink some international deals for Keisha.

Her model name is K. Cash now. They would be gone for a month. King G didn't like it, but he understood. King G had 23 dozen tiger lillies delivered to their hotel for LUV on her birthday. King G used this alone time to fly to New York to visit K9 on Rikers Island. K9 came through the visiting room door and sat at the table and greeted King G.

"What's gettin Bro?" "Dat Cash K9, how you?" "I'm good, you know me."
K9 said with a shrug of his shoulders.

"I hear dat, so what's it looking like?" "Man, I'm bout to cop out to a 15 piece. They trying to push for 25. The lawyer haggled with them and got it to 20. I turned that down and they came back with 15. The lawyer says they ain't gonna budge, so I'm gone go with that, I aint'got no choice really. They got like 5 eyewitnesses, who are gonna testify. I'm good though." "Damn! So, what you need from us?" "Nothing really. Just keep a nigga with packages and pics. I got plenty on my commissary. I think it's like $26K up there. I need y'all to take my bread and put it somewhere it can make money for me. I've got a few kids out there. I want to make sure will have something when they're older." "You got kids?" Why we never knew about this or them?" "Just something I never got around to. Don't worry Gauge gonna take care of them financially." "Yeah ok, whatever"
King G couldn't believe how deep this person, he used to think of as his brother, fakeness went!

"Chill King G, I don't make my issues everyone else."

King G had heard enough.

"I'm gonna put your money somewhere safe by the time you touch, you will be very well compensated. We got you on the packages and pics. Don't worry. By the way, you're welcome for the commissary and the lawyer."

King G got up to walk off.

"Hey, Yo King G."

King G turned around.

"What's up?" "Crash or get Cash Bro."

King G chuckled then looked at K9 seriously and said.

"Forever Cashin never crashin!"

Then walked away never looking back.

Chapter 35

It was now July 30, 2003; King G had been up since 3am securing his wives anniversary presents. Butterfly decided even though she and King G were married in January she wanted to celebrate it with her other sister's wives. They all agreed. Once King G received the call that his wives presents had been dropped off outside, he went to wake them up.

"Wake up y'all."

King G yelled then sang, "It's our anniversary.

"My King it's 6:30 in the morning. Where you get all this energy? Yes, Happy Anniversary!" LUV said, as she went to the bathroom to get herself together.

Empress and Butterfly went straight to their bathrooms, without a word, to get ready. Brandy was still in the bed with a pillow over her head. King G hopped on the bed tickling her.

"Wake your sexy ass up, Lil mama. We got some celebrating to do." "Ha ha-ha, Daddy stop you're gonna make me piss on myself."

Brandy hopped up completely naked, King G slapped her ass as she ran in the bathroom. When they finally came down dressed, he was sitting at the table with four small jewelry bags in front of him. He handed each one a bag and said:

"You ladies have made me the luckiest man in the

world. You are all a blessing from Allah. I appreciate you and cherish what we have for eternity! This is just a small token of my appreciation."

They all opened the bag and removed the ring boxes. When they opened them, they all gasped!!

"Oh my God, Daddy, I love them!" "Yes, my LUV they are beautiful" "Boo, our original rings are nice, but these are niiiice." "Thank you so much, Papa Bear. You sure know how to pick out jewelry," "Ha ha. Well, I'm glad y'all approve. Just so y'all know those engagement rings are 3 carat, princess cut, solitaire diamonds set in a platinum band. The wedding bands are 1.5 carats on a platinum band. Now let's go get your other gifts."

As King G walked away all his wives looked at each other and smiled. When they got to the door, he blindfolded them and slowly walked them outside. Once they were in position he said.

"Take your blindfolds off."

They all snatched them off immediately and screamed.

"Oh my God!!!"

Parked right in front of their home was 4 2003 Mercedes-Benz S550's, fully AMG Kitted, painted a burnt orange with black flakes going through it, no chrome or rubber siding. The grills were painted all black, even the Mercedes-Benz emblem. Each car had 20" momo rims on them, 1 set was all chrome, another all black, then one, the same color as the car and the last one had a chrome lip and black and burnt orange on the face of the rim. The Lady G's were jumping up and down and high-fiving each other. They all ran and kissed and hugged King G. Back inside after the ladies calmed down, they let him know.

"Each one of us is gonna get you to ourselves starting at 8am. I will be going first, my King. Then Empress followed by Brandy and last but not least Butterfly."

LUV went into the kitchen and grabbed 4 bottles of Ginseng, 4 bottles of Magnum and 4 bottles of Baba roots and gave it to King G.

"You gonna need all your energy my King" and walked away.

All King G could do was laugh. As she made it up the stairs she shouted.

"Get dressed me and you going to breakfast!"

LUV came down dressed in a Chanel crop-top, Chanel skirt, Chanel sneakers and Chanel earrings. Her hair was in a high ponytail to the side just for her husband. King G was wearing a Polo Teddy Bear Hat, Polo Teddy Bear T-shirt and shorts to match and some Prada low top sneakers. They hopped in her Benz truck. They arrived at the Marriott and entered their suite. Ten minutes later, a chef came to the door with a full-on breakfast platter. After eating LUV said:

"My King being married to you has been amazing.

You're a true Protector and Provider. You love me how I need to be loved and allow me to love you the best way I can. Happy Anniversary."

She handed him a gift-wrapped box and walked up to the bathroom. King G opened his present and found a Cartier Box. There were a pair of iced out Cartier Rimless frames with diamonds all on the wood grain handles and the bridge of the glasses. There was also an iced-out Cartier rimless watch the bezel and band were completely flooded. "Thanks, my LUV" King G said excitedly as he tried them on. As he was admiring, the look he called out:

"My LUV. What are you doing? Get your sexy ass in here."

Just then, LUV walked in the room with what appeared to be a halter dress made out of gift-wrapping paper and some 6" stripper heels. Her toes and nails were French manicure, she looked insatiable to King G.

"Come and open the rest of your present, my King." King G didn't need to be told twice. He walked over and tore the paper from LUV's body, while pulling her to him and passionately tonguing her down. He stepped back to admire his wife, as he walked around her constantly caressing her body. Her ass had swelled to a mean 50 inches which had him completely swollen. Her skin was so smooth. Her wide areola and thick firm nipples excited him. He had loved this woman since childhood! She was all his. He loved her stance and her bandy leg. The way the heels accentuated her stance, and her ass, was almost too much for him. He quickly stripped, approached his wife again and gently cupped her breast. Gliding his tongue over her hard nipples; she let out a slight moan. He kissed down her body as he spread her legs apart, then dipped his head between her thighs to lick at her firm swollen clit. He sucked on her love button until she erupted in a body shuddering orgasm! Her legs went weak, and he held her. She smiled and said:

"My turn" wickedly!!

She pushed him onto the bed and got on her knees. Aggressively pushing his legs apart and began eating his dick up. Slurping and drooling all over it. King G grunted and mounted at the pleasure she was giving. She tried her best to get every inch down her throat! She used her hand to work his dick up and down as she licked and sucked him; the whole time staring in his eyes.

"You like that my King? Huh. I belong to you show me I'm yours."

With that, King G grabbed her hair and started to fuck her face, loving the gagging sounds she was making. Then he pulled her up, sucked on her pussy again. then made her straddle him, while he entered her, in one deep long stroke. Kissing her, making her taste her own sweet juices. He could feel her pussy squeezing him, like she wanted to pull the nut out of him, as she screamed.

"Yess, my King give me dat shit!!" "Oh, you want it? I'm gonna give it to you."

He flipped her over, laid her on her stomach and pulled her hands behind her back. She arched her back, pushing her ass into the air and he entered her and began pounding her!

"Oh shit, Fuck me. Fuck me! Fuck me. Shit. Shit. Yesss my King."

King G was in a zone. He pounded her until she came again and begged him to stop.

"Nah, you belong to me! Let your King own this pussy."

She started throwing it back, until he nutted all in her. They both lay there breathing heavily. LUV got up.

"Where you going my LUV?" "I gotta go, or I will fall asleep. Don't worry this day is far from over," she said with a wink. As she was leaving out the door she said,

"Get some rest you gonna need it."

At noon, he is awakened by Empress.

"Hey Boo get up. You hungry?" "Hell, yeah Boo" "Good I Brought you some Curry Goat, Cabbage and Boil dumpling. Oh, yeah and Irish moss." After King G ate, he jumped in the shower. When he got out, he noticed Empress had her hair in two ponytails. He loved it when she did this. She had on a halter top by Louis Vuitton with matching maxi skirt, and some Louboutin sandals. King G sat at the table admiring his wife.

"Why are you looking at me like dat, Boo? You see something you like?" "Nah, I see something I love" "Stop, you are making me blush."

She handed King G a gift-wrapped box. As he tore it open, he was smiling with anticipation. In it he found a high-rise ring dat had a G with a crown on it. The crown was all yellow diamonds, and the G was all white diamonds, the rest of the ring was platinum. There was also a platinum custom chain that had the letters GGC all around it. The letters were yellow and white diamonds.

"I love it Boo. This shit real icy."

Empress stripped her clothes off and walked to her husband completely naked. She got on all fours and slowly started giving him head. She was making love to his dick and moaning all over it! She would start going fast until she had to stop to gasp for air. Then she would go right back. She stopped abruptly, stood up, and walked to the middle of the room, calling King G. over with her finger. He knew she liked to see him walk around with his dick hard. When he got to her, she kissed him, while massaging his balls. She dropped into a side-split and started sucking him off, aggressively! King G's mind was gone. The sight of her in a split and the way she was working her mouth, had his knees weak!!

"Stand up Boo, keep dat dick in your mouth."

She did as she was told. King G grabbed her by the waist and flipped her upside down and began to eat her pussy, while she was still giving him head. The blood rushing to her head and King G working his tongue sent her over the edge! She began cumming, which only made her suck on him harder!!

"Damn Boo, you trying to make me cum," King G said. When she stopped for air she said, "Fuck me Boo. I need it now."

King G laid her on her stomach on the bed and then put her legs in a side spit and entered her from the back holding her two ponytails.

"Oh yesss, Boo, fuuuck! Give me dat dick. Oooh, you in my fuckin stomach" "You like that, huh? You love this dick. Tell me. I love this dick." "I love it. I love it" "You love what?" "That dick Boo. I love that dick! ooooh shiiit."

He snatched his dick out of her as she collapsed. He could see her pussy hole spasming. He laid her on her back, put both of her legs behind her head and long stroked her.

"Fuck Boo. Fuck Damn you all in my stomach. Shiit King G take it out."

King G slowly pulled it out til his head was at the entrance; and dove right back in.

"Aaaargh. Fuck I'm gonna cum Boo. I'm cumming! I'm cumming."

This made King G go harder. He let her legs go and he continued to pound her through her orgasm until he came. She licked his dick clean which had him at attention and ready to go again.

"Save some for Brandy and Butterfly Boo. We ain't done with you yet!"

Empress left him in the room with 2 more magnum drinks and 2 more ginseng. King G said himself,

"What the hell do they got planned for me?"

King G hopped in the shower, then made sure to offer his salaat.

At 2:30pm Brandy came in wearing a Prada mini dress and some Prada heels. Her toes were painted white, which instantly turned King G on.

"Hey Daddy. You save some energy for your Lil Mama?" "You already know Lil Mama. Brandy instantly grabbed King G by the hand and led him to the bed. She stripped him out of his clothes and then took off her dress. She was completely naked underneath! She pushed her husband onto the bed and straddled his face for a 69. King G immediately latched on to her sweet pussy. He began to lick her clit and suck her pussy. At the same time, Brandy was deep throating him and slapping her face with his dick as she spit all over it! She began gagging on the dick, as if she was choking. Every time, she pulled it out, King G could hear her making a popping noise, that turned him on. He was tongue fucking her and sucking her pussy so good she couldn't concentrate. She just kept popping her mouth on his head while she enjoyed him." "Yes, Daddy suck dat pussy. You got me so fuckin wet." King G slapped her ass and then thrust his hips to get more dick in her mouth. "Yes, fuck my face, Daddy. Ack, Ack, Ack!!!" she said as he began hitting the back of her throat. He latched onto her clit, and she started to cum. "Can I cum please Daddy please?" "Mmm, Hmm Mmm Hmm." "I'm cummin Daddy. I'm cummin you makin me cuuuum." After she came, she spun around to ride him. She rocked back-and-forth and bounced on his dick rubbing her clit along his shaft, while he sucked on her titties. "Oooh yeah, Daddy give me dat dick. Choke me choke me" He started to choke her. The lack of oxygen and the mass amount of pleasure had her cummin again! King G slid her to the end of the bed still, on his dick then said, "hold on to my neck." He stood up and began fucking her. Standing up, thrusting in her, while pulling her to meet his thrust.

"Ooh shit! Ooh shit Daddy fuuuuck me!"
King G pounded her til they came together. They showered together. Then she came out and gave him his present. It was a 3-D pendant for his chain. It was a King sitting on his throne with an iced-out crown. The piece was all platinum. King G knew the chain and piece together would be heavy on his neck. Then she handed him a piece of paper with a number written on it.

"What's this Lil Mama?" "It's the pager I got just for you. Anytime you want me to come suck dat dick or you want some of this pussy, page me and I'm coming asap! No talking, no questions asked. Your wish is my command." "Damn Lil

Mama now that's an original gift. I love it" "I thought you might. Now rest up. Your meeting with Butterfly will be here soon enough."

King G had fallen asleep and woke up; he prayed again and still Butterfly hadn't shown up. He decided he would take control of this episode, like the King he was. Around 6:30pm, he heard the door opening. Butterfly came through the door, holding a bag. King G came to the door naked, grabbed Butterfly and slammed her into the wall! He kissed her passionately while caressing her, loving the feel of her body. She was wearing a Fendi tank top, and Fendi monogram shorts with matching sneakers. He pulled her tank top over her head, removed her bra and squeezed her breasts while he sucked on her nipples. He knew this would drive her crazy. She began kicking off her sneakers as she moaned; then he began pulling her shorts down. They were so tight around her juicy ass. Once he got them off, he kissed his way to her clit, tasting her sweet juices! He spread her legs further apart and blew on her clit as he fingered and massage her G-spot. Her body shuddered and she said:

"I need you in me Papa Bear" "Not yet Mama Bear." He put one of her legs on his shoulder as he ate her to an orgasm, while tickling her G spot.

"Aww Fuck Papa Bear."
He stood up with her leg still on his shoulder and plunged into her, hard and deep.

"Oooh shit Papa Bear. Yesss, right there in the back of my pussy."

He slow stroked her enjoying every inch of her walls. She moaned:

"Faster."

He gripped her other leg and put it on his other shoulder; then pressed her into the wall and began pounding her:

"Oh, oh, oh shiiit, Papa Bear. Oooh fuuuck!"

She started to cum again. He walked her to the bed and sat down with her on his dick. She kissed him and then got off and turned around. Reverse cowgirl.

"Keep your eyes on this ass Papa Bear."

She began bouncing her ass up and down making her ass clap, as King G's dick went in and out of her.

"Damn Mama Bear, ride this dick!" "Mmmm, Mmmm Yesss Papa Beeeaaarrr. Fuck!"

She put her hands on the floor and bounced some more, then came back up and reached her hands back.

"Grab my arms, Papa Bear and beat my guts up." King G did exactly that. Pounding her like a jack rabbit!

"Oooh Papa Bear. You fucking…The...Shit...Outta... Meee! Tell me when you gonna cum pleeease." "I'm bout to cum Mama Bear. I'm bout to cum!"

Butterfly hopped off the dick then knelt in front of her husband. She deep throated his dick. She worked her mouth ferociously til she felt his balls tighten up; then she took his nut all over her face, then sucked him dry! After they took a shower, she gave him his present.

"Happy Anniversary, Papa Bear."

He opened the bag and pulled out 2 jewelry boxes. The first one had a platinum custom bracelet that spelled out King G, with all white diamonds. Then the other box, contained a platinum Cuban link chain, with an iced out Skeleton Key.

"Thanks Mama Bear. What's the skeleton key for?"

"That's the key to all our hearts Papa Bear. You're the only one with it."

King G really loved the sentiment in that gift.

"Come here Mama Bear!"

As she came to him, he kissed her and then proceeded to eat her to another orgasm. Leaving out of the hotel with Butterfly wearing all his new jewelry. King G looked like a rap superstar! He made it home to find the rest of his wives standing in front of a large rectangular object wrapped in Brown paper. They ripped off the paper and yelled.

"Surprise!"

It was a picture of his wives posing like Charlie's Angels and Empress in a full side split in front of them. They were all completely naked.

"Don't worry Daddy, the photographer was a female. She gave us back the originals." King G laughed, "That's good and I love it y'all. It's going right in the bedroom. I really enjoyed today y'all outdid yourselves. Thank you." "We enjoyed it to my King, but it ain't over. Tonight, you get to be entertained by us all."

LUV said with a wicked smile that she shared with the others.

"Well before we do that let me give y'all something." King G replied. He went upstairs and came back with four bags. His wives opened them up. He had gotten them each an Audemar wristwatch with iced out Bezels. They all screamed and were showing each other their watches. They kissed and hugged King G. Brandy said:

"We got you tonight, Daddy."

King G was sure they would. After today, he was trying to make that cash back and figure out his next moves. Getting cash was the motto and the motive!

Chapter 36

A week later, King G was in his office talking to Bobby on the phone. He was letting him know how all GGC business earnings were going, from NC to New York. King G's $2 mil was on track to hitting $5 mil in the predicted time frame.

"That sounds good Bobby. Can we meet up in about an hour? I wanna discuss some other ventures." "No problem, King G see you soon."

Flex called King G letting him know he wanted to start a label.

"I'm telling you Bro; I'm making some fire beats. I been studying the business, all we need are some artists and we can Boom!" "I'm down Bro, I'm meeting with my accountant in about an hour, then I will call you back." "Cool. Crash or Get Cash" "Crash or Get Cash."

King G had nothing to do until Bobby arrived, so he decided to test out Brandy's gift. He remembered her note that said #1 for head, #2 for sex. He paged her, his office number and put in #1. Fifteen minutes later, she walked in wearing a Valentino maxi dress and heels.

"Hey Daddy"

She instantly dropped to her knees and got to work.

"Slow down a Lil Mama, you ain't gotta rush! She started slowly making love with her mouth. Fifteen minutes later, the phone rang, and Bobby said he was pulling up. King G tried to get Brandy to stop, and she said.

"No, I'm not finish yet."

She scooted under the table and pulled King G's seat under. Luckily, he had a big desk that couldn't be seen under. He turned on the radio and awaited Bobby's entrance. Bobby came in shook his hand and sat down.

"So, what did you wanna discuss King G." "Well, Bbbobby. Excuse me I had a frog in my throat. I'm interested in starting a record label. Do you know anything about that?" "Yeah King G. It's a good way to make a maximum earning, with the right push. Are you doing this on your own or with partners?" "Mmm Hmm… Uhh yeah… With partners. My man Flex to be exact." "Well as long as you have artists, producers and an engineer it can work. Do you need a location?" "Yesss... Absolutely Bobby. Is it something you can do?" Uhh, sure King G, are you ok boss? You're sweating a lot. You need some water?" "No, I'm cool. Do me a favor though, let's finish this over lunch. Wait for me in my car and I will be right with you."

King G tossed him the keys and Bobby walked out, eyeing him suspiciously. As soon as Bobby left, King G could no longer hold back and came down Brandy's throat! She got up smiling.

"Brandy Greene at your service Daddy."

As she walked away, King G could only smile and shake his head.

After lunch, King G received a package in his P.O Box. When he opened it, it was 10,000 credit cards. He immediately called Lil Kenny.

"What's getting big Bro?" "Dat Cash Bro. Hey Lil Kenny, you sent me a package?" "Yeah, big Bro just some appreciation coming your way." "You don't owe me nothing Bro," "Yeah, I know big Bro but that's from the heart! It's something small anyway." "Thanks Bro, I appreciate it. Listen I been thinking bout a record label. How you feel bout that?" "That's what's up. You know me and my homies fuck around. You remember my 3 Homies who you put on? They go by Pocketful, Big Face and Add It Ip." "Yeah, I remember them. So y'all still rocking?" "Hell yeah! Dem my day ones! We call ourselves Cheddar Mafia. My rap name is K. Dollars." "Ok well we gonna talk. I might have Flex hit you up. "Crash or Get Cash" "Crash or Get Cash."

King G called P-Nut to get the Dominican Mami's to hit the road with the cards. Then he called Hitman to inquire about some chicks, that can do the same.

"I will let you know big bruh but listen swing through here before you go home. We got something for you." "Aight cool Hit."

On the way to meet Hit, King G called Bobby. He has him meet him on New Bern Ave, at the Bojangles. He asked Bobby did he have any people that will go out with the cards.

"Hell yeah, King G. I got a whole bunch of female cousins who don't care. As long as they gonna get paid, they're with it." "Ok set that up, ASAP!"

As King G pulled up on Quarry St. He saw Hitman and the crew posted up. It's a whole different look about them now! They still thuggin, but now they got on starched Diesel jeans and Polo tees, with Fresh Jordan's on their feet.

"What's getting Quarry St.?" "Dat Cash," they all answered. "Hey King G, we just wanna thank you for changing our lives," said Killa. "I just gave y'all the opportunity. Y'all did the work!" "Well, here's for the opportunity." Web said throwing a bookbag into King G's Chevelle. "What's this?" King G asked. "That's $240k. Just a lil something big bruh. Don't insult us, by not taking it!" said Hitman. King G laughed. "You got it Bro. I appreciate y'all. Look, I'm thinking bout starting a label. If y'all want to invest, that will give you something else to focus on besides the block." "Yeah, we can dig that. It's over for this block end of the year, anyway. We probably open up in the country. Can't stay one place with the same people, too long." "Aight we gonna talk. Crash or get Cash" "Crash or get Cash, big bruh."

King G reached the Royal Palace and pulled his Chevelle into the garage. He noticed the Benz trucks were gone. He didn't really think nothing of it. He figured his wives probably went to get the kids. He put the money up then hit P-Nut to come over and chop it up. An hour later the ladies stepped in with the kids in tow.

Daddy!!! His kids all run to him and hug him. "Y'all miss Daddy?" "Uh Huh," they all say. "I missed y'all too. Go put y'all stuff up so we can get some food." "Yaaay," they all say running to their rooms. "Hello my beautiful Queens." "Hello, our handsome King" "P-Nut on his way over. He probably bring K. Cash with him." "Ok my King." The doorbell rings. "I got it Papa Bear" after a minute Empress says, "What is Butterfly doing? C'mon on Brandy and LUV lets go check on her."

This got King G's attention, he shouted upstairs to the kids.

"We gonna be in front of the house. Y'all chill and play" "Ok Daddy!"

King G walked outside and saw his wives, K. Cash and P-Nut staring at him smiling. Behind them is a Mercedes-Benz G550, same color as his wives S550's, with 20" black Lexani rims, blacked out grill and 50% tint all the way around with a bow across the hood.

"Your wives had a little late surprise anniversary gift for you," says P-Nut. "Man today must be my day! Allahu Akbar. Y'all got me good!" "Me and Empress sold our trucks and Brandy gave Candy hers, so we can make room in the garage. We going to cop 4 X5's tomorrow." "I hear that! I'm gonna cop us some storage space. It's getting deep round here. Let's go eat," says King G.

Chapter 37

King G copped the 4 BMW X5's for his wives. That was everyone's birthday presents out the way. Everything was going well. King G, Flex, P-Nut, Lil Kenny and Hitman started GGC Records. They signed Cheddar Mafia. Hitman brought in a group called O.O.K, for "Only Our Kings." Everything was cruising along just the way King G liked it. Years passed by smoothly. In 2006, Butterfly announced she was pregnant. King G welcomed their new son Emir G., on August 31, 2006. King G's son name meant Ruler of an Islamic Country.

Bobby had come through as an accountant, and multiplied King G 's money as promised. He multiplied the rest of the crew's money as well! As promised, King G gave Bobby $500k and the crew matched that! Cheddar Mafia and O.O.K were selling records and Booking shows. GGC was in a zone. Then in 2008 the snakes started to show their ugly heads…

Chapter 38

King G had just upgraded all him and his wives luxury cars to the 2008 models. Then he flew to New York for a meeting with Flex and Cheddar Mafia. After the meeting, Lil Kenny pulled King G to the side.

"Hey King G, check it out. Word on the street, is K9 got all them niggas he put down, screamin GTC, Gotta Take Cash." He supposed to be having Gauge run them until he gets back. He got them recruiting. Preparing for a war with our crew. He wants us eliminated by the time he comes home! Gauge just submitted a bounty on your head for $100k. I only know this cause Gauge don't think I'm loyal to K9." "Ok Bro then you know what it is. Y'all stay strapped and keep on point! We gonna continue to do what we do. If they come to holla at us, we gonna holla back! I will let the rest of the crew know what's up." "Aight King G, stay safe. Take this with you though."

Lil Kenny threw King G a military grade bulletproof vest. King G looked at it and shrugged.

"I guess better safe than sorry, huh?"

King G met up with the crew to let them know what was up.

"Man, Fuck dat Bro, let's take it to these niggas now! I ain't waiting on them to strike first." TEC Barked. "Word King G, niggas must think we soft." Stated Nutso. "Listen y'all, first we gotta know who we are up against. I'm not saying we do nothing, but let's plot and plan. Y'all follow the ones we know around to see who they link up with and where they hang at. We need all the info possible. Then when it's time to strike, we on them!" King G replied. "Bro is right. We gotta play it smart. We got too much money to be moving reckless." LT stated. "Y'all just stay on point. We know they out for me, but they don't know where to find me. Let's get this homework done. I'm bout to holla at Vino for some nice tools out the hardware store."

King G met Alvino in Long Island City and let him know what was going on.

"So, you mean to tell me, hermano, that this low life bendejo has the nerve to try and bite the hand that fed him?" "Basically, yeah Vino. So, I need you to put in a special order for me. I need everything high-powered. A few silenced weapons and a bomb expert. Once it's time for war, I wanna be thorough with them!" "What did you have in mind Hermano?" "Well definitely those Mossbergs, some MP-5's, AR-15's, some military grade scopes, a few grenades and a couple of 9mm calicodes. You know the ones that hold 100 rounds." "I got you Hermano. I will let you know when they're in. If you need me my men are available to you." "Thanks Vino, I will let you know."

In the meanwhile, King G was content in carrying his trusty Beretta, and wearing his vest. Which reminded him, he called Alvino and ordered some of those too.

He drove through the Bronx looking for Gauge in the uptown section, where Lil Kenny told him he would be. As soon as King G spotted him, he spun around the block, then parked up and watched him. After a couple hours, Gauge jumped in his Escalade and drove off. King G followed him and noticed he was headed upstate. A few hours later they were in Binghamton, NY. Gauge got out of his car on 2nd Street. King G watched as he greeted a group of niggas with a special handshake and heard them yell "Take Cash." He could tell this was their trap or where they hung out. King G slowly pulled off, headed back to Brooklyn. He had seen enough.

TEC was watching one of the trap spots in Brooklyn that was robbed. He could see about 12 niggas in and out the spot. They all had "Free K9" shirts on. TEC wanted to shoot them right then but remained cool. He watched them make money, but they didn't appear to have much else going on. As he was about to leave, he noticed them picking on a young kid with glasses. They were pushing him around and giving him wedgies. When they were done, they all laughed, as the kid walked away crying with his head down. TEC followed the kid and then pulled up alongside him and got out.

"Hey kid."

The kid looked around wondering who this man, that was driving a 2008 Range Rover was talking to. The kid pointed at himself and said:

"Who me? "Yeah, yeah. Why them niggas was fucking with you and why you let them do it?"

The kid looked down and said:

"They pick on me because I always wear the same thing all the time. I can't beat them, so I let them get away with it. It's really nothing. They're only messing with me." "What's your name kid?" "Tommy" "How old are you, Tommy?" "15" "Aight Tommy, I'm T. In order to get respect, you have to demand it! Don't let nobody fuck with you! Why are you always wearing the same thing anyway?" "My mom has 5 kids; she works, but all that does is pay rent. I go out and steal candy. I sell it at school, but that's to help mom pay bills."

TEC immediately got on an idea.

"You see them niggas every day?"

Tommy shook his head up and down.

"Ok Tommy, I'm gonna help you but I need your help."

TEC pulled out $2,000.

"Here Tommy this is $2,000 take it. I want you to give $1,500 to your mom then I want you to take $500 and go get a cell phone and a new outfit. Here's my number. After you take care of that call me. I will bring you $5,000. All I need you to do is tell me what them dudes got going on. How many of them be out here and if you hear bout them all going somewhere." "That's it T?" Tommy asked. "Yeah Tommy.

Can you handle that?" "Yeah, I can do that." "Ok this is between me and you. Don't say nothing! You can tell ya mom you work for me unloading and loading trucks. Don't worry, if them niggas fuck with you anymore; I promise to make them pay!" "You got it T."

TEC pulled off smiling. He knew that these niggas would be easy pickings. The rest of the crew had all done their homework equally.

After they all sat down discussing things; King G remembered Chips plan for Mama LUV.

"I gotta go y'all."

King G pulled up at the diner. He ran inside and saw Mama LUV behind the counter, with a man playing her close.

"Mama LUV what's up! You good?" Mama LUV and the man turned around. King G noticed; it was LUV's Dad. He had been deported back to Trinidad in 1991. "Mr. Jameson, you're back?' "Yes, King G. You sure have grown since I last seen you." "He just got back. He hasn't been here 15 minutes. He surprised me." said Mama LUV. "Ok, that's what's up, but check it, Mama LUV. It's time for your retirement, effective immediately! I will be here every day, all day until you find a manager for the diner." "What's going on King G?"

King G proceeded to tell Mama LUV. Mama LUV called her sister and offered her the job. When she accepted, she told her she would start tomorrow. King G stayed until closing time. He handed Mr. Jameson $10,000 before he left and said,

"Welcome back Mr. Jameson."

King G made it to his car and had second thoughts of leaving before he seen Mama LUV and her husband pull out. He sat behind the tint in his Navy-Blue Jeep Grand Cherokee SRT8, Alvino had given it to him. He noticed a man approaching the diner as Mama LUV was locking up! The man was looking around nervous, his hand was in his pocket. Alarm bells went off in King G's head! He jumped out of his whip and ran towards the diner, screaming "Fuck GTC!" The man spun around, gun in hand, with a grimace on his face. When he raised his gun; King G's silenced Beretta was already pointed at him Ta-Ta-Ta! King G unloaded 3 rounds into the would be gunmans face and throat. The body dropped instantly. Then King G heard a fusillade erupt! Boom, Boom, Boom! King G 's body spun, and he hit the ground. He knew the gunman was behind him cause he was shot from behind. King G raised his gun and sent his own Fusilade in the direction he thought the shots came from. At the same time, he heard tires screeching; he saw Mr. Jameson unload on the shooter as he drove away. Boom Boom, Boom, Boom! Mr. Jameson had picked up the first gunman's gun. Mama LUV ran over "

Oh my God, King G are you ok? Oh gaaawd." "Mama LUV get us to my whip!

Mr. Jamison and Mama LUV helped King G to his whip. They put him in the backseat. Mr. Jameson jumped in the passenger seat while Mama LUV drove. King G tried to lift his arm to open the stash spot and pain shot through his arm.

"Aaarrgh!"
He told Mr. Jameson how to open the stash to hide the guns. Then he called LT.

"Yo Bro I been shot get the Doc and meet me at the Warehouse. Aaarrgh, hurry up Bro!"
King G hung up Mama LUV got him to the warehouse.

"Mama LUV pull the Jeep inside. Go in my phone and call Vino. Let him know I've been shot and where we are."
Mama LUV did as she was told. Mr. Jameson checked King G's body once they were inside.

"Your vest picked up two shots, but one went through your left shoulder." Mr. Jameson said. "You're losing a lot of blood King G. I need to put pressure on it." "There are some towels upstairs in the bathroom."
King G said trying to bear the pain. Mr. Jameson ran to get the towels. When he got back King G. had passed out!!

Chapter 39

King G woke up two days later in a bedroom he didn't recognize: with his wives sitting around him with tears in their eyes.

"Where am I!" "He's up, he's up!" They yelled simultaneously. "You are in one of my bachelor pads hermano."

King G was happy to see Alvino.

"The doctor took very good care of you, then gave you something to sleep, so you could regain your strength." I will leave you with your wives, I'm sure you have much to discuss. I will also call LT for you Hermano. He asked that I do so when you woke up." "Thanks Vino." Daddy, how are you feeling?" "I'm ok, little Mama. Just a lil sore." "My King, we were so scared when Mommy called us to say you got shot. We took the first flight up here." "Where are the kids, my LUV?" "Brandy's Mom has them." "Boo I can't believe someone tried to take you away from us." "Don't worry bout that Boo. Real G's die hard!"

King G noticed Butterfly in the corner with her back turned.

"Mama Bear, what's up with you?"

When Butterfly turned around, she looked possessed.

"Now that I know you're good, I want to kill every last one of them motherfuckers Papa Bear!" "Chill out, Mama Bear. We will handle it. Look I need y'all back in NC. Tell all the Bros to put it out there, that I died in the hospital! Have Lil Kenny say that to Gauge. Have everyone come down to NC. As a matter of fact, like if, that's where the funeral will be. We gonna give these niggas 30 days to celebrate. Then we at their front door like a doormat!" "What about you Daddy?" "I'm flying down too, but I'm gonna have Vino get me there on a PJ."

Two days later, everyone was together in NC, at the Gentleman's Club before opening hours.

"Listen y'all, we got 28 more days and we at these Niggas! It should take us 1 day to eliminate these bitch ass niggas. I got someone who will get us around, so that we don't have to worry about the police. I've been mapping this shit out. Alvino has a gunsmith right now making silencers for 20 Glock 19's. Lil Kenny you responsible for kidnapping Gauge. Since you're the closest one with access to him! How did he take the news of my demise?" "Well big Bro, he was excited to say the least! He's supposed to be going to visit K9 to give him the good news," "Aight bet. Once you grab that nigga Gauge, you gonna bring him to one of Alvino's storage spots. We gonna get all the info out of him. We hitting these spots with head shots for everyone! We have got to make a statement. Alvino's boys will leave another kind of message, which I already discussed with him. We are leaving the money in each spot for Alvino's boys for their services. This ain't bout money for us." "Hold on King G. One of the spots in

Brooklyn: I want to go to the little kid Tommy, that been giving me info on the niggas there." TEC stated. "Ok, that's fine Bro. I can appreciate your mind on that one. Anyone got anything to add?" "I know Gauge picks up money every 2 weeks from his spots." said Lil Kenny. "Ok cool. When you get back find out his next pickup and we will time our move around that. Let's focus y'all. After this I expect to have no more problems!" After the meeting King G pulls LT to the side. "Where is Polo at Bro?" "Man, King G; when I told that nigga, we was going to war with K9's people, before you got shot, he said he ain't want nothing to do with that! He just wanna get money." "Well, he gonna have to find somewhere else to get it cause he ain't gettin it with us. He is just another phoney homey. He must have forgot about us coming to his aid when his moms was robbed, and when you put food on his plate! Cut that nigga's water off Bro! It's over for him!" "Say no more King G. I was already on that anyway. Can't eat with us, if you can't work with us!"

Chapter 40

On the 28th day King G, P-Nut and the Quarry St. Gangsters were getting ready to fly out on the P.J. King G kissed and hugged his wives and kids.

"I love y'all. Y'all stay safe. If Bobby needs any help with the club, lend him a hand." King G stated, "We love you," his family said.

Butterfly was visually upset cause she wanted to ride, but King G wasn't hearing it! Once in New York, they all rode in a Limo to Alvino's storage spot.

"Welcome back hermano. You're looking well."

"Thanks Vino. Is everything ready?" "Of course, hermano." He showed them a suitcase with all 20 silenced Glock's and ski masks and all black fatigue suits. King G gave him everyone's shoe size and Alvino sent one of his workers to purchase combat Boots.

The next day Lil Kenny called Gauge.

"Yo Bro what's da word?" "Ain't shit Lil Kenny, how you?" "Cooling Bro listen I got some money to give to you and I got one of my people trying to spend with you." "Aight Bro, where you trying to link at?" "Stop by my spot. When you get the chance." "Shit I'll be there in an hour. What your people tryna do?" "I ain't get into all of that with him. I know he is holding. I figured y'all could work that out, cause I ain't know what price to quote him." "Aight Bro, check you in a minute." Lil Kenny gets a text from Gauge that's he's pulling up. Lil Kenny says, "Right on time."

He has Pocketful there to help execute the plan. As he looks out the window, he sees Gauge coming to the door. He opens it and greets him.

"What's up Bro?" "What's good?" Gauge says as he walks in.

Lil Kenny, while turning to close the door says,

"This my homie I was telling you bout."

Pocketful approached to give Gauge dap. Lil Kenny pulls the taser out and shocks Gauge until he passes out!

"Zip tie this nigga up Pocketful. It's time to move!"

One of Alvino's men open the garage door, as Lil Kenny pulls in. Only after the door is closed does Lil Kenny step out. King G steps in and says,

"So, where this hoe ass nigga at Bro?" "He in the trunk, King G." "Well let's go say hello."

As Lil Kenny pops the trunk, Gauge looks up. His eyes go wide at recognizing King G! King G is enjoying the look on Gauge's face as well as seeing him gagged and tied up.

"Yeah, you bitch nigga. It's me King G in the flesh! See you and ya big homie fake asses thought it would be easy to get rid of me. But real G's die hard! Get this nigga out of there, so we can have a real heart to heart."

Lil Kenny and Alvino's man pull Gauge out and tie him to a steel chair in the middle of the garage. King G walks off and comes back with a cart that contains a car battery, jumper cables, and electric drill. He takes another chair and sits in front of Gauge and removes his gag. Immediately he tries copping a plea!!

"King G, man listen, I ain't have nothing to do with this. It was all K9!"

King G delivers a quick right hook, that shakes Gauge to his core!

"Shut your bitch ass up! You talk when I ask questions and only then. Your phoney ass quick to sell out your big homie. I got no love for phoney homies or fake friends! Nigga, you were better off riding this out to the end like a gangster!! Now I'm gonna ask you some questions. Depending on how you answer, will determine how painfully you die! Nod your head if you understand me." Gauge nods in the affirmative. "Good that's good. Now let's get down to business. I already know you pick up your money on a schedule. When is the next pick up due?" Gauge hesitates then says, "I just made a pickup yesterday." King G shakes his head in disgust! "Guess you gotta learn the hard way how to play this game." King G grabs the drill and drills straight through Gauge's ankle. "Aaaaarrgh, shit man! King G what the fuck! "Aaaarrrgh." Ever so calmly, King G looks up at Gauge, and says, "Now we know when your last pick up really was. I just wanted to start with something simple, to see if you would come correct! Now answer the question correctly."

"OK, OK, OK man fuck! I am due for a pickup tomorrow."

"See now that's better. Now, how do you run your pick-ups? Is it a certain time? Are there certain roles?"

Gauge is still wincing in pain but manages to answer.

"I pick up from the traps. I make sure there is no traffic at the spot, until after I get the money. I have the key to each spot. I have the crew meet me there for a meeting on any upcoming agendas. They never know when I'm coming. That way, they are totally focused on the pickup and drop off."

"How much is in each spot?" "Man, King G, you want money? I got $300k in my duckoff spot right now! Just let me go and you can have it."

King G is obviously vexed by this outburst. He walks off and comes back with a bottle of vinegar and saltshaker. Lil Kenny looks at him confused and so does Alvino's worker. King G takes the top off the vinegar and the saltshaker and throws both into the wound he created with the drill.

"Aaaargh Aaaaargh, Fuuuuck! Fuuuuck. Ok, ok, ok," screams Gauge. Now I told you, only to speak when I ask questions. Not only do you speak out of turn, but you insult me as if need money. "Pussy nigga. I'm King, motherfucking G! I don't need nothing from you but ya soul pussy. Now answer." "Ok yo, fuuuck! The spot in the Bronx will have $210k. The two Brooklyn spots will have $80k and $60k. The same for the two spots in Queens." "Tsk, tsk, tsk. Aren't we forgetting something? What…. About…. Binghamton? Huh." With every word in his last question King G splashes more vinegar into Gauge's wounds. Gauge is now shaking furiously and gasping for air! King G chills to let him gather himself. He doesn't wanna send him into shock. Finally, Gauge replies weekly,

"I pick up $70k a week from them." Then hangs his head. "Ok you're gonna tell me where that $300k is in your Lil spot. Then you're gonna show me which key is for which spot. If any of them are wrong… When I get back, I'm gonna drill through your other ankle, then your knees, your elbows, your shoulders and your jawbone. After I'm done putting extra holes in your body; then I will pour a gallon of vinegar mixed with salt over your head and watch you squirm like the dying snake you are!!"

Gauge tells King G everything he needs to know. King G smiles then signals Lil Kenny to follow him out of the garage. When they reach outside, King G tells Lil Kenny to get everyone together and have them meet up at the storage spot at 3am.

"I got you King G. Yo, that was some wicked shit you did back there to that nigga." "You ain't seen shit Bro."

Lil Kenny just smiles as he watches King G walk back into the garage. As King G enters the garage, he takes out his phone and makes a call.

"Hello… yeah, everything is in place. Be here at 3am and don't forget the vests and badges…Ok see you then."

Chapter 41

The whole crew arrives at 3am. Gauge is tucked away, waiting for the outcome of the night. King G wanted to end his life! He realized, just in case anything went wrong, he could exert some more torture on his counterfeit opponent. Everyone was dressed in their all-black fatigues and Boots. King G gets a call,

"Hello…Ok."

He hangs up then says,

"Open the door."

In steps a white woman, who was quite good looking. She is carrying 2 large duffle bags. As she drops them on the floor, she comes over and gives King G a friendly hug. The crew is wondering who this white woman is. King G can sense their curiosity and does an introduction.

"Everyone this is Agent Webster. Agent Webster this is everybody." "Well, hello everybody." Agent Webster says. "Bro don't trip she is on our side. She will get us to and from our destinations tonight with no worries. Open them bags and everyone grab one of each item inside." King G states.

LT opens the bag and finds bulletproof vests that say "FBI" on it and badges attached to chains. LT shrugs and goes with the flow. They load everything into the tinted 16 passenger black van. The crew gets in the van. Agent Webster jumps into the driver's seat. King G steps into a back office, where one of Alvino's men are sitting. He hands King G a bookbag with 6 GPS trackers in it. These will be used for Alvino's men to locate each spot after King G and his boys do their thing. King G gives him a head nod then makes his way to the van and hops in the back with his crew. Three hours later they are in Binghamton. As they pull up on the first spot King G says

"Everyone pull your masks down, keep y'all badges out over your vests. Agent Webster will lead the way. Once we are in, fan out and leave everyone stinking! Agent Webster, once we get in, you get back in the van and wait for us."

Everyone nodded in the affirmative. They pulled up outside the spot. Agent Webster had been given the keys by King G. Each key was marked for each spot. As she reached the door, the crew jumped out, moving tactically. Like a real SWAT team! She opened the door, and they pushed in. "

"FBI. Don't move. Everyone on the floor!"

The crew had caught these posers lacking. Most of them were sleep and the others just lollygagging around. King G was the first one in. He put 2 in the face of the first man to jump up, killing him instantly! TEC and Nutso ran straight to the back, clearing the house, killing three men in the back. While LT killed 2 in the front room at the same time. Everyone gave the all clear. LT noticed a duffle bag under a table. He opened it and signaled it was cash. King G nodded and then pointed to the door and dropped the GPS. They exited, leaving the cash.

One down, five more to go! Now, on the way back to the city, King G was proud of the efficiency that they executed with. They were in and out in under 30 seconds and because of the silenced weapons; there were no nosey neighbors to notice what had went down. Once they made it to the Bronx there was no need to speak. They already knew the drill. The spot would be a little different because it was an apartment building. It was obvious that someone would see them go in. This didn't worry them because they would appear to be FBI. Agent Webster got out, gun drawn and badge in full display. She opened the lobby door and then made it to the 3rd floor apartment. She proceeded to open the door to the spot. This time P-Nut and Hitman and his crew took the lead. They rushed in with the same entrance as before. This time, some of the occupants of the apartment tried reaching for weapons and were cut down with several headshots. King G and his crew were the ones to clear the backrooms. They only found one dude hiding in a closet. Illy shot him in between the eyes, splattering his brains everywhere! The money was located. The GPS tracker was dropped, as they made their exit. A few nosey people were standing around, but when they didn't see nobody being arrested, they figured the feds hit at the wrong time. As the crew pulled out, they could see people pointing at them laughing. King G laughed himself, at the thought of the people thinking, the feds had failed and taking enjoyment out of it. The two spots in Queens went off without a hitch.

Pretty much, just like the Binghamton spot. Now they were gonna tear down the two spots in Brooklyn. These would pose a bit more difficult, because of the amount of people in the traps, the time of day and just because these were Brooklyn niggas. These niggas were liable to do anything whether they thought it was the feds or not! King G had come up with the perfect plan to avoid all this. Both locations were private houses that had backdoors. The crew would hit the front and back doors at the same time. Agent Webster was carrying 4 tear gas canisters. They would be tossed into the spots to disorient the enemy. Then King G and the homies would do their thing." First, they had to stop at King G 's warehouse, where Alvino had left gas masks for them. After retrieving the masks, they were ready to move. The first spot they hit was the one, TEC had been watching. As planned, they hit the front and back doors simultaneously. They tossed the tear gas canisters and went in killing anything that moved!! When the smoke cleared, twelve men lay dead. TEC snatched a bag of money as King G dropped the tracker. They had to lock the doors on the way out. Of course, people noticed the onslaught of the federal agents rushing the spot. But with nobody being taken out, they pretty much kept it business as usual. Not to mention most people on the block were hiding or running. They weren't looking to be involved with no feds! The last spot was the easiest. As the crew was pulling up, they saw 5 people leaving out the spot. When they rushed it, there were only 3 people there. Instead of killing the 3 and leaving; King G and his men waited around in the back room with the 3 dead men. They heard the 5 men re-enter enter the home. They clearly were looking for their homies, as they yelled out,

"Yoo, yo what the fuck y'all niggas doing back here?" As soon as the first victim walked in the back, King G dropped him, as his homies rushed to the front and terminated the other 4. As King G made it to the front; he noticed the many bags of different fast foods and figured this is what drew the men out. He dropped the tracker, and they locked up and made a quick exit.

Back at the warehouse, they stripped out of their clothes and burned them in the metal barrel. After changing King G collected all the vests and badges. Everyone got ready to leave. King G let them know he would meet them all back at the airport.

"I gotta make a stop first." TEC said, holding up the bag of money.

King G nodded in agreement. Agent Webster drove King G back to Alvino 's garage. On the way, King G thanked her.

"Thanks for your help, Agent Webster. It's greatly appreciated."

Agent Webster laughed then said.

"Cut the Agent Webster crap King G! We are more familiar than that." "Yeah, you're right Lauryn. I do appreciate you though." "Well, that's what you been paying me $100k a year for, ever since you had me quit being a stewardess, to join the FBI. I was wondering when I was gonna earn all that money. You know you done paid me $900k already. All you ever want is info on your name or any of your associates' names coming up. The funny thing is y'all ain't on nobody's radar!" "It's still money well spent Lauryn. By the way, the last key will get you into one of Gauge's spots. There is $300k in it. That's all you for coming through for us. I also need you to find me other agents of cops that will play ball. I need them in other states all over. My homies are thinking of expanding. I will let you know what areas. Take your time I don't wanna put you in harm's way and I need you to be sure. Right now, I need someone in North Carolina, just for info!" "Damn King G, you know I got you! $300k. That means because of you, I will actually be a millionaire. Whatever you need, I'm gonna get it for you!"

King G smiled and then handed her Gauge's address. They exited the van once inside the garage. Lauryn took her duffle bags and went about her business.

King G walked inside and called Alvino.

"Hola, hermano" "What's up Vino? Everything is well on my end. Tell your barber to meet us late tonight for our haircuts." "Say no more hermano. He will be right on time."

After hanging up, King G walked into the back room, where Gauge was still in the chair. He had pissed and shit all over himself. King G didn't even have the energy to drag this out. He put the silenced glock to the back of his head and leaned into whisper in his ear.

"Phoney Homies die lonely my nigga. Tell your GTC homies I said, suck a dick, when you get there!!!"
King G stepped back and put one round through his head. Alvino's man stepped out of the office smiling at King G, then stuck out his hand for the gun. King G gave it to him and left to go to the airport.

While King G was completing the mission, TEC was meeting Tommy on Utica Avenue at McDonald's on Avenue H. As Tommy got off the bus, he spotted TEC and walked to his car and got in.

"What's up Tommy?" "What's up T?"
TEC looked Tommy over and smiled. Tommy had a new aura about him. He seemed more confident! He was wearing some 501 Levi's, some Jordan 1's and Jordan Tee, that matched his sneakers.

"How's your family doing?" "My mom is good especially since I gave her that money. I kept a thousand to buy me and my brothers and sisters some clothes. My mom paid the rent with most of the money and bought groceries."
"That's good Tommy. Listen I'm gonna give you something"
TEC handed Tommy a Bookbag. "It's $80k in that bag. I want you to keep $30k and give your mom the rest. Let her know I gave it to you to give to her. She can call me to verify it. I'm

gonna be gone for a few weeks. When I get back, I'm gonna have a job for you and your mom." Tommy just said there stuck. Then he said, "$80k?" Man, I can't get on the bus and walk home with all this! Wait, I'm sorry. Thank you, T. I forgot my manners." "It's ok kid. I know that money is shocking! I'm gonna put you in a cab. Call me as soon as you get inside your house." After seeing Tommy off, TEC went to the airport. The whole crew hopped on a PJ back to NC. Mission 1 completed!!!

Chapter 42

It didn't take long for news to spread about the dead bodies all over New York City and Binghamton. The news was calling it the worst massacre the state has every scene! 48 decapitated heads found in total. The police had no clue as to what happened. The only common denominator between all the spots, was that a group of hispanic men, looking like a cleaning service had been seen around the different locations. Nobody heard anything, which made no sense to the investigators or the news crews.

King G kept the crew out of town for a couple of weeks just to play it safe. Then it was back to business! Everything was running smoothly as usual. Cash was coming in steadily. Everyone around King G had to be eating, it was only right. Brandy's parents had just built a new house in place of their old one and they both were driving 2008 Cadillac EXT's. Candy and Andy each had their own homes built. Candy was driving a 2008 Range Rover HSE. Andy had a 2004 Dodge Ram SRT-10 and a 2007 Ford Mustang Shelby GT500. Bobby and his wife Angela were now the proud owners of a 4-bedroom house in Apex and matching 2007 Mercedes Benz CL500's. Yeah life was good! King G decided he would invest all his time into his family until the day he could complete his final mission.

Year after year, King G kept his word to himself. He spent all his time with his wives and kids. He taught his children how to be go-getters and to achieve greatness. He gave them lessons in business and in life. He taught them the golden rule; that whatever they do, they gotta get cash! But there was another rule that he had to leave them with. That was tolerate no phoney homies and to never become one! Every month GGC made sure to load K9 up on packages and commissary. He still didn't know of Gauge's whereabouts and figured that he ran off with the money. Gauge was his only connection to the world, outside of his day ones. Even though he heard of the massacre on the news, he still didn't know what was going on. He still believed King G was dead. Around June 2017, King G had LT start to write K9. The letter consisted of LT telling K9 that he was at the end of his bid and couldn't wait till he touched. He asked K9 to call him and sent a number to a burner phone. He didn't want any jail or prison calls coming to his personal or business phones. When K9 finally called he had a lot on his mind.

"Yo LT, what's getting Bro?" "Dat cash, long time no hear from." "Ain't bout nothing Bro. I know I have been out of touch. That's just how I do my bid. What's up with y'all tho?" "We making it the best way we know how. Still missing Bro, but besides that we striving!" "I hear that. Yeah, I'm sure it's different without Bro around. But I see y'all managing. Anybody run into the nigga Gauge?" "Nah Bro, niggas ain't even heard nothing about him. It's like the nigga vanished off the face of the earth." "Damn that's what I was thinking too. Maybe he somewhere locked up, Out of Town or something. Anyway, what's up with the bitches out there?" "Same old shit Bro. They gonna be what they gonna be. Every one of them out here looking like a good Whole Foods plastic bag with all these plastic bodies. That's for sure!" "Ha Ha. Whole Foods plastic bag though, Bro? Ha, Ha, Ha you a fool for that! Well, I need a couple of those when I touch them. How the rest of the team?" "They are good. Illy and Princess G got three grown ass kids. TEC and Nutso still ain't settle down, but they got a couple pickney running around. Jungle still going hard with the porn company. He even got him a little one. I got one too. Speaking of kids. Send me the info for yours, so we can put something together for them." "That's a bet Bro, that's what's up, everyone is doing them. How's LUV and them?" "They making it, you know. King G had them set! His kids are basically grown and pushing hard like their pops." "True. Aight Bro, I'm bout to hit the yard. Catch you on the come out, if you don't hear back from me." "Aight Bro and don't worry you coming home in style! King G made sure your money did gymnastics like Simone Biles. We sending a limo to get you. Wherever you come home from." "That's a bet LT. Crash or Get Cash." "Crash or Get Cash."

K9 hung up, feeling good about coming home in style. If his money flipped the way, he thought; he knew he was a wealthy man. It burned him that King G was responsible for that, but he figured that was minor. Since he knocked him off the board, like a chess piece! All the way to the yard K9 was smiling. LT sat there looking at his phone in awe at how one of his day ones could be so fake. He called King G up,

"Yo LT was getting Bro?" "Dat cash King G. Just got off the phone with this snake ass nigga K9. Can you believe he was all on some what's getting shit. Before he hung up the line, he said crash or get cash. That shit had me tight Bro." "Don't stress Bro. What can you expect from a snake, but for it to slither and hiss. Besides that, how it go?" "Pretty much as you expected Bro. He wants a couple Broads on the come out and he is excited about the limo and all that. So, everything is set. Ball is in your court now." "It always has been Bro! I'm Jordan, LeBron, and Kobe all in one. Crash or get Cash Bro." "Crash or get Cash."

King G set back lost in his thoughts. He couldn't wait till the day came to bust his move. January 2018 came around fast. King G checked the offshore accounts set up for K9, and seen it was at $23mil. Since King G name was also on the account, he transferred $3 mil to his account. He would wire the rest to K9s kids, equally. They deserved their cut of cash. King G went to the Cadillac dealership, already knowing how he would spend the money on the team. He had Bobby meet him there and they went in on a mission.

"Hello gentlemen welcome to your local luxury

Cadillac dealership. How may I help you?" the salesman asked. "We are looking to buy some cars. My name is King Greene and this is Bobby Teller." "Nice to meet you gentlemen. My name is Edward Sanderson. What might I interest you in today?" King G smiled at Bobby and said, "I like this guy's attitude already." Bobby nodded in agreement. "Ok Edward check it, I'm prepared to spend $2.5 mil right now here today. I need 30 2018 CTS-V's top of the line and 3 2018 Escalades top-of-the-line."

King G stated confidently. Edward was astonished at the sound of the request but managed to say.

"Let me check with the manager." Then Bobby jumped in, "I used to work for Ford I know your manager will agree and can do the sale. Tell him if he doesn't, we will walk with this cash and find somewhere else to spend it!"

Edward quickly walked away. In less than 3 minutes he was back saying,

"We would absolutely love to make you the proud new owners of the Cadillac's you requested."

With a smile King G and Bobby walked to the manager's office.

It was now March 1st., the 2018 H2 Hummer Limo pulled up outside of Sing-Sing Correctional Facility. Inside Keisha and Candy sat waiting, wearing mini dresses and 4-inch Christian Louboutin heels. When K9 exited the prison, he was dressed in a Givenchy sweatsuit with a pair of Nike

Vapor Max sneakers on. He spotted the limo and smiled, as he saw the hispanic driver standing at the rear door, waiting to let him in.

"Hola Senor K9."

K9 nodded and proceeded to step into the limo. When he spotted the two beautiful women he almost passed out! Their makeup and hair was done so well. He didn't even recognize them!

"Hello ladies. Is all this beauty for me?" "Of course. You are the famous K9 aren't you. Anything less wouldn't do." stated Keisha.

As the car was pulling off K9 made it all the way over to the ladies, who were sitting with their backs to the partition. K9 sat in between them and put his hand on their thighs. They smiled at him. The car stopped and the ladies started to caress K9's body to distract him. The back door opened and in jumped King G, holding a small crossbow with a look of indignation. K9 was stuck not knowing what to do. Keisha and Candy jumped away from him. King G fired the crossbow through K9's chest. As K9 was slowly dying, King G looked at him and said,

> "$100k wasn't enough homie. You thought I was dead. But as always, Real G's die hard! Phoney Homies die lonely!"

With that King G, Candy, Keisha and the driver exited the limo. They jumped in a black Dodge Durango SRT8 and peeled out. After putting a quarter mile between them and the limo King G said,

"Now Amigo."

The Mexican pressed a button on a remote control and the limo exploded, KABOOM! Mission complete!!!

www.ingramcontent.com/pod-product-compliance
Lightning Source LLC
Chambersburg PA
CBHW070222260626
47160CB00002B/645